Haunted Toronto

John Robert Colombo

OTHER BOOKS ABOUT MYSTERIES BY THE SAME AUTHOR

"They are the best collections of their kind
being produced by anyone, anywhere, so far as I can see."
(Hilary Evans, on the "Personal Accounts Series")

Colombo's Book of Marvels
(Toronto: NC Press, 1979)

Windigo
(Saskatoon: Western Producer Prairie Books, 1982)

Mysterious Canada
(Toronto: Doubleday Canada Limited, 1988)

Extraordinary Experiences
(Toronto: Hounslow Press, 1989)

Mysterious Encounters
(Toronto: Hounslow Press, 1990)

Mackenzie King's Ghost
(Toronto: Hounslow Press, 1991)

UFOs over Canada
(Toronto: Hounslow Press, 1991)

Dark Visions
(Toronto: Hounslow Press, 1992)

The Little Blue Book of UFOs
(Vancouver: Pulp Press, 1992)

The Mystery of the Shaking Tent
(Toronto: Hounslow Press, 1993)

Strange Stories
(Toronto: Colombo & Company, 1994)

Ghosts Galore!
(Toronto: Colombo & Company, 1994)

Close Encounters of the Canadian Kind
(Toronto: Colombo & Company, 1994)

Ghost Stories of Ontario
(Toronto: Hounslow Press, 1995)

HAUNTED TORONTO

John Robert Colombo

Hounslow

Haunted Toronto

Hounslow Press
A member of the Dundurn Group

Publisher: Anthony Hawke
Editor: Liedewy Hawke
Designer: Sebastian Vasile
Printer: Webcom

Canadian Cataloguing in Publication Data

Colombo, John Robert, 1936-
    Haunted Toronto

Includes bibliographical references.
ISBN 0-88882-185-9

1. Ghosts - Ontario - Toronto.   2. Haunted houses -
Ontario - Toronto.   I. Title.

BF. C3C65 1996   133.1'2'09713541   C96-930606-7

Publication was assisted by the **Canada Council**, the **Book Publishing Industry Development Program** of the **Department of Canadian Heritage**, and the **Ontario Arts Council**.

Printed and bound in Canada

Hounslow Press	Hounslow Press	Hounslow Press
2181 Queen Street East	73 Lime Walk	250 Sonwil Drive
Suite 301	Headington, Oxford	Buffalo, NY
Toronto, Ontario, Canada	England	U.S.A. 14225
M4E 1E5	OX3 7AD	

CONTENTS

To the Memory of William Kilbourn
Historian, Torontonian, Humanist

Canada needs ghosts, as a dietary supplement, a vitamin taken to stave off that most dreadful of modern ailments, the Rational Rickets.

Robertson Davies, Preface, *High Spirits* (1982), a collection of ghost stories set in Massey College.

The character of a place is often most perfectly expressed in its associations. An event strikes root and grows into a legend, when it has happened amongst congenial surroundings. Ugly actions, above all in ugly places, have the true romantic quality, and become an undying property of their scene.

Robert Louis Stevenson, "Legends," *Edinburgh: Picturesque Notes* (1879)

There is nothing supernatural about ghosts. They are part of the world in which we live and they follow laws which we are beginning to understand more fully as more and more research into parapsychology continues to be done.

Robin Skelton and Jean Kozocari, from their book about ghost-busting, *A Gathering of Ghosts* (1989)

I've not seen a ghost. They've never been able to capture one, you know. But I've been one — I've haunted a lot of lives.

Allan Lamport, Metro's Goldwyn Mayor, *obiter dictum*, 8 July 1995

$\mathcal{P}$reface

Haunted Toronto: A Ghosthunter's Guide?

Yes, of course!

This is the first book to be researched and written about the city's spirits and haunts. There have been newspaper stories and magazine articles a plenty, but so far no books. This book deals with ghosts and spirits, apparitions and poltergeists, wraiths and spectres, haunted houses and shunned sites, folklore and urban lore, strange events and peculiar experiences, the supernatural and the parapsychological. It deals with the eerie. It gives locations, descriptions, and sources. It covers all of Metropolitan Toronto, not just the City of Toronto. It begins in prehistory and continues through the historical period right up to the New Age of the 1990s.

Author John Robert Colombo, shown in this photo taken in 1987, is leaning against a stone marker which bears the explanatory words "The Birthplace of Modern Spiritualism." The marker identifies the site of the Hydesville Cottage in Upstate New York where two Upper Canadian farm girls, Maggie and Katie Fox, inadvertently launched the Spiritualist movement on 31 March 1848, and thus embarked on careers that made the two of them the most — famous or infamous — mediums of the nineteenth century.
[Hawkshead Services]

Toronto is interestingly named. The official meaning of the name is "place of meaning" in the language of the Huron Indians. Toronto may thus be said to be a place where human beings encounter the known — and the unknown.

Why Toronto?

There are ancient places that have been continuously occupied for thousands of years. Records show that such sites as Babylon, in present-day Iraq, and Third Mesa, the traditional home of the Hopi in Arizona, have been occupied for six thousand or more years. Toronto is not among such ancient places. Yet neither is it a newcomer among communities. It is no Brasilia. Well before the Renaissance in Italy, there were people living on the northern shore of Lake Ontario. All established cities have their own resident spirits, or at least their own traditions of hauntings. Toronto is an established city and has them too, as the entries in this book show. Perhaps it is time that Torontonians paid attention to them.

Some early inhabitants of today's Toronto were people of sensitivity, sophistication, and worldly experience. They were comfortable with the cultures of the Old Country and the possibilities of the New World. For instance, the prose and poetry of the great German poet Goethe were being read in their original language with sympathy and understanding in Little York within four years of the poet's death in Weimar in 1832. The Goethe-reader was the colonial writer Anna Brownell Jameson who enjoyed the poet's works and showed a fine appreciation of how Goethe made dramatic use of legend and myth in a haunting ballad like "The Erl King" which he based on local supernatural lore. Mrs. Jameson was sympathetic to the arts but also to the beauty and wonder of the new land, especially the traditional lore of its native people. Indeed, the Indians of Manitowaning Reserve on Manitoulin Island granted her that rare distinction, an Indian name. They called her *Was-sa-je-wun-e-qua* which means "Woman of the Bright Stream."

Well before the arrival of the Europeans, the Mississauga Indians were encamped at the mouth of the Credit River — present-day Etobicoke and Mississauga. How long they were there is anyone's guess. Then came the French. Brûlé Gardens in the city's west end was named after the explorer Etienne Brûlé, who traded in the region in 1615. The French military erected Fort Rouille, remains of which may be examined today on the grounds of Exhibition Place. The first British soldiers arrived following the conquest of New France in 1759, but it was not until 1794 that the area began to assume familiar social form. That year John Graves Simcoe sailed across Lake Ontario and pulled up into the fine harbour where he established a naval yard and garrison base. Four years later he founded the Town of York to serve as the capital of the Province of Upper Canada.

SIMCOE LANDING AT TORONTO 1793
The view of the Harbour is from a sketch by Mrs Simcoe

Indians were present to greet John Graves Simcoe, Lieutenant-Governor of Upper Canada, as he stepped ashore in 1793 to inspect the future site of York, later Toronto. It is interesting to note that Simcoe's settlement was originally named York, after England's walled city, reputed to be the most-haunted city in Great Britain. The drawing is from C.W. Jefferys' *The Picture Gallery of Canadian History* [1950].

[Metropolitan Toronto Reference Library]

A Simcoe Ghost Story

John Graves Simcoe left a number of marks on York. A British career officer, he served as the first Lieutenant-Governor of Upper Canada from 1791 to 1796. Historians depict Simcoe as a practical person, a man of propriety, yet his marriage to Elizabeth Posthuma, an orphan who possessed no particular means apart from her remarkable abilities as diarist and artist, suggests otherwise. His sensitivity to emotion and words is evident in the verses he wrote to celebrate the love of his wife. A vivid portrait of Simcoe painted by the contemporary artist Charles Pachter gives a glimpse of the breadth and depth of the man's feelings and interests. No reports suggest that Simcoe's ghost lingers here, even around the sites of the two buildings that he caused to be erected, Gibraltar Point Lighthouse and Fort York. Yet Simcoe does figure in a ghost story. It took place before he met and married Elizabeth Posthuma.

In 1778, Simcoe was a young bachelor officer in command of the Queen's Rangers on Long Island, New York. He billeted himself in Raynham Hall, Oyster Bay, where he fell in love with Sally Townsend, the young and beautiful daughter of the family then in possession of the glorious Hall. One evening he proposed to Sally in the parlour of the mansion; the next evening in the same parlour he met with the British intelligence agent Major John Andre. There they secretly plotted to bribe General Benedict Arnold, the commandant of West Point, to surrender the garrison to the British. The sum mentioned was twenty thousand pounds. When she learned of the British plot, Sally informed the authorities and the plan came to naught. Arnold made good his escape to British North America. Andre was caught and hanged as a spy.

Lieutenant-Governor John Graves Simcoe, known to historians as a sober-sided administrator, was a "man of mysteries." The officer and gentleman's somewhat meditative nature surfaces in this evocative acrylic painting, completed by the Toronto artist Charles Pachter in 1984.

Simcoe broke his engagement to Sally and returned to England. There in 1782 he married Elizabeth Posthuma, and in subsequent years they were instrumental in bringing British institutions to Upper Canada. Meanwhile, on Long Island, to this day, the ghost of John Andre is said to haunt Raynham Hall. From time to time witnesses claim to see or sense the presence of this unhappy, unfulfilled British officer. Modern-day visitors to the Hall also learn about the romance of Simcoe and Sally and how it changed the history of North America. American history is made of romance; Canadian history is made of sterner stuff — "Graves" stuff.

From York to Toronto

The Town of York was named after the walled city of York in Yorkshire, England. To this day the original York is said to be the most haunted city in England if not in the world. (Toronto may well be the most haunted city in Canada; but on a *per capita* basis that distinction could be claimed by the residents of Niagara-on-the-Lake, a small community in the Niagara Peninsula with innumerable old homes and a long tradition of hauntings that extends well into the present.)

The Town of York was a frontier community that came into its own during the War of 1812. It could boast but seven hundred residents, but they were loyal and true men and women, and they had as their leader John Strachan, who would be appointed first Bishop of Toronto. When the American expeditionary force took Fort York, occupied the town, and proceeded to plunder and sack its public and private buildings, they were opposed by the redoubtable Strachan. York survived and thrived and grew in size. In 1834 it was incorporated as the City of Toronto, capital of the Province of Upper Canada and later of the Province of Canada West. That year there were nine thousand inhabitants, and one of them, William Lyon Mackenzie, served as the first Mayor of Toronto.

Sites saturated with history survive from the earliest of days to the present day. Taber Hill Park exemplifies the early and continuing native presence. Gibraltar Point Lighthouse and Fort York represent the beginning years of York. Mackenzie House recalls William Lyon Mackenzie's term as Mayor of Toronto as well as the part he played in the Rebellion of 1837.

As Toronto grew in size, it began to act as a magnet for visitors from the United States and Europe, many of whom were bound for or back from the cataract at Niagara. There must have been something strange and wonderful in the sky in those days. For instance, on his visit in 1804, the Irish poet Thomas Moore was inspired to compose a poem, which he called "To the Lady Charlotte Rawdon." It includes a surprising description of "the blue hills" of Toronto:

I dreamt not then that, ere the rolling year
Had fill'd its circle, I should wander here
In musing awe; should tread this wondrous world,
See all its store of inland waters hurl'd
In one vast volume down Niagara's steep,
Or calm behold them, in transparent sleep,
Where the blue hills of old Toronto shed
Their evening shadows o'er Ontario's bed...

A "pillar of light" was seen to rise over Toronto Bay and into the sky on 8 May 1837. It moved slowly northward, disappearing in the northeast ten minutes after its first sighting. It was described in detail in the article "Aurora Appearance" in *The American Journal of Science* which appeared later that year. The eye-witness account was prepared by Sir Richard Bonnycastle, who held a commission in the Royal Engineers. At first Bonnycastle thought the illumination was caused by a meteor. Then he changed his mind:

> ... my attention whilst regarding the heavens was forcibly attracted to the sudden appearance due east of the shining broad column of light ... I was convinced that the meteor was an effluence of the sky, as I now saw it extend upwards from the eastern water horizon line to the zenith, as a well-defined, equal, broad column of white strong light, resembling in some degree that of the aurora, but of a steady brightness and unchanging body.

Naturalists found objects of scientific interest in the natural harbour and in the Scarborough Bluffs. But Sir Charles Lyell, the widely travelled Scots geologist, described the vision that greeted him as he approached Toronto by water. It is now known as the Toronto Mirage.

> June 14, 1842. — From Queenstown we embarked in a fine steamer for Toronto, and had scarcely left the mouth of the river, and entered Lake Ontario, when we were surprised at seeing Toronto in the horizon, and the low wooded plain on which the town is built. By the effect of refraction, or "mirage," so common on this lake, the houses and trees were drawn up and lengthened vertically, so that I should have guessed them to be from 200 to 400 feet high, while the gently rising ground behind the town

had the appearance of distant mountains. In the ordinary state of the atmosphere none of this land, much less the city, would be visible at this distance, even in the clearest weather.

Lyell's account appeared in his book *Travels in North America in the Years 1841–42 with Geological Observations on the United States, Canada and Nova Scotia* (1845). The Toronto Mirage has not been reported in many years.

In 1867, with the Confederation of the Provinces of British North America, Toronto became the capital city of the newly formed Province of Ontario. Toronto's fortunes rose and fell alongside those of the new Dominion of Canada. Montreal served as the country's financial, social, and intellectual capital for the first hundred years of Confederation. Then Toronto surpassed Montreal in population, business, and finance, as the Québécois turned their attention to the preservation of their language and cultural identity. By 1967, Metropolitan Toronto was the country's most populous and prosperous city, and it was soon recognized as the social and intellectual centre of English Canada. That year there were an estimated 1,925,985 Torontonians. For the year 2010, the city's population is projected to lie between 2.5 and 2.7 million. But these figures understate the number of people who live in the area. It is widely maintained that the Greater Metropolitan Area, the hub of southern Ontario's Golden Horseshoe, has a population today of 3 million.

Back in 1953, amalgamation of neighbouring municipalities to supply uniform, city-wide services took place. Today the Municipality of Metropolitan Toronto represents a workable amalgam of the City of Toronto and four other cities — Etobicoke, York, North York, and Scarborough — and East York which continues to describe itself as "Canada's only borough." Since the 1960s Toronto has been called the New City, the City that Works, the International City, the World's Newest Great City, etc. It is a forward-looking place. As former mayor and malapropist Allan Lamport is fond of maintaining, "Toronto is a city of the future and always will be."

Many of the city's haunted sites may be imaged in the guise of historic plaques to mark the pathway that goes from frontier fort through provincial capital to cosmopolitan centre. The plaques bear the names of important sites and the dates that refer to construction or tradition of haunting: Taber Hill (A.D. 1250), Fort York (1793), Gibraltar Point Lighthouse (1806-09), University College (1857-58), Don Jail (1858), The Grange (1871-1910), Queen's Park (1893), Massey Hall (1894), Old City Hall (1897), Casa Loma (1911-14), Grand Opera House (1919), Soldier's

Memorial Tower (1923), Royal Ontario Museum (1957 to the present), Massey College (1963-81), Ontario Science Centre (1969). It is easily concluded that there is a long tradition of hauntings in Toronto.

Stories and Tales

What are "ghost stories"?

Ghost stories are accounts of events or experiences that are supernatural or paranormal in nature. Here are some of my own thoughts on the subject.

An account of a ghost or spirit that haunts a person, a place, or a thing is properly called a "ghost story." There are two types of ghost stories. The first type is most aptly called a tale. A haunting that is legendary or traditional is a tale. The story of the University College Ghost is certainly a tale. It is a traditional account. One tells it with a grin or a grimace, and hears it with a smile or a scowl. Does anyone really *believe* that Reznikoff, the stone carver of University College, ever lived? Such tales correspond to a deep-seated human need. They enrich our present lives by encouraging us to re-experience the past through our imaginations. These tales are most often told in the third person: "He saw this, she felt that."

The second type of ghost story is the story that is told in the first person and is told-as-true: "I saw this, I felt that." It is a direct account of personal experience. The listener may question the informant's intelligence, credulity, or integrity. Indeed, the listener may question the informant's interpretation of the event or experience, yet there is always the assurance that the account is "the truth, the whole truth, and nothing but the truth." The listener is not called upon to believe that such things happen, only that the informant is rendering an account that is not false to his or her experience. Such told-as-true ghost stories are not tales like secondhand accounts. Nor are they supernatural in nature. Instead, they are paranormal. They may be called "memorates."

To the folklorist, a memorate is a first-person account of an event or experience that is told as true. It is not a work of the imagination; it is not a work of fiction; it is presented as something that actually occurred. A number of the accounts in this book are actually memorates or are accounts based on memorates. For instance, the disturbances that took place at Mackenzie House in the late 1950s are based not on the will-o'-the-wisp of legend; instead, they are personal experiences as recorded in affidavits that folklorist would call memorates.

So the term "ghost story" may refer to either a tale or a memorate. Which is which? It should be clear to the reader from the entry itself whether the haunting is part of the lore of everyone, or part of the experience of someone. Pretty soon someone's experience becomes someone else's experience and then most people's. It is not really important to distinguish the one from the other. At least it is not important to the reader of a book of ghost stories. The reader has the opportunity to absorb history, lore, and a measure of human experience.

The accounts themselves, whether based on objective events or subjective experiences, or both, may be divided in another way. They may record occurrences that are supernatural in nature or paranormal in nature. Supernatural occurrences are miracles and hence are beyond all reason and will never be understood. Paranormal occurrences are events or experiences that will be explained some day when we know more about the workings of human nature and the natural world.

Some of the accounts in the present collection are genuinely mysterious; others are simply puzzling. The haunting of Mackenzie House is genuinely mysterious; at least no single explanation accounts for all the manifestations that are reported to have taken place within those walls. The disappearance of Ambrose Small is a strange event, largely because of the absence of information. Pieces are missing from the puzzle. It is unlikely there will ever be a satisfactory explanation for all the effects that are said to have taken place in Mackenzie House — members of the Committee for the Scientific Investigation of Claims of the Paranormal (CSICOP) take note! Even at this late date it is possible that new information will turn up concerning the whereabouts of the remains of Ambrose Small — psychical researchers and ghostbusters, keep a weather eye open!

Documentation

Where did ghost stories originate?

They come from here, there, and everywhere!

It is rare that one meets a Torontonian who does not have a story to tell, even if the story is someone else's — that of a relative or friend, about a strange experience with a "presence" in an old house or public building.

There is no single source for all of these ghost stories. Some were told to me by friends and associates and appear here for the first time. Some I found in newspapers, magazines, and books; I have tried to trace each one back to its original appearance in print, as writers are inclined to repeat one another's accounts (mistakes and all) in print versions in a way that parallels the oral transmission described by folklorists. Others I heard from the lips of friends and associates. As different as these sources are, they may not be as distinct as they seem. Oral traditions are often beholden to words in print, just as printed versions often record oral testimony. Both may arise phoenix-like from personal experience. Tale-telling knows few bounds.

When ghost stories first appear in print in the columns of daily news-papers, it is rare that they make their début as news stories; they usually appear as entertainment features. Until the Second World War, at least, the daily press in Canada was markedly uncritical when it came to claims of miracles or bizarre occurrences. Since that time reporters have shown more reserve and have attributed paranormal claims to claimants rather than reporting them at face value. With the rise of the skeptical organiza-tion CSICOP in the 1970s, there is good reason for members of the media to balance claims with counterclaims, although journalists have an instinctive distrust of an account that is perfectly balanced. The appeal of the outrageous story knows no limit. Outrageous stories are characteristic of "tabloid" journalism and "tabloid" television; the supermarket "tabs" are meeting their match in pseudo-documentaries on TV.

Many of the stories in this book are hoary with age, having been told and retold, written and rewritten, so that they exist not just in one but in many forms. Inessential, and even essential, details vary from account to account. For instance, there is the tale of the bank teller who committed suicide in the Bank of Montreal building; she now haunts the corridors of the Hockey Hall of Fame built on its site. All accounts agree that the teller's name is Dorothy, but no one now recalls her last name, so there is little chance any researcher is going to be able to identify her. There is also the question of her term of employment. When did she work for the bank? Was it in "the early 1950s," as one early and enthusiastic account has it; or was she an employee in "the early 1900s," as a later but more critical account puts it? Perhaps these are not the questions to ask. Perhaps one should leave well enough alone and enjoy the story as it is told.

I have retold the standard versions of these stories wherever and when-ever they exist. I have resisted the temptation to romance the reader by romanticizing the stories. I believe the details are riveting enough without relying on adjectives like "gloomy" and "scary."

Do Ghosts Exist?

I think the reader has the right to ask the author this question. The answer I always give is short but thoughtful. "Ghosts belong to the category of experience, not to the category of belief." I am not waffling when I make this statement. Throughout history, many responsible people — and many irresponsible people — have reported uncanny events and experiences, and in many instances they have described what they have seen or felt as "ghosts" or "spirits." One does not need a parapsychologist to account for these weird happenings; the psychologist is well able to do so. Yet individ-ually and collectively the happenings and the records we have of them seem much more than the sum of their parts. The sense or feeling persists that "there may be something in it," and this is what drives psychologist and parapsychologist alike. Skeptics who say "there is nothing in it" seem never to leave the stage of denial. Credulists who maintain "it's all connected" never advance beyond the sense of wonder. It should be possible for someone to enjoy the stories without taking sides.

Skeptic and supernaturalist alike have likened ghosts and spirits to cigarettes: "They Are Dangerous to Your Health." The skeptic argues from science that unfounded belief is dangerous to your mental health; the supernaturalist argues from scripture that such belief is injurious to one's spiritual well-being. One argument holds no water, the other is all wet! My maxim goes like this: "Ghosts are good for you." They are good for us because they lead us to ask questions. Asking questions about ghosts and spirits means speculating about the unknown. The unknown surrounds us; we are immersed in it; indeed, it pervades us. We forget to include it in our calculations. We ignore it at our peril.

There is no need to "take sides" on the existence or the non-existence of ghosts and spirits. Such beings or such non-entities run throughout recorded history; they are the subject of reports in all cultures and countries; and they will continue to haunt the future as they have the past and as they do the present. We should keep our options open.

The poet Earle Birney once wrote that "it's by our lack of ghosts we're haunted." He had in mind mankind's reluctance to face the unknown with equanimity, humanity, and humility. Ghosthunting offers everyone a popular way to approach the unknown, and to learn a little about history and society, literature and architecture, people and principles, along the way.

People find a good ghost story frightening. Indeed, the good ones seem to bring about all manner of physiological and psychological change. They induce shuddering, they send shivers up and down spines, they raise goosepimples, they account for rises or falls in temperature, they result in clammy hands and feet, they cause sinking feelings in stomachs, they drain blood from cheeks, they quicken pulses, they make hairs on heads stand at attention, they induce nervousness and fear! Good ghost stories do all of these things, and all the while they make us feel more human.

Perhaps ghosts are very simple creatures. Perhaps they *were* us. Maybe they *are* us. Possibly they *will be* us. They could be our abstractions of ourselves: *They* may be imagining *us*. It may be that the poet and singer Leonard Cohen had such matters in mind when he wrote the song titled "This Is What You Wanted" which includes these lovely lines:

And is this what you wanted
to live in a house that is haunted?
by the ghost of you and me?

"Ghost Walks"

If you pay your fee you may go on "ghost walks" around a number of the world's major cities. It seems the world's first "ghost walk" was organized in 1973 in York, England. By the 1990s the "ghost walk" has become a standard if somewhat offbeat service for tourists. By day or by night, guides lead small groups of visitors through the older quarters of York, Edinburgh, London, New York, Chicago, Salem, New Orleans, and other cities in the Western world. There is general agreement that the walk around the French Quarter of New Orleans is the most colourful and scary, but veterans of ghost tours maintain that the walk within the walled city of York is the most rewarding of all. It should be for a number of reasons. York is often described as the "most haunted" city in the world; the city introduced the very idea of the "ghost walk" in 1973; and there are so many different walks for visitors to take — seven different walks in all were given in summer 1995. (In passing, it is worth nothing that Toronto was originally named after York.) York's rival for number of walks is New York City, which currently advertises six different ghostly tours through six different districts of Manhattan.

In Canada, there are seasonally scheduled tours of the older parts of Halifax and Toronto as well as an irregularly scheduled tour of Victoria. Local groups in smaller communities often arrange "haunted tours" to celebrate Halloween and raise funds for charities. (One notable "haunted tour" occurs in Penetanguishene.) Halifax, a port city, has many ghosts associated with land and sea; there is no connection other than name with the title of the most popular collection of British ghost stories, *Lord Halifax's Ghost Book,* published in 1936 and still in print. In the past, in the 1960s, Canadians who wanted to travel abroad could take advantage of the Psychic Tour of Great Britain. BOAC (now British Airways) offered a two-week excursion. For $629, one could visit the Old Country's cursed castles, spend nights in haunted inns, check out a psychic healing centre, and wander around Stonehenge. There is nothing comparable in Canada. Perhaps in the not-too-distant future, Europeans will be flying to Canada to visit its peculiar sites, including the "phantom ships" of the Maritimes, the haunted houses of Toronto, the "medicine wheels" of the Prairies, and so forth.

The city's first publicized ghost walk was sponsored by the Royal Ontario Museum and held as a public service and a fund-raiser. It was organized and conducted by Bette Shepherd, a seventh-generation Canadian with a passion for local history and lore who was then with the Royal Ontario Museum. Bette's walk was held once and once only on 23 April 1980. She led about sixty people through ROM's Bishop White

Gallery, and then they went by bus and on foot to visit a dozen other sites in the downtown area. Press coverage of the first walk served the city's ghosthunters well. Every Halloween, it seems, the newspapers retell Bette's stories.

It is not widely known that sixteen giant heads look down upon the City of Toronto, like wise guardians of old.

They do so from the tower of the old Canadian Imperial Bank of Commerce building which stands at 25 King Street West. The building, erected in 1931, underwent a major renovation in 1976, and is now part of the complex known as Commerce Court North.

Each giant head juts out ten feet from the structure and measures twenty-four feet from brain to beard. The four basic designs represent Courage, Foresight, Observation, and Enterprise.

Marilyn McKelvey, writing in *Toronto: Carved in Stone* [1984], observed that the gargoyle-like heads look down upon the city from the thirty-second floor of what was once "the tallest building in the British Empire." The carved granite heads, designed by the architectural firm of Darling and Pearson, served as guardian spirits during Toronto's middle years.

This photograph, taken by architectural historian William Dendy, shows the tower's arcade and the top half of one of the sixteen giant heads.

[Willian Dendy Collection, University of Waterloo Library, Waterloo, Ontario]

The city's first regularly scheduled ghost walks were introduced as a tourist attraction on 1 May 1994 by Danielle Urquhart, a graduate in history from McGill University. Throughout that first summer, rain or shine, twice a day, at 1:00 p.m. and at 7:00 p.m., she met people with a fancy for ghostly lore in front of the Royal Ontario Museum. She then led them on foot for a walk of two and a half hour's duration. There were thirteen stops en route between ROM and the Old City Hall. Danielle told her own lively versions of stories from newspapers and also stories based on her own research which often began with nothing more complicated than rapping on a likely door and asking the person who answered about "the disturbances" inside. More often than not, she was invited in and told a story or tale or two. She has so many tales to tell that she has organized specialty walks, including one that focuses on the city's theatrical ghosts. I like to call Danielle Urquhart "the Ghost Lady." She has agreed to share with readers of this book some of her favourite stories.

Danielle Urquhart is known as "the Ghost Lady." She has conducted daily "ghost walks" of Toronto since 1994. The photographer took this picture of her standing in front of the Keg Mansion, a haunted restaurant.
[Jack Kohane, *Toronto Voice*]

24

Areas of the City

Metropolitan Toronto covers an immense region of 632 square kilometres. For the purposes of this book, the city has been divided into five geographical areas: South, East, Central, West, and North. The areas lend themselves to the following display:

The areas are bounded by the following city streets:

North
The area north of Davenport Road.

East
The area east of Sherbourne Street.

Central
The area bounded by Queen Street in the south and Davenport Road in the north;
Sherbourne Street in the east and Bathurst Street in the west.

West
The area west of Bathurst Street.

South
The Islands and Lake Shore Boulevard.

The entries are arranged by areas in the table of contents. The city boasts a first-class public system of subway, streetcar, trolley, and bus transportation. Driving or walking from site to site is a fine way to sense and feel the city, especially if the traveller bears in mind the fact that there are so many other sites to explore along the way: historical, cultural, and literary places. What the visitor to the city (as well as the resident) could use is a general cultural and artistic guide to place these attractions in an urban perspective.

Generally, the sites clustered in the Central area of the city may be visited on foot in under three hours. Sites in other areas of the city require transportation of one sort or another.

Important Notice

Many of the sites described in this book are private residences, and they are so identified in the entries. Private residences are houses that may be owned or occupied by people who do not wish to be informed or reminded of reports of disturbances or resident spirits in their buildings or on their properties. Private residences are precisely that — private. Do not disturb the occupants!

Public buildings are also identified. In most cases, visiting hours are given, but it is prudent to check by phone in advance of a visit to make doubly certain about details. Having travelled to a site that is a public building, the visitor may be disappointed that the guides and attendants, although informed about historical matters and courteous in manner, are less than knowledgeable about hauntings on their premises than they might be. Often the guides, interpreters, and attendants are students, part-time employees, or volunteers who have memorized carefully researched and thoughtfully written scripts. The scripts will be long on political and social history and short on folk and ghostly lore. The result is that the visitor may know more about a haunting than the guide or attendant. In the past it has been the policy of some historical boards to downplay if not deny the tradition that a building is haunted. There are many reasons for this defensive practice. One reason is that the authorities do not wish to discourage visits from prospective visitors who may have religious or cultural objections to walking through a site that may exhibit "the work of the devil." Yet it is impossible to imagine what harm, if any, has been done to the bodies or souls of the millions of tourists who each year, year after year, visit haunted Edinburgh Castle in Scotland or haunted Winchester House in San Jose, California.

Acknowledgements

In the preparation of this book I have benefitted from the assistance from a number of friends and associates — kindred spirits, so to speak. As in the past, so in the present, Alice Neal acted as my helpful, tireless researcher. Philip Singer of the North York Public Library ran down otherwise elusive references, and Jeanne Hopkins of the same library system volunteered additional information. Dwight Whalen was at my beck and call with many suggestions.

Librarians are helpful and cheerful people, especially when it comes to responding to offbeat requests for information on haunted places. I conducted most of my research at two public libraries — the Barbara Frum Branch of the North York Public Library and the Locke Branch of the

Toronto Public Library — as well as at the Metropolitan Toronto Reference Library and the John P. Robarts Research Library of the University of Toronto. Research was also conducted at the City of Toronto Archives and the Metropolitan Toronto Archives and Records Centre. I was able to make good use of the resources of the CBC Reference Library, Cinematheque Ontario, and the libraries of the three Toronto newspapers, the *Globe,* the *Star,* and the *Sun.* (Their names suggest a binary solar system!)

I am grateful to the following men and women who were particularly helpful: Joseph Cartan, former manager, Massey Hall; Irma Coucill, artist; David Creelman, genealogist; Ted Davy, researcher; Mary Dixon, former parishioner; Elise Delbianco, librarian, Trinity College; Don Evans, artist; Mike Filey, archivist and author; Edith Fowke, folklorist; Sandra Fuller, archivist, St. James' Cathedral; Margaret Harmer, former chorister; Tom Hyland, photographer; Julie Kirsch, librarian; Michael Lucas, occupant, Friendship House; Sharon MacDonald, Metropolitan Toronto Police Museum and Discovery Centre; Mary Mason, daughter of the late Healey Willan; Gerald Pratley, film historian; Michael Roth, manager, Keg Mansion; Aldona Satterthwaite, creative services, Art Gallery of Ontario; Ivan Semeniuk, astronomer, Ontario Science Centre; Patricia Sculthrope, media relations, Royal Ontario Museum; Craig Urquhart, anthropology student; Robin Shepherd, former historic-site interpreter; Raymond Souster, poet; Beatriz Zeller, librarian.

I am also grateful to Bette Shepherd who read the first draft of this work and suggested ways to improve it. I am indebted to Danielle Urquhart who, the hot afternoon of 2 May 1994, led me around the centre of the city on one of her popular "ghost walks" and then agreed to share with me some of her lively ghost stories. I was touched when artist Don Evans contributed his "Isaac Bickerstaff" sketches and Charles Pachter his painting of J.G. Simcoe.

I have been collecting information on hauntings in Toronto and in Canada since the Centennial Year in some out-of-the-way places. In the late 1950s, when I was an undergraduate at University College, I first learned of the tragic tale of Diabolos and Reznikoff. I heard it from the lips of its most impassioned teller, the late Dr. Humphrey Milnes. At the time I prevailed upon Professor Milnes to write out the tale so that I could print it in *The Undergraduate,* the student literary magazine which I then edited. I was a literary ghosthunter even then! Since that time I have written about the UC ghost and even discussed it on radio and television. For the account in these pages, some additional details were kindly provided by Professor Douglas Richardson of the University College Archives. The college archives are housed, appropriately, in the Humphrey Milnes Room.

Information about the trance medium Thomas Lacey was supplied by Stuart MacKinnon, Coordinator, Collections Management, Dana Porter Library, University of Waterloo, Waterloo, Ontario. The story of Simcoe's ill-starred romance is a staple of American ghost books; it appears in two resourceful works: *Haunted Houses U.S.A.* (N.Y.: Pocket Books, 1989) by Dolores Riccio and Joan Bingham, and in *The National Directory of Haunted Places* (Sacramento: Athanor Press, 1994) by Dennis William Hauck.

David J. Burnside, Chairman of the Toronto Historical Board, encouraged the folkloristic aspects of the present work. D. Scott James, the THB's Managing Director, co-ordinated the Board's response to first-draft entries, intelligently dissected by Diane Beasley, Carl Benn, Eleanor Darke, and Betty Roodhart. Both the Toronto Historical Society and the North York Historical Society published my appeal for information on hauntings in the area. James Randi answered questions about his early Toronto years. One tale yet to appear in print came orally and unbidden from Professor Jon Redfern, who attended the University of Toronto's School of Graduate Studies in the 1970s and who now teaches at Centennial College, Scarborough. William Toye, M.T. (Terry) Kelly, and Elizabeth and William Kilbourn generously shared with me their subtle sense of the city's history — in Terry's case, its aboriginal past. Other contributions were made by two friends, Dr. Cyril Greenland and Dr. David A. Gotlib. A good many of the photographs were taken for this book by Josh Goldhar, who spent part of the summer and fall of 1995 driving around the city, camera in hand.

Radio hosts love to interview guests about ghosts, especially around Halloween time, so I have happily chatted with a number of Toronto-area radio personalities, including Bill Carroll of Q-107 and AM 640, Andy Barrie of CFRB, and on CBC Radio with Kathryn O'Hara of "Later the Same Day" and Christopher Thomas of "Radio Noon." Newspaper reporters and columnists also acknowledge Halloween. I am in the debt of the newspaper reporters, magazine editors, and freelancer writers who contributed the stories, columns, and articles that appeared in the *Toronto Star*, the *Globe and Mail*, the *Toronto Sun*, not to mention the old *Toronto Telegram* and community papers like *Toronto Voice* (formerly *Toronto's Midtown Voice*).

I consulted a number of books while working on this one. A useful general guide to sources is George M. Eberhart's *A Geo-Bibliography of Anomalies: Primary Access to Observations of UFOs, Ghosts, and Other Mysterious Phenomena* (Westport, Conn.: Greenwood Press, 1980). Details of buildings were checked against Patricia McHugh's outstanding *Toronto Architecture: A City Guide* (Toronto: Mercury Books, 1985). There are two anecdotal collections of ghost stories. The first is Eileen Sonin's *ESPecially Ghosts: Some True Experiences of the Supernatural in North America* (Toronto: Clarke, Irwin & Company, 1970); it was reprinted as *More Canadian Ghosts* (Markham, Ont.: Pocket Books, 1974). The second is Sheila Hervey's *Some Canadian Ghosts* (Toronto: Pocket Books/Simon & Schuster of Canada, 1973). Mention should be made here of the two historical studies that survey supernatural and parapsychological occurrences in this country: R.S. Lambert's *Exploring the Supernatural: The Weird in Canadian Folklore* (Toronto: McClelland & Stewart, 1955) and A.R.G. Owen's *Psychic Mysteries of Canada: Discoveries from the Maritime Provinces and Beyond* (New York: Harper & Row, 1975).

Above all, I am pleased to draw attention to the continued presence of my own "familiar spirit" in haunted Toronto, my wife, Ruth Colombo.

South

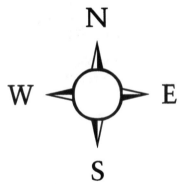

The Gibraltar Point Lighthouse Ghost

Is our oldest historical landmark the haunt of our oldest historical ghost? Let a lighthouse shed some light on the matter!

Site: Gibraltar Point Lighthouse

Locale: Gibraltar Point, on the spit of Ward's Island, one of the Toronto Islands

Period: 1815 to the present

Sources: Jane Widerman, "The Haunting of Toronto," *The Toronto Star's City Magazine*, 29 October 1978

Sally Gibson, *More than an Island* (Toronto: Irwin, 1984)

Sally Gibson, "Visiting John Paul's Ghost," *Canadian Heritage*, October-November 1987

Additional information supplied by Diane Beasley, historian, Marine Museum, 27 June 1994

Further information supplied by Michael Moir, archivist, Toronto Harbour Commissioners, 15 July 1994

Gibraltar Point Lighthouse is the oldest historical landmark in Toronto that still stands on its original site. For many years the lighthouse was the first sight to greet those settlers and travellers to York and Toronto who arrived by sea. It overlooks Lake Ontario but no longer functions as a beacon. It is owned by the Municipality of Metropolitan Toronto and is maintained by the Metro Parks Department for architectural as well as historical reasons.

Governor John Graves Simcoe issued orders to establish a military works at "the Point" in 1796. The Point was once a peninsula of the mainland but today is an extension of Ward's Island in Toronto Harbour. Initial construction of the lighthouse to seventy feet took place in 1806-09, and twelve additional feet were added in 1832.

It is widely held that the lighthouse is haunted by the ghost of its first keeper, a morose individual named John Paul Rademüller who resided in the shadow of the tower in a pioneer cabin built by soldiers from Fort York. The cabin has long since disappeared. Rademüller was appointed keeper of the light on 24 July 1809.

The story goes that on the dark and stormy night of 2 January 1815, the keeper's repose was disturbed by two carousing guards from nearby Fort York. John Henry and John Blowman demanded that Rademüller share with them a keg of his homebrewed beer. He refused and fled, climbing the lighthouse's spiral staircase. They climbed up after him and catching hold of him on the top-deck they hit him on the head with a rock and heaved the unconscious body over the side to his death. To hide their villainy, they chopped up the body and buried its parts here and there on the grounds. Henry and Blowman were arrested, imprisoned, indicted, then acquitted of the crime on 31 March 1815.

In 1893 some bones were unearthed by George Durnan, a later keeper of the light. They have never been proved to be Rademüller's, and there is some evidence that the area had been used as a burial site by aboriginal peoples. Durnan maintained that on cold nights he could hear the sounds of a man moaning, and that on misty nights he could see Rademüller's spectre seeking its lost limbs. Later visitors to the lighthouse have alleged that they have seen the ghostly keeper ascend and descend the spiral staircase in order to light the lamp on dark and stormy nights.

In her account of the lighthouse, Sally Gibson noted that in 1984 two "ghostbusters" or psychics visited the Gibraltar Point Lighthouse and essentially confirmed the truth of the oft-told tale.

Gibraltar Point Lighthouse guided many a ship's captain in and out of Toronto Harbour. It was erected in 1806-9 and has been said to be haunted by the ghost of its former keeper since his tragic death in 1815. In this photograph it looks today much as it must have looked in the 1830s.

[Annabelle Cooper]

The Haunting of Historic Fort York

Will "spectral sentries" stalk the barracks of Historic Fort York until the Yankee threat is no more? Or do the ghosts of Yankee soldiers who were killed attacking the British fort linger among its battlements?

Site: Historic Fort York

Locale: Garrison Road, off Fleet Street, between Bathurst Street and Strachan Avenue

Hours: Mid-May to September, Tuesday to Sunday, 9:30 a.m. to 5:00 p.m. October to Mid-May, Tuesday to Friday, 9:30 a.m to 4:00 p.m.; weekends, 10:00 a.m. to 5:00 p.m. Phone (416) 392-6907

Period: War of 1812

Sources: Wendy Herman, "Ghost Town Toronto," *The Toronto Star*, 27 April 1980

John Robert Colombo, *Mysterious Canada* (Toronto: *Doubleday Canada*, 1988)

Carl Benn, *Historic Fort York, 1793-1993* (Toronto: *Natural Heritage*, 1993)

Interview with Robin Shepherd, high-school principal and former guide at Fort York, 26 June 1994

Additional information supplied by Carl Benn, historian at Fort York, 27 June 1994

Historic Fort York, one of the city's major tourist attractions, has been open as an historic site since 1934. It has been administered by the Toronto Historical Board since the THB was established in 1960. The fort is a restoration of the original buildings and defences that survived into modern times. It is a national architectural treasure as well as the birthplace of Toronto and an important battlefield and archaeological site. It recalls the small palisaded garrison that was erected by the Queen's Rangers under Governor John Graves Simcoe at the entrance to Toronto Bay in 1793.

The fort saw action on three occasions during the War of 1812: 27 April 1813, 31 July 1813, and 6 August 1814. The Americans captured

Past Fort York's Centre Blockhouse York march a troop of "animators" who represent the eighth [King's] Regiment, circa 1812. This photograph was taken in 1979.
[Collection of the Toronto Historical Board, Toronto, Canada]

John Graves Simcoe served as Lieutenant-Governor of Upper Canada. He was also early Toronto's "man of mysteries." There is a ghost story associated with Simcoe that predates his arrival in York, now Toronto; once on these shores, he caused to be erected structures [notably Gibraltar Lighthouse and Fort York] that have enduring reputations as haunts. In the portrait reproduced here, he appears appropriately grave. The head-and-shoulders was painted from life in 1791 by Jean-Laurent Mosnier.
[Metropolitan Toronto Reference Library]

35

the fort the first two times and destroyed the barracks and defences during their brief occupations of York. The British began the rebuilding of Fort York, the fort we know today, in August 1813, and its defences were adequate to rebuff the Americans when they tried to enter the harbour in August 1814. "Fortifications and buildings were altered over subsequent years," noted historian Carl Benn. "Of special interest was the re-arming and upgrading of defences in 1838 during the Rebellion Crisis, and in 1862 as a result of Anglo-American tensions during the Civil War. Fort York's defences and guns were at their most impressive and its garrison its largest during the 1862-66 period."

To tour Historic Fort York is to hear the music of fife and drum, to imagine cannonades and the swirl of battle, to ponder acts of bravery and camaraderie. Gunpowder magazines, blockhouses, barracks, parade grounds, and officers' quarters give rise to tales and stories. Interpreters and visitors say they have observed spectral sentries in British uniform standing guard at entranceways, as well as ghostly soldiers in American uniform standing at attention at the base of the flagpole as the American flag is lowered. Maintenance personnel have said that on stormy nights they may hear the sound of stomping feet in the former sleeping quarters. On a number of occasions the sounds of little children, the pitter-patter of tiny feet, racing through the barracks have been described. This is not as farfetched as it might seem because in the early nineteenth century regular soldiers lived in the barracks with their wives; their children slept under the bunks.

Interpreters have complained that invisible hands have tried to push them off defensive walls and parapets. Robin Shepherd, now a high-school principal, worked in the fort's kitchen between 1977 and 1980 where she had a number of unusual experiences. "There are two doors that lead from the kitchen through the pantry to the officer's mess. There is no breeze there and the doors open in opposite directions. Yet one door would shut by itself, then the other, as if somebody was walking right through. There were two cats, called Mrs. Simcoe and Fred, and they reacted instantly to these disturbances. Their claws would come out and they would streak away. The fort was never empty. Some guides and maintenance people claim they watch full regiments at drill and witness flag lowering and raising ceremonies. I myself saw a soldier looking out the second-floor window of the big block house when I know there was no one there."

Carl Benn noted, "Although Fort York is a battlefield site and a logical place for hauntings, all the ghost stories about Fort York are inventions by young tour guides a generation or more ago. They developed these tales for the Girl Guide, Boy Scout, and school groups that stayed overnight at the fort on educational trips. Since then, we replaced those stories with the authentic songs and folktales that the soldiers and their families at Fort York knew. We did this in order to provide visitors with a more historically appropriate experience. Alas, none of these authentic stories has any reference to ghosts at Fort York."

Do British and American "forces" still occupy the old fort? Apparently old soldiers' tales never die.

The Spectral Horses of Clarence Square

Are the Colonel's spectral horses to be heard clopping along the street at night?

Site: Clarence Square

Locale: East side of Spadina Avenue, south of King Street West, opposite St. John's Park

Period: About 1814

Sources: Wendy Herman, "Ghost Town Toronto," *The Toronto Star*, 27 April 1980

Interview with Bette Shepherd, former ROM worker, 27 June 1994

Residents of the old houses on Clarence Square, off Spadina Avenue, have long reported hearing the sounds of a pair of horses clopping along the street late at night. When they look out their windows or step out onto their porches, they look around and see nothing.

According to journalist Wendy Herman, who accompanied Bette Shepherd on the city's first-ever "ghost walk" in 1980, "There are records of two horses being buried [here] around 1814 and their deaths were traumatic. They were shot by their owner Colonel Battersby when he didn't want to take them back to England."

The Second Garrison Burial Ground

Are the dead restless in St. John's Square with its tiny burial ground? Residents nearby seem to think that they might be ....

Site: Second Garrison Burial Ground

Locale: St. John's Square, Spadina Avenue, south of King Street West., opposite Clarence Square

Period: About 1814

Source: Wendy Herman, "Ghost Town Toronto," *The Toronto Star*, 27 April 1980

                  Interview with Bette Shepherd, former ROM worker, 27 June 1994

Over the decades residents of the houses located in the vicinity of the Second Garrison Burial Ground, which is part of St. John's Square off Wellington Street West, have reported hearing strange sounds from this cemetery. The sounds are said to be the cries of the British officers and men who died around the time of the War of 1812 whose remains rest here.

Metrosaurus

Did "a queer thing" some fifty feet in length laze along the shore of Lake Ontario and startle Torontonians? Does the city have its very own ... Metrosaurus?

Sites::   "Garrison common," "Exhibition wharf"

Locale: Shore of Lake Ontario south of Exhibition Place, possibly the present site of Ontario Place

Period: 21 August 1882

Source: Anonymous, "A Marine Monster," *The Daily Mail* (Toronto), 22 August 1882

Sea serpents are associated with the coastal waters of the Atlantic and the Pacific. Lake monsters are spotted in lakes and rivers everywhere else in the country. Although Toronto is spread for dozens of miles along the north shore of Lake Ontario, sightings of lake monsters are few and far between. Here is a verbatim description of the city's very own creature of the deep, its Metrosaurus, from the columns of a leading newspaper of the day.

A Marine Monster

Which Some of the Markers Saw at the Ranges Yesterday
Another Edition of the Sea Serpent

The sea serpent is not dead by any means, and the only thing to be wondered at (apart from its existence) now is that it is able to appear at widely separated points within comparatively short intervals. A few months ago it was seen (!) in the Indian ocean by a jovial party of pleasure seekers. It next turned up in the Mediterranean, but was frightened off by the prospect of a collision with one of the ironclads. It was again heard of in a creek in the vicinity of Hog[g]'s Hollow, and yesterday morning turned up in the lake in the neighbourhood of the Garrison common. The monster appears to have the power of altering its size to suit circumstances also. Sometimes if any faith is to be placed in the veracity of those who profess to have seen it — it is of brobdingnagian proportions. The locality also seems to have an effect on its size. In the Mediterranean and other warm latitudes it swells out, while further north it dwindles down from the size of an ordinary saw-log to a ship's hawser. This may be attributed to the witnesses, as the tropical heat of low latitudes has such a magnifying effect on some brains that they see everything "double." Further north this is not so apparent, and hence the size of the monster diminishes.

METROSAURAS

Sightings of a "marine monster" in Lake Ontario appeared in newspapers in August 1882 and gave many a Torontonian pause to wonder. Dubbed "Metrosaurus," the creature is given a light-hearted look by artist and illustrator Isaac Bickerstaff.

Yesterday morning was cool, and perhaps this was the reason why some of the workmen engaged at the targets on the Garrison ranges say the serpent they saw was not more than fifty feet long, and the size of a man's body. The story as told by one of them is in substance as follows: — Between eight and nine o'clock, while placing the targets in position on No. 1 range, a boy rushed up saying that there was a queer thing floating near the shore. Some of the men were curious enough to leave their work and hasten down to the shore. There sure enough was a large, blueish-grey mass floating lazily near shore. It had every appearance of being asleep, as its body yielded to every ripple. Part was submerged, but the upper portion of the head floated just above the water. That part which was visible was covered with short stiff bristles in front, which increased in length towards the sides, and extended for a distance of about ten feet on each side. The back, or at least that portion of it which appeared above the water, was lighter-coloured than the head. A good view was had of the monster for upwards of three minutes, when suddenly raising its head out of the water, it gave a swish with its tail and started directly south in the direction of one of the steamers. Its head, as it raised it above the water, was very much like that of an eel, with the exception of the long trailing hair or whiskers. Its eyes were small, and he thought he heard it give a short, sharp bark. A line of foam marked its progress out into the lake for about half a mile, when, turning sharp around, it dashed towards the Exhibition wharf, and again out into the lake, where they soon lost sight of it.

The men did not appear at all anxious to speak of the matter, as they feared their veracity would be questioned. As it is, their story is given for what it is worth, but surely the word of three men who saw it is worth that of thirty who did not see it.

The Demise of Golden Eagle

The demise of Golden Eagle sounded the death-knell of the traditional beliefs of the Mississauga band of the Ojibwa Indians. Henceforth, symbolically at least, Christian beliefs and practices would replace the traditional shamanistic beliefs and practices.

Site: Mississauga Indian encampment

Locale: The flats of the Credit River, Mississauga

Period: War of 1812

Sources: Peter Jones, *Life and Journals of Kah-ke-wa-quo-na-by (Rev. Peter Jones, Wesleyan Missionary)* (Toronto: A. Green, 1860)

Peter Jones, *History of the Ojebway Indians; With Especial Reference to Their Conversion to Christianity* (London: A.W. Bennett, 1861; Freeport, N.Y.: Books for Libraries Press, 1970)

Donald B. Smith, *Sacred Feathers: The Reverend Peter Jones (Kahkewaquonaby) and the Mississauga Indians* (Toronto: University of Toronto Press, 1987)

A tragic event of symbolic importance took place on the flats of the Credit River at the time of the War of 1812. The flats were the traditional home of the Mississauga band of the Ojibwa. Loyalists and other immigrants moving into the area forced the Indian band to resettle. By 1828 they were living near the mouth of the Credit River, and by 1847 they were relocated on the Grand River Reserve outside Brantford.

The tragic event was witnessed by a young man named Peter Jones (1802-1856). Kahkewaquonaby (or Sacred Feathers) was his native name, and he was the son of a white surveyor and a Mississauga woman. He worked as a farmer and he owned a log house in the vicinity of the flats of the Credit River. He was wrestling with the competing claims of the Old Ways and the new Christian ways. In 1823, Christianity won and Peter Jones became The Reverend Peter Jones, his people's first Wesleyan missionary.

The factor that led to his conversion was the fate of Golden Eagle (or Quinipeno), the band's elderly chief and religious leader. Seeking guidance during the War of 1812, Golden Eagle fasted and prayed. He dreamed that he had acquired special powers against bullets. To prove his invincibility, he instructed a warrior to fire at him when given the signal. He picked up a tin kettle and walked a short distance away, then turned and held the kettle before his face to catch the bullet.

The flow from polytheism to monotheism, from Shamanism to Christianity, for good or ill, may be illustrated in the life and work of Kahkewaquonaby. The Ojibwa brave became the first native Methodist missionary and achieved fame and influence as the Reverend Peter Jones. He is shown here in an etching based on a photographic portrait reproduced in Jones's posthumously published *Life and Journals* [1860].
[Metropolitan Toronto Reference Library]

As the biographer Donald B. Smith wrote: "His followers knew the power of his dreams. Had he not cured the sick? Predicted the weather? Indicated where game might be found in times of scarcity? As instructed, the marksman fired. Golden Eagle fell. To the band's horror when they examined his lifeless body, they found that the bullet had killed him on the spot."

Golden Eagle's death symbolized for the Mississauga band the passing of the Old Ways so rooted in shamanism.

Central

West of Yonge Street

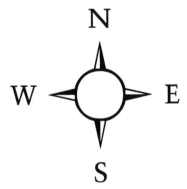

Casa Loma

Here is a frequently asked question: "Is Casa Loma haunted?" The truthful answer is as follows: "Canada's largest castle lacks a ghost to call its own."

Site: Casa Loma

Locale: 1 Austin Terrace, Spadina Road and Davenport Road

Period: Built in 1911-14

Operator: Kiwanis Club of Casa Loma. Phone (416) 923-1171

Hours: 10:00 a.m. to 4:00 p.m., seven days a week

Source: Correspondence with Karen O'Grady, sales and promotions manager, Casa Loma, 27 June 1994

            Sheldon Oberman, *The White Stone in the Castle Wall* (Montreal: Tundra Books, 1995)

This architectural folly of a castle, designed by E.J. Lennox, was erected by the financier Sir Henry Pellatt in 1911-14 who hoped to entertain royalty in its spacious rooms. He never did. Northrop Frye described its twin towers, done in different architectural styles, as seventeenth-century Scotch baronial and 20th-Century Fox.

Not one ghost is said to haunt Casa Loma, despite such splendid structural and architectural features as ninety-eight rooms, a library for ten thousand volumes, secret passageways, and the eight-hundred-foot tunnel that passes under the street to the towered stables, even though for ten years the building was unoccupied, empty, and abandoned (except for a flock of bats). Since 1937 it has been administered as a tourist attraction by the Kiwanis Club of Casa Loma.

Spooks have steered clear of Casa Loma, and so have fiction writers. Not one writer has used the castle as the setting for an adult mystery novel or a ghost story. The poet Earle Birney's remark "It's by our lack of ghosts we're haunted" certainly applies to Casa Loma.

No mysteries may be inspired by Casa Loma, but there is much lore. It is said that when the wall around the castle was being built, Sir Henry Pellatt offered Torontonians one dollar a boulder, as long as they were dun-coloured. Children's story author Sheldon Oberman tells the story of the single white stone in the half-mile-long wall.

Is Casa Loma the only castle in the world without its resident spook? It should have one or more, because it boasts secret passageways and a subterranean tunnel. This vintage photography shows the architectural "folly" almost complete in 1913, with carter and stonemasons in the foreground.

[Kiwanis Club, Casa Loma]

The rumour during the Second World War was that Pope Pius XII was to establish the Vatican at Casa Loma for the duration of the war. In the same vein, King George VI was to move Buckingham Palace to the Château Frontenac in Quebec City, and the incarcerated Nazi leader Rudolf Hess was to occupy an entire wing of Fort Henry in Kingston.

The Toronto Theosophical Society

Here you will find ghosts and spirits, spirit-guides and Himalayan Masters ...
but you will find them — rather like genii in bottles — in books about the
occult, the miraculous, the spiritual, the supernatural, and the paranormal!

Site: The Toronto Theosophical Society

Locale: 109 Dupont Street, east of Davenport Road

Hours: For scheduled lectures and library hours, phone (416) 922-
5571

Period: From 1920 to the present

Sources: John Robert Colombo, *Canadian Literary Landmarks*
(Toronto: Hounslow Press, 1984)

John Robert Colombo, *Mysterious Canada* (Toronto:
Doubleday Canada, 1988)

Correspondence, Ted Davy, researcher, 26 July 1994

The Theosophical Society is an international organization with local
lodges that was founded in New York City in 1875. One its principal aims
has been "to investigate unexplained laws of nature and the powers latent
in man." Helena Petrovna Blavatsky (1831-1891), the leading founder,
was a Russian-born adventurer, occultist, and writer. Her tomes include
The Secret Doctrine (1888), the seemingly exhaustless source of much New
Age thought.

The charter that established the Theosophical Society of Toronto was
signed by Madame Blavatsky on 25 February 1891, and names five once-
prominent Torontonians, including newspaperman and mystic Albert E.S.
Smythe (father of sportsman Conn Smythe) and Algernon Blackwood, a
young remittance man from England. After briefly serving as
Corresponding Secretary, Blackwood returned to England where he began
to write supernatural fiction. From the first he was recognized as a master
teller of tales of terror and horror. *The Lost Valley and Other Stories* (1914)
contains "The Wendigo," his masterful, oft-reprinted story about the
Algonkian spirit of cannibalism.

The Toronto Theosophical Society is the country's largest lodge. From
1921 to 1967, it occupied a three-storey brick residence at 52 Isabella

Street, west of Jarvis Street. Here and at earlier locations, some of the country's leading scientists (Frederick Banting), spiritualists (Albert Durrant Watson), suffragettes (Emily Stowe), socialists (Phillips Thompson), editors (William Arthur Deacon), directors (Roy Mitchell), artists (Lawren Harris), and poets (Wilson MacDonald) met to discuss comparative religion, philosophy, science, universal brotherhood, Eastern religions, karma, reincarnation, revenants, astral travel, and wisdom traditions. The TS sponsored public addresses by visiting Theosophists, notably Annie Besant, the suffragette leader who succeeded Madame Blavatsky as world leader.

This three-storey house on Dupont Street is the home of the Toronto Theosophical Society, chartered in 1891. Members and visitors will find here the city's most impressive collection of books on occult subject and esoteric studies.

[Josh Goldhar]

In 1967, the TS moved from its house on Isabella Street into a old Baptist church (now part of an apartment complex) at 12 Macpherson Avenue, west of Yonge Street. In 1988 the TS relocated to its present quarters in a row house at 109 Dupont Street. Portraits of Madame Blavatsky and other Theosophical leaders hang from the walls; bookshelves are packed with over five thousand volumes of occult interest, including such intriguingly titled books as *A New Model of the Universe, Cosmic Consciousness, Dawn behind the Dawn, Esoteric Buddhism, Human Personality and the Survival of Bodily Death, In Search of Secret India, The Mahatma Letters, The Occult World, Phantasms of the Living, The Phenomenon of Astral Projection, The Third Eye, You Cannot Die,* etc.

In the pages of these books, if not elsewhere in Toronto, the diligent reader will encounter a ghost or spirit or two!

The Ghosts of the Modelling Agency

It seemed that the modelling school and agency was haunted by two ghosts who displayed great concern about their surroundings.

Site: The old Judy Welch Modelling School and Agency, now a private residence and office

Locale: 21 Roxborough Street West, off Yonge Street, north of Davenport Road

Period: 1970s and 1980s

Sources: Jane Widerman, "The Haunting of Toronto," *The Toronto Star's City Magazine*, 29 October 1978

Stefan Scaini, "Buildings that Hold the Souls of the Dead," *The Toronto Star*, 14 January 1984

When the name Judy Welsh is mentioned, visions of wonderful, high-fashion models come to mind, not visions of ghosts.

Today there is a wreath on the door of the private residence on Roxborough Drive, once the offices of the Judy Welch Modelling School, where years ago poltergeist-like disturbance were reported.

[Josh Goldhar]

Judy Welsh, a model turned business woman, established her own agency, naming it the Judy Welsh Modelling School and Agency and later the Judy Welch Model Agency. In 1974, she acquired an elegant, older house at 21 Roxborough Street West, which was to serve as her base of operations. When she moved in, she found that the house had been empty for over a year. Journalist Stefan Scaini continues the story:

> Before she bought the place, people had told her it was haunted. The owners had some trouble with the house and made a point of warning her. They complained of doors that opened or closed themselves, chills and drafts that plagued parts of the house and how pets would act strangely in certain rooms.
>
> Shortly after she moved in, strange things began to happen. Guests would feel peculiar chills in the living room, even though the fireplace was burning brightly. Welch's cats acted nervously in certain parts of the house, and a Tiffany lamp in the parlour would unplug itself.
>
> Welch decided to organize a séance to see if there really was something supernatural going on in the house. Through it, she learned that it did, indeed, have ghosts — two of them, the couple that originally owned the house.
>
> According to the medium, they were unhappy with the previous residents but approved of Welch. They would take good care of her if she took care of their house. And it seems they did. Welch later found out that the wall socket into which she was daily plugging the Tiffany lamp was faulty and could have caused a fire.

There are no further reports of disturbances. Business flourished for close to two decades; then, in 1994, the Judy Welsh Model Agency went out of business. One wonders what the new occupants make of it all.

The Ghost on the Stairs

Did the spirit of Carrie linger in the townhouse and arrange for the delivery of flowers ?

Site: 35 Bishop Street

Locale: Off Davenport Road, north of Bay Street

Period: 1985

Sources: Interview with Andrea Reynolds, 29 July 1995

Additional information supplied by Riki Turofsky, 11 August 1995

Shelley Klinck was the lively host of 640 AM Radio's late-night talk show *Sex, Lives, and Audiotape*. One evening she was kind enough to ask me to be a guest on her show to discuss one of my favourite subjects — ghost stories. As it happened, one of the listeners that evening was Andrea Reynolds, who is a writer and the author of *No Surprises, No More Empty*

There was a "For Sale" sign on the lawn in front of this townhouse on Bishop Street when this photograph was taken in May 1995. When she lived here, writer and author Andrea Reynolds felt the lingering presence of a young women. The previous occupants were opera singer Riki Turofsky and her lovely daughter Carrie, who died tragically in her late teens.

[Andrea Reynolds; Riki Turofsky]

Relationships, and *Let's Do Something Besides Dinner and a Movie.* She is also the publisher of *The Reynolds Report on Romance,* a newsletter designed "to enhance your love life and dating life."

I did not know Andrea, but she was so excited by the program and the topic that evening that she phoned me and asked me if I would be interested in reading an account of a real-life haunting that had occurred to her. I immediately agreed, so she sent me the short manuscript called "The Ghost on the Stairs," the one printed here. Upon reading it, I was startled to realize that not only did I know two of the principals involved in the haunting, but I had also been inside the house in question, the guest one memorable evening of Riki Turofsky and Robert Sunter.

Riki, a popular and appealing opera singer who was born in Toronto and raised in the Yukon, has a career that ranges from performing, recording, and producing to working as an arts volunteer. I had also met her daughter Carrie who died at such a young age in 1985. Before long I also met Andrea, and with the agreement of Riki and Andrea, and thanks to Shelley, here is the true story of "the ghost on the stairs."

> I knew of Riki Turofsky only because her former agent had once asked to represent me. I knew nothing more about her other than she was a very pretty opera singer. I didn't know it was her former home I was walking into, in 1985.

I had recently left my husband and was living in a nice apartment at Yonge and Sheppard. I didn't know what made me buy a *Toronto Star* and look through the rental ads. One ad caught my eye: a three-bedroom, two-bathroom, historic row house in Yorkville. A little pricey perhaps, but I was intrigued.

When I walked into the house for the first time, preceded by the new owner's husband, I found myself saying, "Do you know there's a spirit in the house?" He flinched, but said nothing. I loved the house and wanted to move in right away. But the house was being renovated and some of the former owner's possessions still needed to be removed.

Moving in was delayed because the new owner, an interior designer who was overseeing the work, fell down the stairs and shattered her ankle.

Finally, in October 1985, I moved in. For the first two weeks I was awakened or kept awake nightly by the sound of someone running up and down the stairs outside my bedroom. Not walking, *running*. I stood at the top of the stairs listening to the footsteps approach me, but nobody was there.

I can't describe the fright I experienced, but at the same time I had the sense that there was nothing to fear. Having lived in three other places in which I felt the presence of a spirit, I knew to say prayers of protection ... out loud.

I sensed this was a troubled spirit, and that it wouldn't leave until something that had been left undone was completed. I promised the spirit I would try to figure out what it was and make it right. I wanted it to find peace and move on to where it belonged ... wherever that might be. I also wanted some sleep.

As I met my new neighbours, I learned that Riki Turofsky had lived in the house and Riki's daughter Carrie (I knew her name because she left behind a pair of black rubber boots with her name in each boot) had died — not in the house, but in the hospital — at the age of nineteen. It had been only a year or two since her death. Riki had sold the house and moved to Vancouver for a year.

As I cleaned out the house, keeping some things and throwing out others I couldn't use, I found, behind the washing machine in the basement, a sheaf of newspaper columns written by Riki's former husband, Carrie's stepfather. I found his name listed in the Toronto telephone book and called him to ask if he wanted the clippings. When he came over to pick them up we had a long chat about Carrie, her death, and her presence in the house. The columns had meant a lot to him, but he had figured they were lost forever. He was grateful to have them back and to be able to talk about the loss of his stepdaughter.

Looking back, I believe Carrie wanted me to make contact with both of her parents, perhaps to return significant items and give them peace of mind.

Months later, a beautiful flower arrangement arrived for Riki, who had since fallen in love and returned to Toronto. I tried to get the delivery man to take them to her new address, but he refused and I couldn't reach Riki by telephone. I enjoyed the flowers' beauty and fragrance for almost two weeks.

Eventually I met Riki at a party at the home of a mutual friend. Her first words to me were, "So, you've met my daughter." It was the only occasion we talked, but it was all we needed.

Riki told me it was just like Carrie to run up and down the stairs. She used to run everywhere; she never walked. Riki, in an effort to handle her grief, had sought advice from a close friend who was blind who had been having vivid dreams about Carrie. In her dreams, Carrie was running up and down the stairs of the house, frantically searching for her *chai* medal that she wanted her mother to have. I told Riki I had looked in every closet, drawer, and cupboard, and never came across it.

She also told me that the new owner had treated her unfairly and took advantage of Riki's financial need in her time of grief by pushing down the price to a ridiculously low figure. When I relayed the information that the woman had fallen down the stairs, we were struck by the same thought at the same moment: Carrie had sought revenge by pushing her down the stairs.

As Riki and I ended our conversation, she turned back to me and said, "Carrie wanted you to have those flowers ... to say thank you."

I had always wanted a pair of gum boots. Ten years later, I still have Carrie Doran's black rubber boots.

I moved out in May 1987. In October 1994, the house was for sale again.

The Walmer Road Ghost

Was the suicide of the former tenant being replayed before the new tenant's eyes?

Site: Private residence

Locale: 121 Walmer Road, south of Dupont Street.

Period: 1960s

Sources: Eileen Sonin, *ESPecially Ghosts* (Toronto: Clarke, Irwin and Company, 1970)

             Jane Widerman, "The Haunting of Toronto," *The Toronto Star's City Magazine,* 29 October 1978

It is daytime, yet somebody or something has turned on the porch light of this three-storey, brick house at 121 Walmer Road. Is the kitchen still haunted by the ghost of a man accompanied by his faithful cocker spaniel?

[Josh Goldhar]

The ghosts of a man and his little cocker spaniel haunted the kitchen, bedroom, and living-room of this rambling, turn-of-the-century, three-storey house.

It has new owners now, but in the 1960s the tenant was Ronald Secker, manager of the recording company Hallmark Studios, who lived in the house for a year before he had his first experience with its human and animal ghosts. At 3:00 a.m., he woke with a start. The light was on in the kitchen and he saw a dog running toward him. The dog put his paws up on the bed. As journalist Jane Widerman wrote, "The air was icy and clammy, as though a cloud of cold air had moved into the bedroom. Next Secker saw a man in the kitchen. When he left his bedroom to close the refrigerator door, Secker told the man and dog to leave. The forms went downstairs and vanished through the wall. At the same time, the coldness disappeared."

Two weeks later the ghosts returned, again at 3:00 a.m. This time it was more frightening to Secker. "The ghost was holding a knife over his head, while the dog ran around in circles. The man lowered the knife and stabbed himself, as the dog continued circling him. Then both evanesced, and the room returned to its original temperature."

The next morning Secker phoned the realtor of the property and discovered that a former tenant, a man with a small cocker spaniel, had stabbed himself in that room.

The Ghost of the Recording Studio

*Did two ghostly women haunt the second floor of the old house in Yorkville?
Or was there a poltergeist in the basement?*

Site: Formerly the Ben McPeek Recording Studio

Locale: Private residence, 131 Hazelton Lane, Yorkville

Period: 1969-82

Sources: Jane Wilderman, "The Haunting of Toronto," *The Toronto Star's City Magazine*, 29 October 1978

Kathleen Kenna, "Something Weird," *The Toronto Star*, 26 September 1983

Stefan Scaini, "Buildings that Hold the Souls of the Dead," *The Toronto Star*, 14 January 1984

The late Ben McPeek had a flair when it came to composing sprightly musical jingles and commercials for radio and television. He had a talent for "serious" music as well; one of his symphonic compositions is the well-regarded "Paul Bunyan Suite."

In 1969, the composer bought the old house at 131 Hazelton Lane and converted the basement into a recording studio, using the rest of the two-storey house for offices. Apparently the old house was the home of a resident spirit which was seen many times. Clients who came to the studio described seeing an old woman in a long, flowing dress staring down on them from the second-storey window. There was no old woman on the second floor or anywhere else in the building. Yet the house was the home during World War II of not one but two women. They were sisters whose husbands were serving overseas. The husbands did not return. Thereafter, one or the other of the sisters watches out the window, keeping vigil.

Ben McPeek's two sons Ben Jr. and Jerome opened the downstairs studio under the name Captain Audio. Ben Jr. and Jerome encountered poltergeist activity on one occasion. They said they were driven out of the house during a late-night studio session when they saw record albums suddenly flipping around on their shelves, and they heard a persistent scratching sound at the door. The house was renovated in the summer of 1982 and since then there have been no new reports of poltergeists or ghostly spinsters.

The Haunted Mynah Bird

Was it a male or a female spirit that objected to the "adult movies" being shown in the old artist's studio?

Site: The old Mynah Bird Coffee House

Locale: Site now occupied by a new commercial building, 144 Yorkville Avenue, at Hazelton Avenue.

Period: 1960s

Sources: Hans Holzer, "The Haunted Mynah Bird, Toronto," *Hans Holzer's Haunted Houses: A Pictorial Register of the World's Most Interesting Ghost Houses* (New York: Crown Publishers, Inc., 1971)

Hans Holzer, "The Haunted Nightclub of Toronto," *Where the Ghosts Are: Favourite Haunted Houses in America and the British Isles* (West Nyack, N.Y.: Parker Publishing Company, 1984)

Long gone are the hippies who used to haunt Yorkville, replaced by yuppies. Long gone is the Mynah Bird Coffee House in Yorkville, replaced by a new commercial building. Where have all the hippies gone? Where is the ghost of the Mynah Bird?

A once-popular coffee house, the Mynah Bird had quarters in a narrow house with two storeys and a low attic at 144 Yorkville Avenue. It opened as a coffee house with a small dance floor, but under owner-manager Colin Kerr it found its true *métier* as a *venue* for (to quote a sign on the side of the building in the 1960s) "Beautiful Topless Girls and Nude Films Never Before Seen in Any Club or Theatre in Canada."

Hans Holzer, the New York-based psychical researcher, took an interest in the place when it acquired a minor reputation as a haunt. He explained, "The psychic goings-on started when Kerr changed the club's policy from that of a straight dancing club to the topless entertainment. Possibly the ghosts objected. Lights would go on and off at various times — mostly off, as if someone were trying to put a halt to the proceedings."

The female performers, Kerr found, objected to remaining alone in the upstairs room. They complained of eerie presences and poltergeist-like effects. Musical instruments moved of their own accord. "A male presence spoke ... in the area where the 'adult movies' were being shown at the time. Chairs were thrown all over the place in the upstairs room where there had been no one about."

Upon inquiry, Kerr learned that the upstairs rooms, where the "adult movies" were shown, had earlier been used by an artist for his studio. "One of the girl dancers felt a man standing close to her, whom she could not see — yet she knew he was angry." Another performer "described the entity as an old man with gray hair and a beard. But there may also be a woman ghost on the premises, judging from the smell of perfume that has been observed at times."

Did the hauntings deter the patrons. Not at all, although, as Holzer noted, "They had come to see bodies, not spirits."

Star Centre

The Star Centre may not be haunted by ghosts, but its considerable collection of books about the supernatural and the paranormal makes it a place that will interest all ghosthunters, ghostbusters, and other readers of books about ghosts both factual and fictional!

Site: Star Centre

Address: 87 St. Nicholas Street, Star Centre, P.O. Box 5265, Station A, Toronto M5W 1N5; phone (416) 923-STAR

Locale: South of intersection of St. Nicholas Street and Charles Street, one block west of Yonge Street.

Hours: Centre hours: Monday to Friday, 12:30 to 5:00; library hours: first Sunday of each month, 3:00 to 5:00; or by appointment

Source: John Robert Colombo, *Mysterious Canada* (Toronto: Doubleday Canada, 1988)

Interview with Robin Armstrong, director, Star Centre, 5 July 1994

Whoever enjoys ghosthunting will revel in reading about ghosts at the Star Centre.

The Star Centre is the headquarters of the astrologer Robin Armstrong. Born in Montreal, an alumnus of St. George Williams University, Armstrong began studying astrology in 1970. Now a professional astrologer who teaches the theory and practice of astrology and casts horoscopes with the assistance of a computer, he works out of the Centre which contains the only public astrology library in the world.

The reference library grew out of Armstrong's personal collection of books on astrology, but it is by no means limited to that subject. There are some twelve thousand books and periodicals on all aspects of the supernatural and the paranormal, including rare and out-of-print tomes about ghostbusting, psychical research, parapsychology, channelling, etc. Readers will find everything from Harry Price's books on Borley Rectory ("the most haunted house in England") to popular novels like *The Exorcist* and *The Amityville Horror.*

Mysteries of the Museum

Does the ghost of its first curator roam the halls of the Royal Ontario Museum by night?

Site:　　　The Royal Ontario Museum

Locale:　　100 Queen's Park, southwest corner of the intersection of University Avenue and Bloor Street West

Hours:　　Summer hours from Victoria Day to Labour Day: Monday to Saturday, 10:00 a.m. to 6:00 p.m.; Tuesday, 10:00 a.m. to 8:00 p.m.; Sunday, 11:00 a.m. to 6:00 p.m. Winter hours from Labour Day to Victoria Day: Same hours, except closed Monday. Closed Christmas Day and New Year's Day. Phone (416) 586-8000

Period:　　1957-1980

Sources:　Wendy Herman, "Ghost Town Toronto," *The Toronto Star*, 27 April 1980.

　　　　　　Interview with Bette Shepherd, former ROM worker, 27 June 1994

The main entrance to the Royal Ontario Museum leads to a world of mysteries and treasures. Does the ghost of ROM's founder and first curator stalk the Bishop White Gallery, watching over the safety of its Buddhist sculptures and three Chinese wall paintings which date from A.D. 1300?

[Royal Ontario Museum]

There are six million or so artifacts in the Royal Ontario Museum. Some of them are arresting; others are awe-inspiring. Each one has a story to tell ... from the time of the dinosaurs through the dynasties of Ancient Egypt and China to modern times ... mementos of long-dead civilizations and of the passage of time. One of the ironies of history is that the ROM was formally founded on 14 April 1912, the day the *Titanic* sank!

Bette Shepherd, a seventh-generation Canadian and ROM volunteer, led the city's first reported "ghost walk" on 23 April 1980. It was a one-time affair but a notable one. She took visitors by bus and on foot to thirteen said-to-be-haunted sites in the city. One visitor was the journalist Wendy Herman who described the tour for readers of *The Toronto Star.*

The walk began with a saunter through the museum itself. ROM's McLaughlin Planetarium is a well-equipped "theatre of the stars," and apparently it has its resident spirit. No sooner had the Planetarium opened than volunteer guides who were in charge of school tours reported that, day after day, they saw the same little girl seated in the auditorium. She was about eight years old. She wore a long white dress and had long blonde hair in ringlets. There was a sad, pathetic expression on her face. Noticeably younger than the school children on tour, she seemed lost among the seats and the stars. She was even sighted when the dome-room was otherwise empty on a number of occasions between 1975 and 1980. It is said that her name was Celeste. The domed theatre was closed as an economy-saving measure on 5 November 1995. Where that leaves Celeste is not certain.

Charles Trick Currelly served as first Director of the Royal Ontario Museum of Archaeology. He appears in a heavy winter overcoat in this photograph taken in 1946 on the campus of Victoria College, University of Toronto.

[Royal Ontario Museum]

In the ROM's exhibition halls and corridors, guards at night have reported seeing a gentleman gowned in a nightshirt. It has been suggested that the figure is the ghost of C.T. Currelly, the ROM's energetic founder. Currelly was appointed the ROM's first curator in 1907 and retired as its first director in 1946. He worked so late in his office that he often spent the night in the museum. He died in 1957 at the age of eighty-two but he cannot bear to leave the institution he founded. He is seen in the Bishop White Gallery which displays the priceless East Asiatic Collection of bronzes and ceramics that were collected in China by William Charles White, first Bishop of Honan from 1909 to 1934, who then became keeper of the East Asiatic Collection. Currelly was responsible for the collection coming to the ROM, and some staff members, though scoffing at ghosts and spirits, report strange disturbances in this gallery.

Currelly left his imprint on the outside of the building. He devised the pair of noble inscriptions that flank its main entrance: THE RECORD OF NATURE THROUGH COUNTLESS AGES ... and THE ARTS OF MAN THROUGH ALL THE YEARS.

The Four Ghosts of Queen's Park

Are the stairways, hallways, corridors, and tunnels of Queen's Park haunted by the Old Soldier, the White Lady, the Maiden, and the Hanging Women? If so, our legislators should take note!

Site: Queen's Park

Locale: Ontario Legislative Building, Queen's Park Crescent

Hours: Tours may be arranged between 9:00 a.m. and 4:00 p.m. seven days a week between Victoria Day and Labour Day, five days a week between Labour Day and Victoria Day. Phone (416) 325-7500

Period: 1893 to the present

Sources: Legislative Library, *Grandeur, Ghosts and Gargoyles: The Entertaining History of Ontario's Parliament Buildings* (Ontario Legislative Library, c. 1980)

Claire Hoy, *Bill Davis: A Biography* (Toronto: Methuen, 1985)

Queen's Park certainly looks as if it should be haunted. There are creepy quarters throughout this pink sandstone building which was designed in the Richardson Romanesque style. Stories about its ghostly inhabitants

Queen's Park has served as the seat of the Ontario Legislature since 1893, when it was erected on the site of an old lunatic asylum. Its spectres which date from that period are said to haunt its stairways, corridors, and tunnel.

[Josh Goldhar]

were first collected by journalist Frank Yeigh, author of *Ontario's Parliament Buildings, or A Century of Legislation* (1893), and recalled in 1985 by investigative reporter Claire Hoy.

The Ontario Legislative Building was formally opened on 4 April 1893 in Queen's Park. It was not the first building on this choice property. King's College had once been here and then the University Hospital for the Insane which dated back to 1842. The asylum was demolished in 1886 to make way for the Legislative Building. In many ways the spirit of lunacy pervades the new building as it did the old structure.

Specific reports are that ghosts have been seen descending the Grand Staircase and standing in the darkened Legislative Chamber. They haunt the Lieutenant-Governor's Suite and the offices occupied by the Premier, the Speaker, and the Clerk of the House, as well as the dark storage areas in the basement, near the tunnel which passes beneath Queen's Park Crescent to connect the Legislative Building with the Whitney Block to the east.

Reports of the ghosts of Queen's Park are circumstantial at best, yet it is widely assumed that the building is haunted by a host of ghosts. One of the ghosts is male; three are female.

The male ghost is that of the Old Soldier who from time to time, but usually before state occasions, appears in full regimental dress. He frowns and scowls as he descends the Grand Staircase in the main hall. No one has yet been able to identify his regiment or determine the purpose of his appearances. There may be some truth to the adage that "old soldiers never die."

The three female ghosts are harpies. They are said to be the disconsolate spirits of inmates of the long-demolished asylum. They haunt the basement's corridors and tunnels. The White Lady, as her name implies, is a woman of indeterminate age. She wears a long, wispy white gown and has long, streaming hair. She appears to be grief-stricken.

The Maiden is modesty personified. A wimple conceals her hair. She wears an old-fashioned checkered dress and over the dress she wears a white apron. She holds the apron over her face as if to hide her features. Perhaps she is the ghost of a servant girl who was disgraced.

The Hanging Woman is a gruesome sight. The hag is seen on certain nights dangling from a hook in the wall of the long tunnel in the basement.

About the spirit or spirits of the Ontario Legislative Building, one observer noted, "When you visit Queen's Park, you are likely to observe — taking a leaf from Charles Dickens — the ghosts of New Democrats Past, Conservatives Present, and Liberals Future!"

Tales of the Christie Mansion

Does the spirit of the mistress of a former owner disconsolately stare out of the second-floor window of this mansion?

Site: Old Christie Mansion, now St. Joseph's College, a women's student residence

Locale: 90 Wellesley Street West, northeast corner of Queen's Park Crescent.

Period: Turn of the century to the present

Source: Interview with Danielle Urquhart, "the Ghost Lady," 22 June 1994

The old Christie Mansion has long been a magnet for odd and outlandish stories. The following stories are part history, part tradition, and part

This is the mansion built by William Christie of Christie Biscuits fame. It is maintained that from time to time a mad woman peers from one of its upper-storey windows. The building now serves as a residence for the women students of St. Michael's College.
[Josh Goldhar]

invention. In no way is retelling them here meant to call into disrepute the reputations or achievements of any people, companies, or organizations.

The Christie Mansion was built for his own use by William Christie, "the cookie man." Born in Scotland in 1829, he was nineteen years old when he settled in Toronto. Within five years he was part-owner of his own bakery. In 1868, he joined Alexander Brown to form Christie, Brown and Company to manufacture and sell biscuits and cookies across the country. He lived here with his wife and family when he was not engaged in business travel. He died in the master bedroom of this mansion in 1900. His son, Robert Christie, took over the cookie and biscuit business as well as the family mansion, living here with his wife and their three children. He died in its master bedroom in 1926.

The Christie Mansion is said to be haunted, but not by the the ghost of father William or son Robert. The story (and it is a story) goes that although Robert was devoted to his wife he had a mistress and he kept her in a secret apartment in the house. There were two entrances to the apartment. One of the wooden panels in the hallway swung inside the secret room; the other entrance was by a carved panel in the library. The secret apartment consisted of one room with a bathroom. The mistress had whatever she needed except food which was brought to her quarters by a man servant bribed by Robert.

As Danielle Urquhart tells the story, "The mistress lived in the secret room for years and years, never setting foot outside and seeing no one except the servant and the master. But, gradually, the master's visits grew less and less frequent. The mistress, lonely and jealous, despaired that he was growing tired of her. Finally, the long confinement drove her mad and she hanged herself in the secret apartment. Under cover of darkness her body was secretly removed from the house and buried by the master and the man servant. The master never recovered from the resulting guilt so that by the time of his death the family business had crumbled. The ghost of the mistress is sometimes said to peer out one of the upper windows of the mansion."

Such is the story. Christie, Brown and Company was sold to the giant Nabisco company in the 1920s, and the Christie Mansion was acquired as a residence for women students of St. Michael's College by the Sisters of St. Joseph, the religious order which also founded St. Michael's Hospital. Today the residence is known as St. Joseph's College.

Present-day student residents know all about the tragic story of the mansion's past. There is a "secret room," known as Room 29; because it is attached to the library, it is used as a study room by some students but avoided by others.

As Urquhart noted, "Sometimes, if a student is studying there alone at night, the secret doors (which are both kept propped open for ventilation) will suddenly swing shut. The poor student tugs and tugs at the door-handles, but they will not open. This is strange, as both doors generally open and shut very easily. Eventually, the student is forced to call out for help and someone will come and let her out. Oddly, then the doors can be opened effortlessly — but from the outside! Some students suggest that the invisible ghost of the mistress holds the doors shut to force someone else to experience an approximation of her own long imprisonment."

It should be noted that the Sisters of St. Joseph cast a cold eye on all these stories, tales, and rumours, suggesting that they are student inventions and recent ones at that.

The Spirit of Trinity College

Does Bishop Strachan return once a year on the anniversary of his death? Do the eyes of his portrait follow one around the room?

Site: Trinity College, University of Toronto

Locale: 6 Hoskin Avenue, west of Queen's Park Crescent

Period: Erected in 1925

Sources: Anonymous, "Fatherly Ghost's Yearly Message," *The Varsity*, 16 January 1952

Claire Mackay, *The Toronto Story* (Toronto: Annick Press, 1990)

Interview with Henri Pilon, archivist, Trinity College, 27 June 1994

Trinity College, one of the four original colleges that comprised the University of Toronto, is affiliated with the Anglican Church of Canada. The present building looks ancient, but it dates from 1925, the chapel from 1955. Architectural journalist Patricia McHugh described the present building as a "romantic evocation of England's ivied halls"; she reserved her praise for the chapel: "Built of bright, crisp stone with luminous clear glazed ornamentally leaded windows sparked by brilliant touches of colour, the chapel is almost mystically 'light.'" The style is known as Gothic Revival.

The architectural style of the present building recalls that of the city's first Trinity College. The original building, erected in 1851 in the Gothic manner of the ecclesiastical colleges of Oxford and Cambridge, stood for many years at 999 Queen Street West, at Bellwoods Avenue. The original ornamental gates of that building are the sole reminder of that building. At the beginning of each fall term, "Trin" students may be seen making their ceremonial march from the portals of the new college to the gates of the old.

Trinity College was founded by the blustery John Strachan, first Bishop of Toronto, who commanded considerable political power and spiritual authority in the fledgling Town of York and then the vigorous City of Toronto. He resided in the Bishop's Palace (since demolished) and died there, on 1 November 1867; his remains were interred in the crypt of the Cathedral Church of St. James, 65 Church Street at Adelaide Street East.

One might expect there to be a tradition that Strachan haunts "his" church, the Cathedral Church of St. James, but this is not so. Instead, St. James boasts the Lincoln Imp. During a visit in 1975, the Dean of Lincoln Cathedral presented the Toronto congregation with a replica, the grotesque, carved figure of the celebrated Imp that is identified with Lincoln Cathedral in England. The half-human, half-animal depiction of an impishlooking devil takes its place with other grotesque figures that ornament the Toronto church. The legend of the Lincoln Imp is recalled in a church publication:

> The Legend runs that one day the devil was in a frolicsome mood, and let out all his young demons. One jumped into the sea without getting wet, one rode on a rainbow, one jumped into a furnace, one played with forked lightning, and another went up into the air and was carried by the wind to Old Lindum. The Imp said, "Take me into the Church and I will knock over his Lordship and blow up the Dean, Organist, and singers, and knock out the windows and put out the lights." To this the angel angrily cried out: "Stop! You shall not." The demon replied with decision: "Such as you are better outside. You shall wait here for me till I have finished my fun." He then jumped about the transept, clambered on to the altar, and mocked some angels who appeared with derisive laughter. Thereupon one of the angels commanded: "Wicked Imp, be turned into stone." And there he remains in the Cathedral to this day.

Behind the gnarled branches of an old tree stands Trinity College in all the glory of the Gothic Revival. "Trin" is the home of a secret student society, known as the Episkopon, and the haunt of the college's indomitable founder, Dr. John Strachan.
[Josh Goldhar]

John Strachan may not haunt the Cathedral Church, but tradition holds that, on the anniversary of his death, his restless spirit returns to stalk the halls and walk the corridors of "his" college. As is often noted, the date of his death follows uncomfortably close upon the heels of Halloween.

This arresting portrait shows John Strachan, first Bishop of Toronto and founder of Trinity College. It was painted by the artist George Theodore Berthron from life, in 1865, two years before the subject's death. The portrait hangs in the Provost's office, Trinity College. The subject's eyes are said to follow the viewer's movements about the room. Strachan's ghost is said to stalk the corridors of "his" college on or about November 1st, the anniversary of his death.

[Trinity College Archives]

Hanging in the Provost's Office in Trinity College is a notable oil painting of Strachan. It was painted from life in 1865, two years before the subject's death, by the respected portrait artist George Theodore Berthon. A notable feature of the portrait is the fact that the subject's eyes seem to engage the viewer's eyes ... no matter where the viewer stands or moves in the room. (The artistic feature is known to French artists as "the universal eye.") The gaze of Bishop Strachan is something to behold!

Trinity College has long harboured its own secret society, The Episkopon, the head of which is known as The Scribe. Membership is limited to students and former students of the college, and only members are privy to its rites and rituals. They speak guardedly about it when they speak at all. Some say that the the Episkopon resembles nothing more than a sorority or a fraternity; others mutter that it represents much, much more. To date, little information about the Episkopon has appeared in print. One exception to that rule is the information that appeared in a short article, "Fatherly Ghost's Yearly Message," published over forty years ago in the columns of the *Varsity*, the student newspaper:

A very ancient being, a sort of guardian angel of the Trinity student body, has lived up in the lantern tower of the College since 1925, with only a skull for company.

His name is Father Episkopon, and once a year he descends with a message for his Scribe. This message the Scribe relays to the men of the College at a closed meeting in a subterranean dining room, by the wavering light of a solitary candle. A skull sits at his feet.

Reproduced here is an artist's sketch of the storied Lincoln Imp. The carved stone figure of a devil, half-animal, half-human, has ornamented England's Lincoln Cathedral since the thirteenth century. In 1975, the Dean of the Cathedral, on a visit to Toronto, presented an exact replica to the congregation of St. James Cathedral. The Imp may be seen to squat cross-legged high up between two arches on the north side of the choir.

[Cathedral Church of St. James]

Father Episkopon concerns himself with manners, morals, and misdemeanors in Trinity. His Scribe chastises men of the College verbally for their errors and idiosyncrasies ....

No doubt the exclusivity and secrecy of The Episkopon are eminently agreeable to the spirit of John Strachan who, in his own day, presided over the equally exclusive Family Compact in Upper Canada.

Massey College's Ghosts

The ghosts that frequent Massey College are the ones that first saw life in the rich and bizarre imagination of the college's first Master.

Site: Massey College, University of Toronto

Locale: 4 Devonshire Place, south of Bloor Street, west of University Avenue

Period: From 1963 to 1981

Sources: Robertson Davies's *High Spirits* (Toronto: Penguin Books, 1982)

John Fraser, "Robertson Davies up to 'Mystical Business'?" *The Toronto Star*, 24 December 1995

Anonymous, "Arts Ink," *The Globe and Mail*, 9 January 1996

Robertson Davies, first Master of Massey College, University of Toronto, has been called many things, including the "Merlin of Massey." About the man there always was something magisterial, even diabolical! These contradictory — or complementary — characteristics are caught in this photograph taken by Alicia Johnson of Montreal.

[Alicia Johnson, Moira Whalen]

Massey College is a residential institution for senior scholars within the University of Toronto. For their use, architect Ron Thom created a cloistered space in a bustling city where the passage of time seems less hurried. Robertson Davies, the celebrated novelist and essayist, was appointed the first Master of Massey College and so served from 1963 to 1981. Inspired by the present character and future prospects of the college, he composed a literary composition for each of the Christmas banquets over which he presided. Each "gaudy" took the form of an original ghost story that he set within the precincts of the college. He wrote and recited these stories for eighteen years. These tall tales — amusing, inventive, instructive, scary — were collected and published under the title *High Spirits* (1982).

The tower of Massey College, designed by architect Ron Thom, seems to reach to the very heavens.

[Josh Goldhar]

The literary tribute that Davies paid to a new building must be unique in the annals of literature. Why did he do this? "University College has a ghost, of which it is justifiably proud, and doubtless there are others around the University which have not yet found their chroniclers," Davies explained. "Massey College is a building of great architectural beauty, and few things become architecture so well as a whiff of the past, and a hint of the uncanny. Canada needs ghosts, as a dietary supplement, a vitamin taken to stave off that most dreadful of modern ailments, the Rational Rickets."

Massey College will long remain in the imaginative thrall of Robertson Davies!

In fact, it may remain his personal haunt. Two months before his death in December 1995, Davies assured John Fraser, his third successor as Master of Massey College, that he would write a new ghost story or "gaudy" to enliven the Christmas festivities. Alas, that was not to be. But Davies assured Fraser of something else. "He urged me never to doubt that the college was haunted and that one day he himself hoped to put in a spectral appearance. "Of course, one can't guarantee these things," he said, "but I will certainly try to give some signs."

The Spirits of Soldiers' Memorial Tower

Is it true that the dead are not forgotten within the shadow of this tower ... in more ways than one?

Site: Soldiers' Memorial Tower, University of Toronto

Locale: Between Hart House and University College on the university's Main Campus

Hours: Open on Memorial Day, Graduation Day, and by special arrangement.

Period: Officially dedicated, 11 November 1923

Sources: Interview with Major R.B. Oglesby, Associate Secretary, Faculty of Arts, University of Toronto, 1963-80, 15 June 1994

Interview with Danielle Urquhart, "the Ghost Lady," 22 June 1994

From time to time there are reports of mysterious lights that appear to glow from the Memorial Hall which is located immediately above the arch of the Soldiers' Memorial Tower on the campus of the University of Toronto.

[Josh Goldhar]

The Soldiers' Memorial Tower is dedicated to the memory of those students and alumni who lost their lives in World War I and World War II. The Tower is 143 feet high and encloses a fifty-two-bell carillon, the workings of a great clock, and directly above the central archway, the Muniment Room, renamed the Memorial Room, wherein are preserved and displayed the university's rolls of honour and service, plaques, flags, medals, decorations, and other mementoes of battle. The Memorial Room may be visited on Remembrance Day and by special arrangement.

The Tower was dedicated on 11 November 1924. Since that time, its stone pinnacles have twice been struck by lightning. The second time was shortly before the outbreak of World War II.

Major R.B. Oglesby, the authority on the Tower, maintains that there are no reports of ghosts associated with the Tower. Campus tour guides have another story to tell. Apparently a repairman, while attempting to polish the bells of the carillon, fell from the Tower, landed on the walkway below, and died. The tragedy occurred in the 1930s. Since then, lights at night have mysteriously shone from one of the windows of the Memorial Room, and the poor fellow's ghost appears intermittently in the vicinity of the Tower.

The University College Ghost

The story of the University College Ghost is Toronto's most popular ghostly tale, and Ivan Reznikoff is the city's most familiar spirit. In life, Reznikoff was said to be the master carver of the gargoyles of University College. In death, the spirit of Reznikoff is said to stalk the corridors of the college and the campus of the University of Toronto by night in search of sympathetic listeners to his tale of woe. Scoffers are advised to examine the slash-mark left by his axe on the wooden door immediately east of the Roundhouse ... at midnight!

Site: University College, University of Toronto

Locale: Main Campus, University of Toronto, west of Queen's Park Crescent

Hours: University College is open during business hours; hour-long campus tours which feature the college leave weekdays from Hart House through June, July, and August, 10:30 a.m., 1:00 p.m. and 2:30 p.m. Phone (416) 978-5000

Period: 1870s-1890s

Sources: W.J. Loudon, *Studies of Student Life: Volume V: The Golden Age* (Toronto: University of Toronto Press, 1928)

Douglas Richardson, *A Not Unsightly Building: University College and Its History* (Oakville, Ont.: *Mosaic Press,* 1990)

University College, the earliest and eeriest of the imposing edifices on the campus of the University of Toronto, was erected in the Gothic Revival manner in 1857-58 and restored in the years following the fire of 1890. If ever a building deserves a ghost of its own, it is this "pile" with its medieval trimmings: gargoyles, cloisters, balustrades, leaded windows, flying buttresses, and a roundhouse (known as Croft Chapter House) with its impressive rose window. One may enter the building through the detailed Norman archway that was much admired by Oscar Wilde when he toured the campus on his 1883 visit to Toronto.

Wilde would have relished the story of the ghost that stalks the corridors of University College, had he heard it. There is no record that anyone related to him the tale of the rivalry in love of two stonemasons, Ivan Reznikoff and Paul Diabolos. It seems the burly Russian and the wily Greek from Corinth were suitors for the hand of fair-haired Susie, but she was feckless. She played Reznikoff for the fool and took all his money before she eloped with Diabolos. There is no evidence that the tale was current before 1928, when it appeared in print in *Studies of Student Life: Volume V: The Golden Age* (1928) written by James Loudon, classicist, scientist, and President of the University of Toronto between 1892 and 1906. Yet Eileen Sonin in *ESPecially Ghosts* (1970) maintains that two academics, Registrar Falconbridge, and Bedel McKim saw it in 1866 and 1892 respectively.

University College is a "Gothic Revival pile" if ever there was one. U.C. basks in the century-old tradition that it is haunted by the ghost of the gargoyle-carver Ivan Reznikoff.

The "UC Ghost" certainly stalked the halls of University College in the late 1950s, when the present writer was an undergraduate and listened to Humphrey Milnes, Professor of German, as he recounted the tale with relish. Despite the passing of the decades, the ghost of Reznikoff remains popular with faculty, staff, and undergraduates.

Student affection for the "U.C. Ghost" is shown in the name of the canteen in the Junior Common Room: Diabolos' Coffee Bar. (Its hours are Monday through Friday from 8:30 a.m. to 8:30 p.m., Friday to 4:00 p.m.)

An old stone sculpture of an owl is set in the new north wing of the cloisters. Perhaps it is the handiwork of Diabolos, as the initials "P.D." are said to be inscribed on its back; an inscription explains that the ornamental work survived the fire of 1890 and was preserved by W.J. Loudon (the scholar who told the story of the U.C. Ghost). The owl was presented to the College Archives in 1957.

The owl is not the only reminder of that period. On display in the Principal's Office is the skull that is often said to be Reznikoff's. The

The late Humphrey Milnes displays the human skull that is said to be that of the late, lamented Ivan Reznikoff, Ghost of University College. Milnes was a Professor of German and an amateur archivist who did his best to keep alive U.C.'s traditional ghost story. This photograph was taken in 1980.

[J. Goode, *Toronto Star*]

skull's provenance is cloudy except for the fact that there exists a photograph of it being held by the scholar Sir Daniel Wilson, President of University College (1880-92), who is principally remembered today as the person who coined the word "prehistoric." It is worth adding that the College Archives are housed in the Humphrey Milnes Room, honouring

Almost hidden amid the leafy summer vines is this grotesque face carved in the stonework of the Roundhouse. Is it of Ivan Reznikoff? Is the design the handiwork of Paul Diabolos?

[Josh Goldhar]

Croft Chapter Hall, also known as the Roundhouse, is a distinctive extension of University College. Visible to this day on the massive oak door, which leads from the portico to the passageway that connects the Roundhouse and University College, is the slash mark of the double-headed axe wielded by Paul Diabolos. The gash may be seen to the left of the door-handle.

[Josh Goldhar]

the Professor of German who so enjoyed recalling Loudon's romantic and tragic tale of the UC Ghost.

One misty night in the 1870s, a young student named Allen Aylesworth was walking alone across the campus. Perhaps he was remembering his

United Empire Loyalist forebearers; perhaps he was anticipating the years ahead which would see him being called to the bar of Ontario in 1878, becoming a member of the House of Commons, a member of Laurier's Cabinet, a member of the Senate, and finally Sir Allen Aylesworth.

As he crossed the campus, he encountered the thick-set figure of a man whose bearded head was topped with a tall hat.

"Cold night," said Aylesworth.

"It's always cold with me," replied the figure.

Aylesworth invited the strange man into his student quarters, and as they sat before the fire, the guest introduced himself as a Russian named Ivan Reznikoff. He went on to recount the story of how he and another stonemason, a carver named Paul Diabolos, were engaged in the construction of University College. One afternoon they were busy carving a pair of gargoyles when the Greek pointed to the grotesque face which he had finished and then to the smiling face on which the Russian was still working.

"Does that remind you of anyone?" the Greek asked.

The Russian shook his head.

"It's supposed to be you!" the Greek continued. "See, mine! It's laughing behind your back at your smiling face!"

"Why?" asked the Russian.

The Greek then launched into a wild account of how Susie, the beautiful daughter of the local publican, was inconstant in her affections. She might be engaged to the Russian, but she was secretly seeing the Greek!

The Russian said nothing, but that night he spied on Susie and, sure enough, she was consorting with the Greek outside the Roundhouse. In a rage the Russian picked up a double-headed axe and swung at the Greek. The axe missed but left a gash in the thick oak panel of the Roundhouse door. Later that night the Greek crept up on the Russian and knifed him to death, disposing of the body by dropping it down the unfinished stairwell.

Aylesworth listened to the story with mounting interest. Was this tall mysterious figure the Russian? Was his guest the ghost of the Russian? Aylesworth never found out. When he looked up, the figure had vanished. But proof of the ghostly presence was the half-finished glass of wine on the table before him.

Aylesworth was later to learn that in the aftermath of the fire of 1890, which gutted University College, workmen uncovered in the stairwell the remains of a man — skull and bones — and, inexplicably, a silver buckle. Guides point out to visitors to the college the gash on the door and the twin gargoyles, one grinning, the other grimacing — images of Paul Diabolos and Ivan Reznikoff.

One wonders what Oscar Wilde would have made of the tale!

The Ghost of the Macdonald-Mowat House

Does the spirit of Prime Minister Sir John A. Macdonald stalk the halls on the second floor of his old house on St. George Street?

Site: The Macdonald-Mowat House

Locale: School of Graduate Studies, University of Toronto, 63 St. George Street, south of Willcocks Street

Period: Erected in 1872

Sources: Anonymous, "Some Ontario Ghosts," *The Ottawa Free Press,* 7 May 1898

Interview with Dr. Jon Redfern, Professor, Centennial College, 12 June 1994

Sir John A. Macdonald, as a young lawyer, lived in the imposing residence at 63 St. George Street. It was subsequently acquired by Sir Oliver Mowat who, as Premier of Ontario, frequently sparred with Prime Minister Macdonald over the subject of provincial rights. The residence is now owned and used by the University of Toronto and called the Macdonald-Mowat House. Its second floor is said to be the haunt of the figure of an imposing-looking man.

[Josh Goldhar]

The kindly Sir Oliver Mowat and the stern Sir John A. Macdonald are the subjects of pencil sketches by the portrait artist Irma Coucill. She drew them in 1967 for her "Fathers of Confederation" series.

The Macdonald-Mowat House, an imposing, three-storey brick residence located on the campus of the University of Toronto, serves as the university's School of Graduate Studies. Built in 1872 in the French Second Empire style, it was purchased by Sir John A. Macdonald, future Prime Minister of Canada, who lived here from 1876 to 1878. The Macdonald family owned it for some years thereafter. In 1888 it was bought and occupied by Sir Oliver Mowat, Prime Minister of Ontario, and it remained in the Mowat family until 1902. It was acquired by Knox College in 1910.

It was common knowledge among the university's graduate students in the 1970s that for some years the second floor had been haunted by the ghost of an imposing-looking man who stalked the hall at night. The formidable figure was seen by members of the cleaning staff, all of whom were Portuguese women. If a ghost it was, it could be that of Sir John A. Macdonald who became Canada's first Prime Minister in 1867 and died in office in 1891.

Few people identify Macdonald with the world of spirits (most remember that he was an intemperate imbiber of spirits!) despite the story told by his successor Sir John Thompson. Shortly after Macdonald's death,

Prime Minister Thompson was approached by a young Ottawa man who said that he was in communication with Macdonald's spirit and that the spirit had asked him to convey to Thompson specific information about Cabinet members and proposed Cabinet changes. Thompson was impressed with the incidental intelligence and felt that it could only have come from Macdonald himself.

Perhaps it is the spirit of Sir John A. Macdonald that haunts the Macdonald-Mowat House. Perhaps that is why he was called "Old Tomorrow."

The Police Museum

There is nothing spooky here ... no ghosts need apply. The displays are sometimes shocking ... sometimes grim ... but always fascinating.

Site: Metropolitan Toronto Police Museum and Discovery Centre

Locale: 40 College Street, between Yonge and Bay streets

Hours: Open seven days a week from 9:00 a.m. to 9:00 p.m. Phone (416) 324-6201

Period: 1930s to the present

Sources: Interview with the Director, Toronto Police Museum and Discovery Centre, 21 June 1994

Toronto has a small number of large museums and a large number of small museums. The Metropolitan Toronto Police Museum and Discovery Centre is one of the city's intriguing small museums.

The Police Museum and Discovery Centre may not be haunted, but it has a macabre appeal as well as a reconstruction of a 1929 police station [with a "wanted" poster for Ambrose Small, Canada's most famous missing man].

[Metropolitan Toronto Police Museum and Discovery Centre]

Members of the Metropolitan Toronto Police began their unofficial collection of artifacts connected with police work in the 1930s. It was not until 1967 that these were first put on public display. In 1993, the new Police Museum was opened in the brand-new Metropolitan Toronto Police Headquarters building on College Street. It has proved to be popular with visitors of all ages.

There are about forty display areas that highlight police work in general, including such themes as uniforms, fallen officers, squad cars, motorcycles, investigations, old criminal cases, drugs, and so forth. On display are artifacts like the wooden leg that concealed the saw used in the escape of the Boyd Gang from the Don Jail in 1952 and a noose that recalls Arthur Lucas, the heroin trafficker who was executed for murder on 11 December 1962, the last person hanged in Canada. There is the reconstruction of a 1929 police station that includes an interesting poster. It offers a $5,000 reward for information about missing millionaire theatre owner Ambrose Small, who is thus described: blue eyes, brown hair, 53 years old, 5'6" or 5'7", 135-40 pounds.

The Police Museum has no ghosts, but it has many gruesome tales to tell. It is what the British call a "black museum."

The Haunted Elevator

Would you ride the haunted elevator? Up ... or down!

Site: Malabar Ltd.

Locale: 14 McCaul Street, north of Queen Street West

Period: 1960s

Source: Interview with Danielle Urquhart, "the Ghost Lady," 22 June 1994

Malabar Ltd., the theatrical costumers, was founded in Winnipeg in 1904. The main Toronto operation was established in 1921 and has long been located in the warehouse building at 14 McCaul Street.

Danielle Urquhart, after interviewing long-term employees, has the following tale to tell:

"About thirty years ago, a gentleman was killed when the cable of the shop's freight elevator snapped. The elevator plummetted to the basement and the poor man died instantly, upon impact. Since then, although the elevator has been kept in tiptop condition, employees are still wary of it. Apparently an intense sensation of fear washes over everyone who sets foot in the elevator. For this reason some members of the staff prefer to lug costumes up to the third floor via the stairs rather than tempt fate on the haunted elevator!"

Should you open the door of Malabar's, and climb the stairway, you will find yourself on the second-story landing ... where you will have to choose whether or not to step into the "haunted elevator."
[Josh Goldhar]

89

The Haunted Chinese Restaurant

A ghost inside, evil spirits outside ... will a brace of lions protect the business?

Site: Hsin Kuang Restaurant

Locale: 346 Spadina Avenue, north of Dundas Street

Hours: Has not been open for business for some years

Period: 1960s to the present

Sources   Interview with Danielle Urquhart, "the Ghost Lady," 22 June 1994

Interview with George Prokos, publicist, 27 June 1994

Innumerable tales are told about the building located at 346 Spadina Avenue. It was erected in 1929 and it served as the Labour Lyceum; the body of anarchist Emma Goldman lay in state in its main hall in 1940. The property was acquired in the 1970s by a large company based in Hong

The Hsin Kuang Restaurant on Spadina Avenue has not served as a public restaurant since the 1970s. A brace of white stone lions protects the main entrance. Perhaps the lions are no match for the evil forces or spirits that are said to rush at the restaurant, directed by the arrow-like arrangement of the twin billboards erected on the rooftop across the street.

[Josh Goldhar]

Kong that owns and operates an international chain of quality restaurants. The idea was to turn it into a restaurant for the area's Chinese residents.

The new owners spared no expense renovating and furnishing the building and turning it into a splendid Mandarin-style restaurant. The official opening was a chaotic affair. Right from the start, business was poor. Changes were made, new management was introduced, but every effort to attract new customers to make the operation a success met with failure. Eventually the owners closed the restaurant, and it has remained closed for a good number of years.

The situation in March 1996 was as follows: The handsome building remains unoccupied but it is well maintained. The main sign now identifies it as the Hsin Kuang Centre. In Mandarin Chinese, Hsin Kuang means "New Light." Perhaps the light that did not dawn on the restaurant will shine on the newly renovated commercial establishment.

Danielle Urquhart, "the Ghost Lady," refers to the restaurant on her tour of Toronto's haunted sites. Much of what she says about it is based on information supplied by David Ko of the Toronto Chinatown Walking Tour. Here is her story: "It is said that the site was originally a Chinese morgue and funeral parlour, and that bodies were stored here until they could be shipped back to China. Many Chinese people believe that it is unlucky to erect a new building on the site of a morgue. If so, they are right about the subsequent history of the site.

"People in the neighbourhood say that the restaurant is both haunted and cursed. There is a male ghost who makes occasional appearances in the women's washroom! A Chinese exorcist was summoned to deal with the curse and he identified the problem right away. There are two giant billboards on the roofs of the two buildings directly across the street from the restaurant. The billboards are positioned diagonally, pointing directly at the restaurant. The pointing billboards resemble the tip of a knife or spear or arrowhead, and they act as a conduit for evil spirits to enter the restaurant.

"The company that owned the billboards would not move them. So the Hsin Kuang Restaurant moved its front entrance around the corner from Spadina Avenue to St. Andrews Street! At the exorcist's suggestion, stone lions were placed beside the doorway to guard against the approach of evil spirits. The pair of brightly coloured, imperial-looking lions may have prevented new spirits from entering the building, but they did nothing to evict those that are already plaguing it from inside.

"In the meantime, the restaurant is closed."

The restaurant may be closed for good — or ill. But the building itself, in January 1996, was renamed the Hsin Kuang Centre and will apparently serve as the centre for a number of specialized boutiques.

The Spirit of Henry Scadding

Does the benign spirit of Henry Scadding pervade this lovely house in Trinity Square?

Site: Scadding House

Locale: No. 6, Trinity Square, southwest of the intersection of Dundas Street West and Yonge Street

Hours: Not currently open to the public

Period: Built 1857; occupied 1966-74

Source: Interview with Mary Dixon, parishioner and children's activist, 23 June 1994

One of Toronto's oldest and most historic buildings, Scadding House, is located at No. 6, Trinity Square. It may be overshadowed by today's mammoth Eaton Centre, but observers claim that the spirit of Dr. Henry Scadding, clergyman and archivist, who used to sit on its southern balcony and admire the view of Lake Ontario, resides in the building to this day.

[Josh Goldhar]

Scadding House stands in the serenity of Trinity Square amid the hurly-burly of Eaton Centre and other mammoth modern and post-modern structures. "Eclectic Georgian/Gothic" is Patricia McHugh's phrase for the style of the building which was erected in 1857 by Henry Scadding (1813-1901). Dr. Scadding was the first Rector of Holy Trinity Church. Here he lived, wrote his early histories of Toronto, and died.

If Henry Scadding, first Rector of Holy Trinity Church, does haunt the rectory named in his honour, the spirit is that of a scholar and a gentleman. Some years before the turn of the century, Dr. Scadding posed in a photographer's studio for this portrait.
[Metropolitan Toronto Reference Library]

Mary Dixon was a resident of Scadding House for eight years in the 1960s. A soft-spoken, one-time parishioner of Holy Trinity Church, she helped in the development of community programs for the church and opened the first daycare centre in a Toronto public school.

"I lived in the apartment on the top floor of Scadding House from 1966 to 1974. When I moved in as a parish worker, the house had not had residents for some time; when I moved out, it no longer had any residents at all. In the course of eight years living there, I was aware of Henry Scadding a lot. It is hard to describe. I never saw Henry, nothing like that, but I was aware of his presence. I sensed he was there, writing. There were no scary events; it was a benign presence. I just know that it was one of the safest places in which I had ever lived; one doesn't always feel that safe, especially in this part of the city. Now I'm no expert on ghosts, but I feel about Scadding House the same way I feel about Mackenzie House the first time I visited it. Each place has its spirit.

"In his day Henry would sit by the window or on the balcony and write his books and look out and see the lake. In my day I had the entire fourth floor: one big room plus a kitchen. I used to sit by the window and look out and see ... office buildings! Nobody is living in No. 6 today, but in the 1960s, when I lived there, it was a people-oriented place. I occupied the fourth floor, there were apartments on the third floor, and the second floor was used for church business. On the ground floor there was a meeting place that was a restaurant frequented by business people by day and it served as a coffee house by night. The place attracted street people and especially war resisters. Bands rehearsed in the basement. The Downchild Blues Band got its start here. Scadding House served as the headquarters for the Innercity Angels for some time, but now it is empty and nobody visits it."

Trinity Square always seemed to be "a square out of time." Blodwen Davies caught this quality in a passage from her impressionistic evocation of the early city, *Storied York* (1931):

> But in Trinity Square you enter a little pool of dusk and tranquility. The old brick walls, with their little turrets and groined windows and buttresses, have a quality of perpetual peace. The prayers of a more leisurely age still linger here.
>
> Some one has said that it should always be Christmas in Trinity Square, that there should always be lights in the old stained-glass windows and snow as soft as eiderdown falling about its venerable walls. It has that sort of an air.

The Ghost of The Grange

Is the Ghost of the Grange the spirit of Goldwin Smith returning to consult the books in his library? The ghost of William Chin, the long-time butler? Or the revenant of a celebrated writer of horror stories?

Site: The Grange

Locale: The Art Gallery of Ontario, 317 Dundas Street West, west of University Avenue

Hours: For hours of operation for the Art Gallery of Ontario and The Grange, phone (416) 979-6648

Period: 1871-1910; 1980s and 1990s

Sources: John Lownsbrough, *The Privileged Few: The Grange and Its People in Nineteenth Century Toronto* (Toronto: Art Gallery of Ontario, 1980)

John Robert Colombo, *Canadian Literary Landmarks* (Toronto: Hounslow Press, 1984)

Connie Masters, "Ghosts of the Grange," *The Grange Newsletter,* Issue 59, April 1995

Interviews with Elayne Dobel Goyette, archivist and former guide, 29 August 1994, 13 September 1995

The Grange was built in the style of a Georgian manor house in 1817. It was the Art Gallery of Ontario's first home and was restored in 1973. The celebrated essayist Goldwin Smith held court at The Grange from 1871 to his death here on 7 June 1910. The restorers have succeeded in recreating the appearance of The Grange, using original furniture and furnishings, especially Smith's extensive and well-used library.

Over the years there have been stories that at dusk a gaunt, shadowy figure may be seen to move through the library. The effect may be caused by sunlight and shadow on the floor-to-ceiling bookcases. But if there is a ghost of The Grange, it could be that of Goldwin Smith. One of his many books bears the ominous title *Guesses at the Riddle of Existence* (1897).

The ghost could also be that of William Chin, The Grange's butler for fifty years. Chin kept the household ledger, and his final entry, dated 30 September 1910, reads: "Left dear old Grange at 1:00 o'clock p.m. to be

[a] wanderer." Or the revenant could be that of Algernon Blackwood, one of Smith's assistants. As a young remittance man living in Toronto in 1890-92, Blackwood worked in this study, unhappily assisting Smith in his literary endeavours. In later years in England, Blackwood established a reputation as one of the finest writers of tales of horror and terror.

The Grange is a handsome Georgian residence erected in 1817 that served as the home and study of the Oxford scholar Goldwin Smith. Smith died in 1911 and willed the building to the Art Museum of Toronto, later the Art Gallery of Toronto, now the Art Gallery of Ontario. This "gentleman's house in Upper Canada" was fully restored in 1973.

[Brochure, Art Gallery of Ontario]

In this vintage photograph, Goldwin Smith, skull cap on his head, sits at one of the desks in his book-lined study in The Grange. The view in this turn-of-the-century photograph is not unlike the one the contemporary visitor will see.

[City of Toronto Archives/James 2130]

Connie Masters, editor of *The Grange Newsletter*, wrote as follows in the issue of April 1995:

> Are we sharing the house with others (apart from the resident ants, mice, and moths)? With any house of the age of The Grange supernatural manifestations are not unusual. Does something forever remain of intense emotion experienced by those who have lived happily or unhappily within the walls? Many Grangers have heard the story (and some knew her) of the cleaner who was working alone in the house one day when it was closed to the public. As she was about to go up the staircase to the second floor she looked up, only to see the figure of a man standing at the top staring down at her. Needless to say, she dropped her utensils, and beat a hasty retreat back to the gallery, vowing never to work in The Grange again ... and she didn't.

Elayne Dobel Goyette, now an archivist and records manager, worked as a guide in The Grange in 1989-93. She recalls hearing about — and sensing — the presence of three spirits, not one. There was the Lady in Black whose presence was felt in the young girl's bedroom on the second floor. There was the Lady in White whose particularly scary presence was felt around the main-floor stairwell that leads to the basement kitchen. Finally there was the Gentleman in the Drawing Room who was seen by Dobel herself late one winter evening in 1990. What she beheld was the spectre of a gentleman who wore a yellow velvet coat. She saw him pass through the east wall of the Conservatory, walk right across the room, his velvet coat brushing against her, and then walk through the west wall. His route corresponded to doors and corridors of the Conservatory that existed before the building was remodelled and the room turned into the Drawing Room. The experience left her more surprised than frightened.

The archivist Elayne Dobel Goyette reported a number of unusual experiences. As a university student she worked as one of The Grange's guides.

[Elayne Dobel Goyette]

Past-Life Regression and The Grange

The following account of past-life regression that involves The Grange comes from a letter, dated 29 August 1994, written by Elayne Dobel Goyette:

> I'm so glad that I responded to the "Information Wanted" section of the July-August issue of the OHS (Ontario Historical Society) *Bulletin*.
>
> Historical romance author Jo Ann Ferguson and I met at the banquet of the Romance Writers of America (RWA) conference in either 1988 or 1989, I've forgotten which. We became instant friends and talked of England, Canada, Toronto, and ghosts. I told her of my experiences at The Grange with the Gentleman in the yellow coat who appeared out of a wall, brushed against my arm as he walked through the drawing room, and exited through the wall which was once a corridor. Anyway, we exchanged cards.
>
> A few months later Jo Ann wrote and told me that she and her husband, Bill, would be in Toronto on business. She asked whether I would show her The Grange. I couldn't wait!
>
> That Wednesday evening Jo, Susan (my Day Captain at The Grange), Pauline (another writer), and I began touring the house. As Jo entered each room she'd say, "This isn't right. This room is too big." Or, when she entered what is now the Ballroom, she said, "Wasn't this part of the house all bedrooms?" Jo was correct on all points. At the end of the tour, Susan led us up the stairs and into the attic, which was, and is, strictly offlimits to visitors *and guides.*
>
> It was eerie! I felt that the front of it was untouched and that I was walking, or creeping, into history! Why creep? Simple, I am only $5'3\frac{1}{2}"$ high and my head touched the peak of the roof, which is the highest point in the attic. I recall that I stood, looking out the dirty round window, imagining I was seeing all the way down to Lake Ontario.
>
> Susan pointed out the open-window "shelving" that served as bed-roll and extra-clothing cubbies. All of us decided to bend, and stay bent, in order to enter the space where the unmarried servant girls unrolled their bedding and slept.

I felt peculiarly at home in the attic, as though that confined space had been my quarters in another life. But there was something about the beamed floor that made me uneasy ... but I paid no attention to it at the time.

The time to do something about it came one Sunday evening, when the 1992 RWA conference in Chicago ended. Eleven of us gathered in the hotel room of Janet, one of the writers and someone with experience as a regressionist. I was lying on the floor between the two chairs. Four writers were stretched out on one bed, three on another. Janet sat in a chair, someone sat in a chair behind me, and someone stretched out on the floor between the two beds.

First, Janet regressed us to our happiest past life. I was a temple maiden in Ancient Greece, playing with other toga-clad figures near the small, round, white temple. Janet asked the group to live out that life, from birth to death, but I somehow continued to run and play in the green, green grass. One of the members of the group experienced something really horrible, so while Janet was leading the "discussion" of what we saw, the woman sitting in the chair behind me left the room.

Next, Janet told us to go back in time to the smallest house we had ever lived in. There I was, in Ireland (or so I think), in a one-room thatched cottage. It was white-washed. It had a bright red door in front, holes for windows on either side of the front door, and a door at the back. That's it.

Janet, who was somehow in my mind, said aloud, "Not a red door. Change the colour of the door." I concentrated. I tried, with my mind, to paint the door white. I failed. All I could do was imagine the door old and withered, with all the bright red paint chipped of.

Then Janet said, "I want you to go upstairs to bed." Upstairs? My house had no stairs. Only then ... I was no longer in the little thatched cottage in Ireland. I was walking up the stairs to the attic in The Grange, with nothing but a candle to light my way.

Next, Janet said, "Go to the window and look out at the moon and the stars." I blew out the candle and stared at the little round window in the peak of the attic roof, *but couldn't see anything but smoke!* The beams under part of the roof were smouldering.

All I remember next was my mind screaming, "Help! I've got to find a way to stop the fire!" Then, suddenly, the smoke detector in the room went off! Not the fire alarms within the hotel, mind, just the smoke detector in the room. Needless to say, none of us was smoking. The harsh buzzing of the alarm brought me back to reality.

Jo jumped off the bed on the other side of the room. She ran over and grabbed hold of me and hugged me. We held onto each other. "You did it. You saved my life," she kept repeating. "I was burning and couldn't save myself." We hugged and rocked back and forth while Jo added, "I've always, always, been afraid of fire .... "

At the next conference in St. Louis in 1993, Janet set up a regression for just Jo and me. As we relived that life, I learned that Jo was married to one of the Boulton sons and that I was her personal maid. The fire, we discovered, was in 1843, two years before Toronto Mayor William Henry, the oldest Boulton son, married and brought his Boston heiress to The Grange.

That's the gist of it.

Toronto General Hospital

One does not normally consider hospitals to be haunted. Yet if there is a spirit that separates itself from the physical body at the point of death, it would surely be observed in flight in a hospital, especially in an operating room, where people sometimes expire, sometimes suddenly, under the eyes of well-trained observers. As it happens, there are *reports, subjective accounts, of near-death and out-of-body experiences, even in medical journals. But they originate with the patients, not with the medical staff. Here is one of those accounts ....*

Site: Coronary Unit, Toronto General Hospital

Locale: 200 Elizabeth Street, near College Street West and University Avenue

Period: 1971

Source: R.L. MacMillan, M.D., F.R.C.P.(C), and K.W.G. Brown, M.D., F.R.C.P.(C), "Cardiac Arrest Remembered," *Canadian Medical Association Journal,* 22 May 1971

What does the conscious person experience at the moment of death? In the absence of a scientific answer to that question, folk beliefs abound. Traditionally, the dying person watches as scenes from his or her life unfold (the life review); then the spirit separates from the body and surveys it dispassionately (autoscopy); finally, there is the voyage into realms of radiance (the soul's flight).

Something approaching the traditional pattern of the near-death experience was recorded by a patient in the coronary unit of the Toronto General Hospital. The details were set down by the patient himself at the request of his two physicians who then added their own observations. They published the account under the heading "Cardiac Arrest Remembered" in the correspondence column of the *Canadian Medical Association Journal,* 22 May 1971.

The two physicians contributed the two paragraphs which appear here; in the journal, these preceded and succeeded the patient's own narrative. For present purposes the 68-year-old man has been identified as Patient X.

A 68-year-old man who previously had suffered no symptoms of coronary artery disease awoke with aching pain in the left arm. Squeezing retrosternal pain developed several hours later and persisted until his admission to hospital in the late afternoon. He was transferred without delay to the coronary unit, where his general condition was found to be satisfactory. Blood pressure was 126/78, heart sounds were normal, and there were no signs of cardiac failure. A 12 lead electrocardiogram was normal. The heart rhythm was monitored continuously and only an occasional ventricular premature beat was seen that followed the T wave by a comfortable distance. Ten hours after admission, the chest pain became worse, and the patient was given 50 mg. of meperidine. Suddenly a ventricular premature beat fell on a T wave, causing ventricular fibrillation. One of the coronary unit nurses recognized the cardiac arrest and immediately defibrillated the patient. After this there were no further serious arrhythmias, and convalescence was uneventful apart from an episode of pulmonary infarction. The ECG was normal the morning after defibrillation, and it was not until the tenth day that changes of anterior sub- endocardial infarction became evident. Changes in SGOT and CPK levels, however, were diagnostic of recent myocardial infarction from the first day in hospital. The patient remembered in detail the events surrounding his cardiac arrest, and the following account is his own vivid description of the experience. (The right leg mentioned was badly scarred from osteomyelitis suffered in childhood.)

*

It is unusual for patients to remember the events surrounding cardiac arrest. More often there is a period of amnesia of several hours duration before and after the event. This description is extremely interesting. The patient saw himself leaving his body and was able to observe it "face to face." This could be the concept of the soul leaving the body which is found in many religions. The delightful feeling of floating in space and the tranquillity, the yellow light, the rectangular shape with holes in it, associated with the wish of not wanting to be brought back again, may provide comfort and reassurance to patients suffering from coronary artery disease as well as to their relatives.

R.L. MacMillan, M.D., F.R.C.P.[C] and
K.W.G. Brown, M.D., F.R.C.P.[C]

Coronary Unit
Toronto General Hospital,
Toronto 2.

As I promised, I am setting out my experiences as I remember them when I had the cardiac arrest last May.

I find it hard to describe certain parts — I do not have words to express how vivid the experience was. The main thing that stands out is the clarity of my thoughts during the episode. They were almost exactly as I have written them and in retrospect it seems that they are fixed in my memory — more so than other things that have happened to me. It seems at times that I was having a "dual" sensation — actually experiencing certain things yet at the same time "seeing" myself during these experiences.

I had been admitted into the intensive care ward in the early evening. I remember looking at my wrist watch and it appeared to be a few minutes before 4:00 a.m. I was lying flat on my back because of the intravenous tubes and the wires to the recording machine. Just then I heaved a very, very deep sigh and my head flopped over to the right. I thought, "Why did my head flop over? — I didn't move it — I must be going to sleep." This was apparently my last conscious thought.

Then I am looking at my own body from the waist up, face-to-face (as though through a mirror in which I appeared to be in the lower left corner). Almost immediately I saw myself leave my body, coming out through my head and shoulders. (I did not see my lower limbs.) The "body" leaving me was not exactly a vapour form, yet it seemed somewhat transparent, for I could see my other "body" through it. Watching this I thought, "So this is what happens when you die" (although no thought of being dead presented itself to me).

Suddenly I am sitting on a very small object travelling at great speed, out and up into a dull blue-grey sky, at a forty-five-degree angle. I thought, "It's lonely out here. — Where am I going to end up? — This is one journey I must take alone."

Down below to my left I saw a pure white cloud-like substance almost moving up on a line that would intersect my course. Somehow I was able to go down and take a look at it. It was perfectly rectangular in shape (about the same proportions as a regular building brick), but full of holes (like a sponge). Two thoughts came to me: "What will happen to me when it engulfs me?" and "You don't have to worry; it has all happened before and everything will be taken care of." I have no recollection of the shape catching up with me.

My next sensation was of floating in a bright, pale yellow light — a very delightful feeling. Although I was not conscious of having any lower limbs, I felt something being torn off the scars of my right leg, as if a large piece of adhesive tape had been taken off. I thought, "They have always said your body is made whole out here. I wonder if my scars are gone," but though I tried I could not seem to locate my legs. I continued to float, enjoying the most beautiful tranquil sensation. I had never experienced such a delightful sensation and have no words to describe it.

Then there were sledge-hammer blows to my left side. They created no actual pain, but jarred me so much that I had difficulty in retaining my balance (on whatever I was sitting). After a number of these blows, I began to count them and when I got to six I said (aloud, I think), "What the ... are you doing to me?" and opened my eyes.

Immediately I was in control of all my faculties and recognized the doctors and nurses around me. I asked the head nurse at the foot of my bed, "What's happening?" and she replied that I'd had a bad turn. I then asked who had been kicking me, and a doctor pointed to a nurse on my left, remarking that she really had to "thump" me hard and that I would be black and blue on my left side the next day. (I don't think I was.)

Just a few comments as I think over what happened to me. I wonder if the bright yellow surroundings could have been caused by someone looking into my eyes with a bright light?

I have read about heart transplants where it is claimed the brain dies before the heart stops. In my case, my brain must have been working after my heart stopped beating for me to experience these sensations.

If death comes to a heart patient in this manner, no one has cause to worry about it. I felt no pain (other than what I had when I entered hospital), and while it was a peculiar experience it was not unpleasant. The floating part of my sensation was so strangely beautiful that I said to a doctor later that night, "If I go out again, don't bring me back — it's so beautiful out there," and at that time I meant it.

The Queen Street Haunting

What was inside the closet that so upset the tenants of the two flats in the building on Queen Street?

Site: Second-floor and third-floor flats

Locale: Friendship House, 280 Queen Street West, west of Beverley Street

Period: 1968

Sources: Eileen Sonin, *ESPecially Ghosts* (Toronto: Clarke, Irwin and Company, 1970)

Stefan Scaini, "Buildings that Hold the Souls of the Dead," *The Toronto Star*, 14 January 1984

Interview with Michael Lucas, President, Concerned Friends of Soviet People, 27 June 1994.

Kitty McCaulay and Bruce Cockburn were a young married couple in need of an apartment. With another married couple, Patti and Murray, they went hunting for an apartment close to the Ontario College of Art where they were students.

In 1968 they found flats that seemed to meet their needs. One was on the second floor and the other was above it on the third floor of an old building on Queen Street West. There was — and still is — a bookstore on the ground floor. Patti and Murphy took the third-floor flat, Kitty and Bruce the second-floor flat.

Patti found her flat strangely depressing, and so did Kitty, who told Eileen Sonin, author of *ESPecially Ghosts.* "Even then, I was aware of a strangeness about the place. I put it down to the depressing green paint which covered everything, but even after we had repainted the walls, hung up happy curtains and filled the windows with flowering plants, there was still an oppressive atmosphere which was so noticeable that friends would comment upon it when they visited us. They said that they sensed a drift of unpleasantness between the two flats."

Kitty felt that another mind was trying to dominate her. "The first concrete thing that happened occurred one day when I was pouring myself a glass of water. I suddenly realized that I must not drink it because it was poisoned." She drank it anyway. "The next time it happened the threat seemed stronger, and I knew that I must not touch the water with my lips."

"Then, about a week later, I was standing in the bathroom when a sudden vivid mental picture appeared, and as quickly disappeared." The vision was "extremely gory and frightening. I saw myself — or an image of myself — with my throat cut, and the whole bathroom a shambles as if there had been a fight with blood everywhere."

Kitty began to feel that someone else was in the room with her although she was alone in the flat. "I knew someone or something was tampering with my thoughts, and began to feel as though I were living in a nightmare. It seemed incredible that outside my home I was a normal, rational, well-adjusted being, while in my home I was becoming the victim of someone who needed to take control of a human mind and body. It seemed as though something was testing me by trying to control my reactions to certain events.

"Suddenly I remembered that several months previously when walking with Bruce in the yard of St. Patrick's Church on McCaul Street, I had become aware of something trying to reach out to me, as if it were trapped in the yard and wanted me to take it home. At the same time, I received a mental warning that I should not listen to or tamper with this spirit, and so I asked my husband if we could leave at once.

"Next day, I talked myself into believing that the whole episode had been a mental association of churches, cemeteries and graves and, as it was a bright sunny day, I made up my mind to revisit the place, this time alone. I walked to the same spot where I had the strange feeling the evening before, and almost at once I heard a soft voice say, 'Take me with you, take me with you.' I turned and ran from the yard into the sun-filled street where children played and traffic passed by. But the reality of my surroundings could not dispel the unreality of my experience."

When Kitty shared her experiences with Patti, she found Patti was having her own misgivings. She too felt that there was poison in the drinking water. She too had experienced a vision. In fact, Patti had experienced two visions. In the first, she saw herself with her throat slashed; in the second, it was her husband who had been slain. Then Murray admitted to waking up in the middle of many a night with irrational fears and bathed in a cold sweat.

Aroo, Kitty's dog, was also affected. Kitty said, "Aroo had periodically been going to an unused closet under the stairs and sniffing at the door with his tail between his legs, whimpering and looking generally unhappy. I had thought it strange ... But the very night that we had our conversation, Aroo again approached the closet in the hall with his tail between his legs, sniffing at the door. We agreed that we would examine the cupboard, and, armed with a flashlight, we tackled it the next morning.

"We discovered a box of screws and doorknobs, some curious metal household items all covered with the dust of years, some old golf clubs, two sharp fire-pokers and a cane. The cane was abnormally short with a carved hand at its top, the thumb placed between the index and middle fingers. This can mean one of two things — in eastern Europe it is a vulgar and insulting sign; in South America it is a symbol to ward off a demon. Below this hand on the cane was a jumble of several letters which we took to be the demon's name, but none of us dared to try to pronounce it.

"We threw away everything from the cupboard except for the cane, which we replaced, as none of us wanted to be responsible for throwing it out or transporting it from the house.

"My curiosity now thoroughly aroused, I went next door to ask the neighbours — nice, simple people — if they knew anything of the history of the place. They told me they had lived in our building themselves for a very short time, but had moved to their present residence as they needed more space. The tenants who took over from them seemed quiet, sensible folk at first, but as time went on they began to act strangely. They ran down the fire escape, looked carefully both ways and then ran back up again. They yelled at each other and acted as if they were frightened. In time they seemed almost insane, and finally they were evicted by the landlord."

Later that day Kitty and Bruce moved out; Patti and Murray followed a few days later. The two couples had lasted eight weeks in all. Kitty explained, "We reached the conclusion that either someone had come to a violent end in the flats and that the vibrations of panic were still clinging to the rooms, or that it was a conscious and mobile being from another plane who was malicious and evil and thrived on discord and fear."

The Queen Street Haunting took place in 1968. Today the three-storey building is known as Friendship House. Since 1945 the building has been owned by the Society of Carpatho-Russian Canadians. On the ground floor there is a gift shop where there used to be a used bookstore. The second floor has the offices of Concerned Friends of Soviet People (formerly the Canada-U.S.S.R. Friendship Association) where Michael Lucas edits the monthly journal *Northstar Compass*. The third floor serves as a photographer's studio. The interiors are spacious and airy; indeed, the offices served for eight years as the headquarters for the production team that produced CBC-TV's *Street Legal*.

Occupants of the building were surprised to learn in 1994 that twenty-six years earlier it had been the scene of a haunt. Although considerable renovation has taken place since then, there is still a closet on the second floor; it is used for storage. A sophisticated surveillance system was installed that year ... to exclude robbers rather than to enclose ghosts!

Haunted Osgoode Hall

Are there ghosts of women wandering the hallways of historic Osgoode Hall?

Site: Osgoode Hall

Locale: 130 Queen Street West, at University Avenue

Hours: Tours are held Monday through Friday in July and August at 1:15 p.m. Phone (416) 947-4041

Period: From 1829 to 1991

Source: Interview with Elise Brunet, curator of Law Society of Upper Canada, 15 June 1994

It is said that Osgoode Hall is haunted by "nice ghosts." It is also said that the handsome classical stone building, which serves as the seat of the Supreme Court of Ontario, is not haunted at all!

[Josh Goldhar]

Osgoode Hall is a classical building of commanding presence. The east wing goes back to 1829, the west wing to 1844, the centre block to 1856, and additions throughout to 1991. The building was erected as the headquarters of the Law Society of Upper Canada; it also serves as the seat of the Supreme Court of Ontario. Its Great Library, according to architectural historian Patricia McHugh, is "perhaps the noblest room in Canada."

Elise Brunet is Curator of the Law Society of Upper Canada. She works in Osgoode Hall and has a keen sense of the building's history and importance as well as a great affection for the place. She is amused by its tales of hauntings.

"Is Osgoode Hall haunted? We are asked that question all the time. People feel it should be haunted. There are stories of ghosts seen or felt here from the earliest times to the present. Nothing is clear. There are stories of women wandering in the hallways late at night. Another story is of a caretaker who worked here from 1952 to the 1980s who was making his rounds late one night when he heard voices in one of the chambers. Doors are usually left open but this one was closed. He approached it and could hear a discussion that included a number of people. With some trepidation he tried the door, found it locked, unlocked it, only to find that the chamber was dark and empty. There was another exit but it was locked.

"I would not be surprised if I learned that we have some ghosts here. After all, it's an old building. But I have been here late at night and, you know, the building is cozy, not scary. If we have some ghosts, they are nice ghosts."

The Ghosts of Old City Hall

What is there about the Old City Hall that seems to scare people, even those who work there? Do the spirits of condemned murderers haunt Courtroom 33?

Site: Old City Hall

Locale: 60 Queen Street West at Bay Street

Hours: Open business hours; phone (416) 327-6092

Period: 1965 to the present

Sources: Eileen Sonin, *ESPecially Ghosts* (Toronto: Clarke, Irwin and Company, 1970)

Jane Widerman, "The Haunting of Toronto," *The Toronto Star's City Magazine*, 29 October 1978

Kathleen Kenna, "Something Weird," *The Toronto Star*, 26 September 1983.

Stefan Scaini, "Buildings that Hold the Souls of the Dead," *The Toronto Star*, 14 January 1984

Robert Brehl, "Old City Hall Offers Unique Slice of Life," *The Toronto Star*, 30 March 1987.

Few cities are lucky enough to boast a haunted city hall, but Toronto is one of them.

The Old City Hall is a red sandstone building with more than its share of gargoyles and other gothic-style decorations. It is topped with a slender 260-foot clock tower. Built in 1898, the building served as the judicial and municipal headquarters for the City of Toronto and the County of York until 1966. The municipal offices were gradually moved to the modernistic New City Hall after it was opened in 1964. Today the Old City Hall largely functions as a court house.

Like all older buildings, the Old City Hall has its share of creaky stairways, reverberating corridors, and drafty hallways. Perhaps these are what caused Provincial Judge S. Tupper Bigelow to inform the press in 1965 that, as he walked down the hallways, he could hear footsteps behind him and that from time to time he could feel his judicial robe being tugged: "My office was located on the second floor. I began using the staircase which is a convenient way to go downstairs to our common room. On more than one occasion, I have heard these footsteps. I couldn't see anything, but I could feel my robes being plucked. There was no chance that the robes might have caught on anything as I walked downstairs."

Judge Bigelow was not the only officer of the court to report strange sounds on stairways. Apparently Judge Peter Wilch heard the mysterious footsteps on the stairways. He heard footfalls ahead of him on the stairs and raced to overtake them. He reached the top floor of the building and found no one there.

Caretakers who have worked in the building for decades have felt nothing. Others who have worked equally long maintain there are "presences" throughout the building. John Carey, operations manager of the Metro Property Department, told the reporter, "I don't believe in ghosts, but there's something weird about the northwest attic." Other personnel point to the cellars, which are said to reverberate with the moans of former prisoners in the detention areas.

In 1978, journalist Jane Widerman quoted the views of the night foreman Dennis McTernan: "You hear footsteps all over the place, and there's nothing there. Things put on top of filing cabinets are on their sides or on the floor an hour later. The footsteps and noises in the old courtrooms are so bad that some of the women are afraid to work alone in many of the rooms. There's definitely something going on in Old City Hall."

Is Courtroom 33 haunted by the spirits of those convicted and hanged? As reporter Robert Brehl noted, "Canada's last criminals to get the noose, Arthur Lucas and Ron Turpin on December 11, 1962, were sentenced in Courtroom 33. That's the room where most of the 'ghosts' congregate, legend says."

It has become a Halloween tradition for journalists to spend the night of October 31st in Courtroom 33. In the late 1980s, a reporter for the *Star* and her sister decided to test the truth that the building is haunted. They camped out in Courtroom 33. Although they wanted to spend the night there, when the witching hour approached, they were frightened by the "weird sounds" and "cool fogs." At one point they felt their feet were "glued" to the floor. They lasted until 4:00 a.m., when they left for home and for a good night's sleep. The reporter and her sister never did prove one way or the other that the Old City Hall is haunted, only that it feels haunted.

The Strange Disappearance of Ambrose Small

Ambrose Small disappeared under puzzling circumstances. What happened to him? Did he seek a fresh new life under an assumed name in a distant city? Was he kidnapped? Was he murdered? Whatever was his fate?

Site: Grand Opera House (demolished in 1946)

Locale: 9-15 Adelaide Street West, south side, near Yonge Street; today the site is occupied by office complexes

Period: 5:30 p.m., 2 December 1919

Sources: W. Stewart Wallace, "The Mystery of Ambrose Small, *"Murders and Mysteries* (Toronto: Macmillan Company of Canada Ltd., 1931)

Robert Thomas Allen, "What Really Happened to Ambrose Small?" *Maclean's,* 15 January 1951

Charles Fort, *The Books of Charles Fort* (New York: Henry Holt and Company, 1941)

Fred McClement, *The Strange Case of Ambrose Small* (Toronto: McClelland & Stewart, 1974)

Murray Rutherford, "Where's Ambrose Small," *Early Canadian Life,* October 1978

The most famous missing person in Canadian history has to be Ambrose Small. The man's life was interesting enough, but his disappearance earned him enduring if posthumous fame in the form of an ongoing legend and in the following cryptic paragraph which appears in Charles Fort's book *Wild Talents* (1932):

> Upon December 2, 1919, Ambrose Small, of Toronto, Canada, disappeared. He was known to have been in his office, in the Toronto Grand Opera House, of which he was the owner, between five and six o'clock, the evening of December 2nd. Nobody saw him leave his office. Nobody — at least nobody whose testimony can be accepted — saw him, this evening, outside the building. There were stories

of a woman in the case. But Ambrose Small disappeared and left more than a million dollars behind.

Fort was a collector of such oddities. He noted that Ambrose Small disappeared in Toronto and Ambrose Bierce vanished in Mexico, so he came to this conclusion: "Somebody is collecting Ambroses."

At the time of his disappearance Small was at the height of his career. Born at Bradford, Ontario, on 11 January 1867, he was fifty-three years old, living in a mansion in Rosedale, a self-made millionaire, the owner of theatres in seven Ontario cities, and the controller of bookings in sixty-two other houses. The day before his disappearance, he sold his theatrical holdings for $1.7 million. The payment was in the bank and remained untouched.

Ambrose Small is Canada's most famous "missing man." Despite his notoriety, few decent photographs of the man have survived. This one, which catches the theatre magnate at his desk in the Grand Opera House in Toronto, appeared in Fred McClement's book *The Strange Case of Ambrose Small* [1974].
[McClelland & Stewart]

Ambrose Small's mysterious disappearance in downtown Toronto in 1919 resulted in news stories and articles in newspapers and magazines about his supposed fate. In 1984, Small inspired illustrator Peter Whalley to draw this delightful cartoon.
[Hawkshead Services]

113

The day of his disappearance, he met with his lawyer and friend F.W.M. Flock in his office at the Grand Opera House near Adelaide and Yonge Streets. Flock left at 5:30 p.m., the last person known to the police to have set eyes on Small, except for a newsboy who might have seen Small walking east on Adelaide Street. The disappearance of a prominent businessman under such odd circumstances was guaranteed to catch the public's imagination. An extensive police investigation came to naught. Small was pronounced dead in 1923, but the case remained unsolved and was not officially closed until 1960.

Like Elvis Presley, Small is gone but not forgotten. Over the years he was reportedly seen in a slew of places, including Brampton (Ontario), Montreal (Quebec), and Juarez (Mexico). Psychics tried and failed to locate him. Both Harry Blackstone, the magician, and Sir Arthur Conan Doyle expressed interest in the case. But no traces or clues as to his whereabouts were ever found.

The ghost of Ambrose Small is said to haunt his favourite property, which is not the Grand Opera House in Toronto but the Grand Theatre in London, Ontario. After a disastrous fire in 1900, he had that theatre rebuilt. Perhaps he haunts it to this day.

The Haunted Hockey Hall of Fame

Does Dorothy, the disgruntled ghost of the beautiful young teller of the old Bank of Montreal, haunt the new Hockey Hall of Fame?

Site: The Hockey Hall of Fame

Locale: Corner of Yonge Street and Front Street

Hours: Open seven days a week: Monday through Wednesday, 9:00 a.m. to 6:00 p.m.; Thursday and Friday, to 9:30 p.m.; Saturday, to 6:00 p.m.; Sunday, 10:00 a.m. to 6:00 p.m. Phone (416) 360-7765

Period: The Old Bank of Montreal (1847-1983)

              The Hockey Hall of Fame opened in 1993

Sources: Stefan Scaini, "Buildings that Hold the Souls of the Dead," The Toronto *Star*, 14 January 1984

              William Houston, "Truth and Rumours," *The Globe and Mail*, 19 June 1993

The lovely beaux-arts building on the northwest corner of Yonge Street and Front Street served as a downtown branch of the Bank of Montreal from its opening in 1847 to its closing in 1983. There were plans to turn the building into a museum of photography but these fell through. Restored to the 1885 period, it became part of the Hockey Hall of Fame at BCE Place, when the Hall moved from Exhibition Place to this site in 1993. Perhaps it should be called the Haunted Hockey Hall of Fame.

The tradition is that the old Bank of Montreal building was haunted by the disgruntled ghost of a beautiful young bank teller named Dorothy. She worked in the bank in the early 1900s and had an affair with a married teller. After being rejected, she shot herself in the upstairs washroom.

The ghost of Dorothy has been seen on a number of occasions. Journalist Stefan Scaini interviewed Len Redwood, the bank's chief messenger for twenty-five years, who described Dorothy in these terms: "Lively, full of life and always smiling. She was the most popular girl in the bank." One morning in March 1953, he recalled seeing Dorothy enter the bank around 7:00 a.m. "This was much earlier than she was expected to be in. She looked pretty rough, probably had a night out." According to

Redwood, Dorothy went up to the women's washroom and remained there for some time. She came downstairs for a moment, then went back upstairs. "The next thing I heard was the shot." It seems Dorothy had shot herself in the head with the bank's revolver.

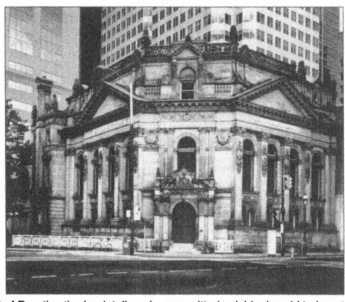

The spirit of Dorothy, the bank teller who committed suicide, is said to haunt the Hockey Hall of Fame. Not for nothing is the place known as the Haunted Hall of Fame! The facade of the Bank of Montreal bank, built in 1847, recalls the distant past. The hall's many displays celebrate hockey's golden years.

[Hockey Hall of Fame]

Scaini noted that "in the weeks that followed, strange things began to happen. Lights would come on and turn off by themselves, doors that had been locked were found wide open. 'We all felt something,' Redwood recalls, 'like there was someone watching us but you couldn't see them.' The cleaning staff became nervous about working in the bank after dark, claiming they heard 'funny noises.' The women refused to use the upstairs washroom, so the bank was forced to build another one in the basement.

"Things settled down after some time, but Dorothy would occasionally remind the staff she was still around by turning on lights or tripping a buzzer. 'Sometimes I got kind of edgy, but most of the time I didn't worry about it,' said Redwood. 'I guess you get kind of used to it.'"

Dorothy is part of the folklore of the Sports Hall of Fame. Columnist William Houston quoted one of the Hall's publicists as saying, "If we've misplaced something, we say, 'Well, it must be Dorothy.'" He also quoted Ron Ellis, a former Maple Leaf, who works at the Hall. Ellis "has heard Dorothy but after playing for Punch Imlach he said nothing frightens him."

Central

East of Yonge Street

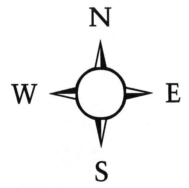

The Philip Phenomenon

If the spirits of the dead prove to be elusive, what about the spirits of the human imagination? Are they elusive too? Is it possible to imagine a spirit into existence?

Site: Private residence in Rosedale

Locale: 10 Sherbourne Street North, north of Bloor Street West

Period: 1970-76

Sources: A.R.G. Owen, *Psychic Mysteries of Canada: Discoveries from the Maritime Provinces and Beyond* (New York: Harper & Row, 1975)

           Iris M. Owen and Margaret Sparrow, *Conjuring Up Philip: An Adventure in Psychokinesis* (Toronto: Fitzhenry & Whiteside, 1976)

The Philip Phenomenon is assuredly the single most fascinating development in the field of parapsychology over the last few decades. It put Toronto on the map of world psychical research.

George and Iris Owen appear in this photograph taken in the lobby of their Toronto apartment in 1987. As one commentator noted, "The Owens are the best-loved and most-active couple in parapsychological circles in this country." In 1993, the Owens moved to Calgary, Alberta.

[Hawkshead Services]

The Philip Phenomenon was the handiwork of a group of researchers associated with the Toronto Society for Psychical Research. Founded in 1970 by A.R.G. Owen and Iris M. Owen, among others, the Toronto Society was modelled on the original Society for Psychical Research, established in London in 1882, and its counterpart, the American Society for Psychical Research, founded three years later.

Some members of the Toronto SPR directed their efforts to the study of the conventions of the séance. It should be noted that these members were not mediums, although a number of them felt themselves to be mediumistic. They made no attempt to communicate with distant spirits or with the spirits of the deceased. Instead, they decided to experiment. They asked themselves the following question: Is it possible, through the use of raps — one for "yes," two for "no" — to communicate not with a spirit entity but with the *idea* of a spirit? After some months they were able to give an affirmation answer to that question: (Rap) "Yes."

The group fabricated a spirit out of whole cloth. In the time-honoured manner of the historical novelist, they created a credible character. They imagined a young Cavalier at the time of the English Civil War, named him Philip, and established him in Diddington Manor, a real country estate in Warwickshire. It was explained that Philip was born in 1624, at twenty he married the beautiful but imperious Dorothea, at thirty he fell in love with the sensuous Margo, and he died in 1654. Such are the bare

The graceful portico is a distinguishing feature of this fine home on Sherbourne Street. In the 1970s, the Rosedale residence served as the home of George and Iris Owen and as a place of meeting for psychical researchers and parapsychologists from around the world. The landmark Philip poltergeist séances were conducted here.

[Josh Goldhar]

bones of the authorized biography. Most intriguing is the fact that when the group began to question Philip through raps, the spirit substantiated the "cover" story and then began to embellish and revise it. New facets of his life began to emerge. Some facts were consistent with what is known of English history; some were contrary to the historical record. The group had contacted a spirit — at times a truthful spirit, but at other times a lying spirit!

The Philip Phenomenon offers proof of nothing, but it does dramatically demonstrate the dynamics of the séance situation — with its physical and mental mediumship and its reputed "spirit communication." It was an experiment in psychokinesis. This episode in parapsychological history offers promise of a better understanding of the dynamics of group interaction, of the psychical consequences of belief, if not of contact with the "spirit-world."

Members of the Toronto Society for Psychical Research and the New Horizons Research Foundation regularly met in the parlour and other rooms of the stately, columned residence at 10 Sherbourne Street North. At the time it was the home of the Owens. Since then it has changed hands and is occupied by a couple who have no particular interest in Philip of Diddington Manor. The residence is in no way haunted — except by the spirits of the past.

The Ghost of the Keg

Was a maid hanged here? Does a child run wild? Why was the armchair stuffed into the windowframe?

Site: The Keg Mansion

Locale: Public restaurant, 515 Jarvis Street, north of Wellesley Street

Hours: Monday through Friday the lounge is open from 4:00 p.m. to 1:00 a.m., dining room from 5:00 p.m. to 11:00 p.m. (on Friday to midnight); Saturday, lounge from 4:30 p.m. to 1:00 a.m., dining-room from 4:30 p.m. to midnight; Sunday, lounge from 4:30 to 11:00 p.m., dining-room from 4:30 to 10:00 p.m. Phone (416) 964 6609

Period: 1950s to the present

Sources: "Halloween Ghosts," *CBC-TV's Newsweek,* 29 October 1987

Mitch Potter, "Halloween Haunts of the Witch and Famous," *The Toronto Star,* 28 October 1988

Brochure titled *The Keg Mansion: Surround Yourself in History* (Toronto: Keg Mansion, 1994)

The Keg Mansion is perhaps the most popular of the twenty or so restaurants in the Keg chain that are found across Metropolitan Toronto. According to architectural writer Patricia McHugh, the mansion was erected by Arthur R. McMaster in 1868. According to the brochure issued by the Keg Mansion, it was erected in 1853 by Lord William McMaster, founder of McMaster University. The mansion was named Euclid Hall in 1860 (brochure) or in 1882 (McHugh) when purchased by Hart Massey, founder of Massey Ferguson, the world's largest manufacturer of farm machinery. King George V and Queen Mary stayed here as house guests. It was the childhood home of Raymond Massey, the actor, and Governor General Vincent Massey. It served as the Massey family home until either 1915 or the 1920s.

McHugh described its architecture as "the quintessential Baronial Gothic ensemble." In the post-Massey period it served as an art gallery, radio station, convalescent home, and popular restaurant called Julie's Mansion with a party bar known as the Bombay Bicycle Club (which advertised itself as "ideal for the type of person who has absolutely no inhibitions or is interested in losing what few he has left"). The period setting made it an ideal set for scenes in the movie *Moonstruck* and episodes in the *Alfred Hitchcock Presents* TV series. The mansion joined the popular Vancouver-based Keg restaurant chain in 1976. As the brochure runs, "Since then the Keg Mansion has established its commitment to quality steak and seafood dinners served in a fun, relaxed atmosphere .... Every superb meal comes with a side order of history."

The old Massey residence, on Jarvis Street, has known many owners and occupants. [It bears a slight resemblance to Borley Rectory, "the most haunted house in England."] Today it serves as the Keg Mansion. In the early 1950s it acquired a reputation as a haunt.
[Josh Goldhar]

Creepy happenings have been reported here since the early 1950s, perhaps earlier. Two stories are commonly told. One story has it that a phantom child runs wild and that on one occasion an armchair was found stuffed into a windowframe. Apparently, one of Massey's young sons, forbidden to play on the Sabbath, argued with his father and in a fit of anger dragged his father's favourite chair noisily across the floor. There have been numerous reports of the sound of children laughing and playing, always coming from the upper floors where the children's quarters were located. The other story that is told is that after Lilian Massey died in 1908 in the second-floor bedroom, a maid was so grief-stricken that she hanged herself in the oval vestibule above the main foyer. A hanging spectre supposedly appears from time to time.

Journalist Mitch Potter interviewed the general manager, Pat Murphy, in 1988. Murphy said that six months earlier he was alone in the building when he heard a little boy's voice calling, "Mommy, Mommy, I'm over here." Murphy continued, "I went straight to the bar and had a martini. And it's not just me, our bartender saw a little boy run by when nobody was around. The music goes on, the lights go on and off — all by themselves."

These days, whenever strange things happen, the staff is in the habit of joking, "Mrs. Massey's back."

The Haunted Theatre

It was reputed to be a "haunted theatre" ... but that was in the days of Toronto Workshop Productions. Now that the building has been renovated and is under new artistic control, will the spirit live up to advance billing?

Site: Site of the old Toronto Workshop Productions, now site of Buddies in Bad Times Theatre

Locale: Buddies in Bad Times Theatre, 12 Alexander Street, off Yonge Street, north of Carlton Street

Period: 1980s

Sources: Andrew Piotrowski, "A Message from the Ghost of Summer to Come?" *The Toronto Sun*, 11 May 1980

Henry Mietkiewicz, "New Lease on Life for Downtown Theatre," *The Toronto Star*, 8 August 1990

Interview with Patricia Wilson, media relations coordinator, Buddies in Bad Times Theatre, 11 July 1994

The city's first alternative theatre was Toronto Workshop Productions, founded in 1959. It flourished under the artistic direction of its founder George Luscombe. Its original home was in the basement of a factory in the city's West End. In 1968, TWP moved to a warehouse-like building on Alexander Street just off Yonge Street. Here, in the centre of the city, in its 320-seat theatre, TWP produced such notable theatrical works as Barry Broadfoot's *Ten Lost Years* and Rick Salutin's *Les Canadiens*.

TWP folded in 1988 and the property was acquired by the Toronto City Council which leased it to a succession of theatrical groups. The building, extensively renovated, is now managed by a company called Buddies in Bad Times Theatre. Under the artistic directorship of Sky Gilbert, it held a gala re-opening of the theatre on 12 October 1994. The company is self-described as "the world's largest gay, lesbian, and innovative theatre."

Theatre history is replete with tragic tales of star-struck understudies, disgruntled stagehands, backstage ghosts, crashing chandeliers, phantoms of operas, and references to "that play" (Shakespeare's *Macbeth*). Theatres in Britain feature their ghosts. In London, Ontario, the Grand Theatre is said to be haunted by the spirit of Ambrose Small, its one-time owner-manager. No one has ever identified the spirit or spirits that were said to have haunted Toronto Workshop Productions.

Christopher Faulkner, long-time TWP associate, recalled an eerie experience he had on the first night he remained alone in the building in order to practise the drums. How heavy he felt the atmosphere was; how heavy were the footfalls he heard. He told researcher Andrew Piotrowski in 1980: "It began with a clatter in the basement. Now that I know more about it, I believe that's the centre of the activity — the costume storage area in the cellar. In any case, that first night was frightening. I mean, think about it. I heard those footfalls, heard them walk up the basement stairs, heard them step up onto the stage and continue moving toward me. But there was no one there! I ran screaming out the back door, the nearest door, in abject fear!"

Piotrowski, intrigued with Faulkner's experience, resolved to spend a night alone in the theatre building. Here is his account of that frightful night.

> Twelve o'clock on a cold Saturday night. With some trepidation, I walk north on the Yonge Street strip, turn left on Alexander, and climb the steps leading to the entrance of the TWP, the oldest and most respected theatre of its kind in all of Canada.
>
> Using the keys so generously loaned to me, I unlock the front door and let myself into the lobby. It's deserted and shadow-strewn, the only light being that of the street lamps shining through the large front windows. I lock the door behind me.
>
> I'm a ghosthunter who likes to work alone.
>
> To guarantee that the theatre is indeed empty, at least of other living people, the first step on the agenda is to patrol the entire building. Although few know about my experiment, I realize that some practical joker may have heard about my wanting to spend the night investigating the rumours of TWP hauntings, and that possibility has to be immediately squelched.
>
> Without turning any lights on, I stroll first through the offices facing the street. No one there. I then cross the gloomy lobby and enter a stairwell leading up into the theatre proper.
>
> The agreement was that throughout the building some lights would be left burning. I know there will be a single lamp dimly illuminating the front stage centre area, but the stairwell itself is uncompromisingly dark, devoid even of the illumination cast by the street lamps.

Stumbling, I slow my pace and cautiously ascend the stairs, each movement forward taking me closer to the psychic hot spot that had distressed so many of the haunting witnesses ....

Stepping out of the stairwell, the theatre unfolds before me, row after focused row of empty seats. Looking down the aisles, the apron of the stage invites me. I walk towards it.

A crude wooden table and chair had been placed for my use directly beneath the single light hanging above. It sways gently on its long black cord. A slight breeze no doubt.

I put my few tools on the table top and continue the initial patrol, walking to the back of the stage, through the ribbon/screen being used in the current production, stepping once again into the semi-dark.

Familiar with the layout of the building, I know the backstage area houses dressing rooms and a workspace for costumes.

Without incident I walk first through the dressing rooms, sensing nothing more than the psychic echoes of past productions, the excitement of opening nights, the triumphs and, yes, despairs of the many performers who had made seriously committed emotional use of the space.

Then I cross backstage from the dressing rooms and into the costumers' workshop. I step a few feet into the room. A single lamp is burning on a corner table top. The room obviously uninhabited, I turn to go and then, out of the corner of my eye, I notice a button on the extension telephone blinking red in the gloom!

Isn't the building empty?

Quickly answering, nothing is heard. No voice, no sound of breathing and, oddly enough, even the familiar hum of a dial tone is absent.

I turn to the Ouija board left on the table top. Now the Ouija board is also a psychic tool, and a potentially dangerous psychic tool at that.

But for me it is a starting point. I set the board on my knees, place my fingers lightly on the planchette, and begin the questioning.

"Is there a spirit present?" Initially there's no movement whatsoever, then the planchette moves.

"Yes," it answers.

"What message do you have for me, spirit?"

Slowly the answer is indicated, single letter by letter. The words given are "the summer."

Is prophecy forthcoming? "What about this summer? What are you trying to say, spirit?" There is a long pause. I sit, all senses straining.

I then hear the distinct sound of a door closing. The sound comes from the direction of the basement. That is definite.

"Spirit?" I ask. And slowly, very slowly, over a period of long minutes, three letters are indicated. A "g." A "d" and then an "h." The planchette stops. It means nothing to me. I ask for clarification and wait.

Then I notice something even stranger. When I remove my fingers to stretch them, the planchette stays firmly and exactly in place. I had expected at least one slight movement. Tentatively touching the planchette, it surprises me in that it's stuck to the highly waved surface of the board itself. Odd. Very odd. To free the planchette, I find it necessary to grip the heart-shaped pointer firmly.

It's time to investigate the basement itself.

Walking down the cellar steps, I see a bit of light shining beneath the crack of the closed door at the foot of the stairs. Nothing unusual there. It was agreed that a few basement lights would be left burning.

Hundreds of dusty, damp-smelling costumes line all the walls of the odd-shaped room, are heaped on tables, are crushed together on rack after overburdened rack. I walk slowly about, taking in the riot of colours, textures, and shapes.

Then in a far corner I notice a grotesque cotton puppet, a distorted face and head impaled on the end of a wooden stick. Recognizing it as a prop used in the theatre's recent production of *The Hunchback of Notre Dame*, I cross the basement floor and touch the puppet's grinning face. It's warm.

Warm?!

Without thinking, I shove the costumes aside, looking past them for a radiator, perhaps, or a furnace pipe, searching for a natural cause for the unexpected heat emanating from the grimacing face of the doll. There are no pipes behind the rack, no radiator.

Then, behind me ... a footfall!

I freeze, visualizing a halo or cloud of protective white light about and around me. I turn.

And suddenly, as though superimposed over the sight of the basement itself, there is yet another and second view.

I find myself standing in a grassy, open field, a beautiful late-summer evening. The night air is cool, refreshing despite the heat. I sense nearby a large body of swiftly flowing water.

Applause is heard. Many people applauding. Turning, I look across the field in a different direction and see in the distance a large, beautiful modern building, its attractive brightly lit lobby clearly seen through the huge glass windows that form the wall looking out into the field in which I'm standing.

The lobby is filled with well-dressed people, evening gowns, tuxedos, expensive suits, and glittering jewelry. I recognize the building and the site.

But the vision changes. Now everything seems to be in closeup. I see faces, soundless mouths opening and closing, silent lips excitedly chattering. The air is rank with hypocrisy and betrayal.

Then, as suddenly as it materialized, the vision fades and once again I'm standing alone in the basement.

I stand stark still, barely daring to breathe, then run across the basement floor and up the stairs, across the stage, gather up my belongings, negotiate the dark of the stairwell, hurry through the lobby, and finally step into the clear, cold, liberating night air, locking the theatre's front door behind me.

Once again I walk down Yonge Street, hugging my greatcoat about my trembling body. It's now slightly after two in the morning, the streets almost deserted.

A taxi stops for me, and as we drive into the night, I can't help but wonder what tragedy, what terrible scandal will strike this summer at Niagara-on-the-Lake. And what did the three disconnected letters (G-D-H) mean? Are they initials? A code of some kind? Counting in from the front of the alphabet, perhaps they're a date: The fourth of July, 1980?

"Where to?" the taxicab driver asks.

"Just drive for a bit, will you?" I tell him. There are so many questions, many more questions than answers. But that's no big surprise.

Hauntings are like that.

The Haunting of Massey Hall

The Phantom of the Opera has haunted Toronto's musical scene for more than half a decade. But the city's real phantom has ... or has not ... haunted the backstage of Massey Hall for ten times ten years.

Site: Massey Hall

Locale: 15 Shuter Street, at Victoria Street

Period: From 1894 to the present

Phone: For tickets to concerts, phone (416) 593-4828

Sources: William Kilbourn, *Intimate Grandeur: One Hundred Years at Massey Hall* (Toronto: Stoddart, 1994)

Interview with Joseph Cartan, retired General Manager, 17 June 1994

It is an open question whether or not Massey Hall, once the city's prime venue for musical performances, is haunted by spirits or spectres. The building's drab exterior belies speculation that the interior is infected with high spirits.
[Josh Goldhar]

129

Massey Hall, the well-loved concert auditorium, served as the centre of the city's musical life for more than a century. Donated to the city by industrialist Hart Massey, it was opened in 1894, and it was the city's principal concert hall until the completion of the Roy Thomson Hall in 1983. It is renowned for its acoustics, not its aesthetics. As Patricia McHugh noted, "Its flat-chested red-brick exterior never had any great architectural pretensions." Today, many Torontonians prefer the ambience and acoustics of the old hall to those of the new.

The Hall has some distant connections with the spirit world. From its podium Sir Oliver Lodge lectured on "Evidences of Survival" on 15 May 1920; Mrs. Annie Besant, head of the Theosophical Society, delivered two addresses in 1926, on November 1 and November 3. She concluded each address with these words: "May the blessings of our Masters rest on us all, illuminating our minds, and filling our hearts with love."

There are rumours (rather than reports) that Massey Hall is haunted. William Kilbourn in *Intimate Grandeur* experienced and conveyed some of the ghostly ambience of the Hall:

> It is late and the Hall is empty, crepuscular. I sit at the gallery's edge, looking down on that great expanse of stage. The old place creaks and rattles a bit and from somewhere far below moans obscurely. The air is alive with silence. The only city sound is a siren's wail, an ambulance for St. Michael's Emergency next door. Its surcease swells the dusk with more ghosts and echoes.
>
> I have never met the Massey Hall apparition, said to be that of a janitor who once lived in the abandoned top flat just behind the stage. I am not sure he is still about; he was never a presence as definite as that of the mild little lady who, after she died, used to visit Healey Willan and various choristers in St. Mary Magdalene's Church.

No one has been associated with the Hall longer than Joseph Cartan, who began as an usher in 1929 and retired as General Manager in 1984. He was the first person to arrive and the last person to leave the Hall at night. Asked about its ghosts, he had this to say:

> In all my years at Massey Hall, I never heard a story of a ghost. There are no ghosts, spirits, or apparitions in the Hall. Nor were there suicides, sudden deaths, or mysterious disappearances in the Hall. If you're looking for Ambrose Small, you won't find him on stage, back stage, or in the audience. People who write about ghosts and

apparitions do so tongue-in-cheek. Reporters are always asking about ghosts and also about the eccentricities of artists. But the ghosts don't exist and most performers are professionals who come to the Hall, perform, and leave. Some of them have mannerisms but few have eccentricities. The strangest event that I recall was renting the hall in 1954 or 1955 for $300 or so to a hospital orderly who billed himself as "Dr. No." He advertised that he would speak on World Federalism. We opened the doors at 7:30 p.m. and at 8:00 p.m. he emerged from the dressing room in a blue cloak with a red lining and approached the stage. But there was not a soul in the house. Nobody came, so we closed the doors at 8:30 p.m. and "Dr. No" went home. That was the strangest appearance at the Hall in my experience.

The Haunted Hospital Ward

Is there a haunted ward in the hospital? Does a ghostly nun make her rounds? What accounts for her appearance?

Site: Ward 7B, St. Michael's Hospital

Locale: 30 Bond Street, north of Queen Street East

Period: 1950s to the present

Source: Interview with Danielle Urquhart, "the Ghost Lady," 22 June 1994

St. Michael's College is owned and operated by the Sisters of St. Joseph. The teaching institution, which embodies Catholic principles of health care, opened its doors in 1892.

There is a story about the haunting of one of its wards. The story will not be found in the books that were written to mark the hospital's centenary — Irene McDonald's *For the Least of My Brethren: A Centenary History of St. Michael's Hospital* (Toronto: Dundurn Press, 1992) and P.A. Kopplin, editor, *On Call in the Heart of the City: 100 Years of Resident and Intern Life at St. Michael's Hospital* (Toronto: Warwick Publishing, 1993). Yet staff and former patients of the institution attest to its truth ... or at least pass on the tradition.

The ward in question is haunted by the spirit of one of the Sisters of St. Joseph. She has a name, Sister Vincenza, and a nickname, Vinnie. "The nun, a most devoted nurse, died in the late 1950s and is still apparently doing her rounds. Lights in Ward 7B are mysteriously switched on and off. The sight of the spirit, though benevolent, is rather disconcerting, as what the witnesses report seeing is the nun's habit with no nun inside. The wimple frames a black chasm where the face should be!"

St. Michael's Hospital is operated by the Sisters of St. Joseph. Sister Vincenza, the nun without a face, is said to make the rounds in Ward 7B. She is shown here by artist and illustrator Isaac Bickerstaff.
[Courtesy: Don Evans]

SISTER VINCENZA

The Haunting of Mackenzie House

Who haunts Mackenzie House? Is it the spirit of the fiery little rebel William Lyon Mackenzie? Is it the wraith of Isabel Grace King, Mackenzie's youngest daughter, the mother of Prime Minister W.L. Mackenzie King?

Site: Mackenzie House

Locale: 82 Bond Street, between Queen Street East and Dundas Street East

Hours: Closed Monday; Tuesday through Saturday, 9:30 a.m. to 5:00 p.m.; Sunday, noon to 5:00. Phone (416) 392 6915

Period: Ghostly disturbances reported between 1956 and 1960

Sources: Andrew MacFarlane, "The Ghosts that Live in Toronto, *The Toronto Telegram*, 28 June 1960.

Frank Jones, "Visiting Our Restless Spirits," *The Toronto Star*, 26 October 1980

Joe Nickell, *Secrets of the Supernatural: Investigating the World's Occult Mysteries* (Buffalo: Prometheus Books, 1988)

Chris Raible, "The Haunting of Mackenzie House," *The Beaver*, December 1989 — January 1990

John Robert Colombo, *Mackenzie King's Ghost and Other Personal Accounts of Canadian Hauntings* (Toronto: Hounslow Press, 1991)

Interview with Robin Shepherd, high-school principal and former Mackenzie House guide, 26 June 1994

Additional information supplied by Eleanor Darke, curator, Mackenzie House, 27 June 1994

Mackenzie House is one of Toronto's most historic homes. Since 1960, the Georgian-style building has been maintained as a museum by the Toronto Historical Board. Mackenzie House has been called the most haunted house in Toronto; as such it is perhaps the most haunted house in all of Canada. It is frequently said that the THB has a policy to deny ghost stories, but as its curator Eleanor Darke noted, "The THB does not have a 'policy' to deny ghost stories. Staff, supported by their managers, simply do not promote a story for which they have no personal or other proof of authenticity." Instead, interpreters dressed in period costume escort visitors through its halls and rooms, which are furnished to recall the period of the 1860s, and offer historical information and interpretation. "They will discuss the ghost story if queried, but will not spend much time discussing what they do not believe to be true."

Mackenzie House is a handsome, gracious building, shown here in a photograph taken in 1985. The historic building was anything but peaceful during the 1960s, when it was described as "the most haunted house in Canada."
[Collection of the Toronto Historical Board, Toronto, Canada.]

The residence bears the proud name of the fiery little Scot William Lyon Mackenzie (1795-1861). Mackenzie was the energetic publisher of the *Colonial Advocate*, first Mayor of the City of Toronto in 1834, the promoter of responsible government, and the leader in Upper Canada of the Rebellion of 1837. When the uprisings were suppressed, Mackenzie fled and found refuge in New York State where he continued his agitation. With the amnesty he returned to Toronto but remained a very controversial figure. He is known to this day as "the firebrand."

The three-storey brick residence at 82 Bond Street, erected in the 1850s, was acquired and presented to him by grateful friends in recognition of public service. He lived in the house from 1859 until his death which occurred in the second-floor bedroom on 28 August 1861. Mackenzie's widow, Isabel Baxter, died on 12 January 1879, but not in this house. She died at 19 Charlotte Street in Toronto where she had moved with her three unmarried daughters, Helen, Elizabeth, and Isabel Grace, in 1871. The Mackenzies rented the Bond Street house to a dentist, Franklin Callender, in 1871, and to Joseph Walker, a merchant, the following year. Isabel Baxter Mackenzie's will left the Bond Street house to any of her daughters who were unmarried when she died. Isabel Grace married John King a month before her mother died, so the property went to Helen and Elizabeth Mackenzie. The two daughters continued to live on Charlotte Street. During most of the next four and a half years, they leased the house to a widow named Anne Davison. On 10 May 1877 they sold the house to a merchant, William Hutchison Sparrow, who lived there until his death in 1883. His family then rented the house to a variety of tenants.

William Lyon Mackenzie was not a man to see ghosts, though he gave members of the Family Compact "the willies." Yet, it is said he haunts Mackenzie House to this day. This photographic portrait shows him in his later years.
[Unknown photographer, Public Archives of Canada; PAC-1993]

Isabel Grace King who lived in the residence died in Ottawa in 1917. She was the wife of the lawyer John King and the mother of William Lyon Mackenzie King (1874-1950) who served as Prime Minister of Canada. Mackenzie King was fascinated by spiritualism and by the question of human survival after death. Indeed, in 1954, one of his friends, the correspondent Percy J. Philip, claimed that earlier that year the ghost of Mackenzie King had joined him and conversed with him for some time on a park bench at Kingsmere, Mackenzie King's country estate in the Gatineau region of Quebec!

Mackenzie King, seated before the shrine in Laurier House, Ottawa, gazes at the portrait of his mother, painted by J.W.L. Forster in 1905. In the portrait, she holds in her hand a copy of John Morley's *Life of Gladstone* which is open prophetically at the chapter headed "Prime Minister."
[Unknown photographer, Public Archives of Canada; PAC-75053]

Psychical disturbances were reported in Mackenzie House between 1956 and 1960. There were no reports prior to 1956; they were concentrated in the four-year-period of transition. And while major reports concluded in 1960, minor ones were noted until 1966. Nonetheless, it is not uncommon to encounter former staff who feel that something "eerie" still lingers in the building. Visitors often comment on the "oddness" of the place.

There are accounts of the appearance of a short, frock-coated man with bald head and wig in the third-floor bedroom ... a woman with long flowing hair in the third-floor and second-floor bedrooms and halls ... phantom footfalls and cold spots on the stairways ... the piano in the parlour playing on its own ... the printing-press in the basement clanking all by itself ....

The earliest accounts come from a responsible couple, Mr. and Mrs. Charles Edmunds. They were the house's first live-in caretakers. They occupied Mackenzie House from 13 August 1956 to April 1960; they left because of the peculiar disturbances. They were followed by Mr. and Mrs. Alex Dobban who arrived in April 1960. The Dobbans, complaining of the same disturbances as the Edmunds, left that June. Archdeacon John Frank of Holy Trinity Anglican Church was called to conduct an exorcism in the parlour, which he did in the presence of reporters on 2 July 1960. Since that time the house's caretakers have lived outside the house, but workmen on the premises and visitors have intermittently complained of disturbances.

The most intelligent discussion — and debunking — of the ghostly happenings at Mackenzie House was conducted by Joe Nickell, a professional stage magician and a licensed private investigator. He has both prosaic and highly imaginative explanations for all the disturbances. For instance, the strange recurring noises that were reported by the caretakers are attributed to the operation of a noisy printing press located in the building next door which in the 1960s was occupied by the Macmillan Publishing Company. Nickell's explanations are a good antidote to credulous acceptance of ghostly phenomena (though they make less gripping reading than the experiences described by members of the Edmunds family!).

Mr. and Mrs. Charles Edmunds, the first care-taking couple, lived in the house for four years. Their accounts are included here, as are the shorter reports of their son Robert and his wife Minnie who were guests in the house. The four reports first appeared in the *Toronto Telegram* on 28 June 1960 as part of a series of articles titled "The Ghosts that Live in Toronto," written by the paper's enterprising reporter Andrew MacFarlane. The series appeared following the refusal of the Dobbans to remain in the house. MacFarlane secured sworn affidavits from all four member of the Edmunds family. They are reproduced here in a slightly edited form.

Twenty years later, journalist Frank Jones wrote about Mackenzie House and its tradition of hauntings in the *Toronto Star:*

> The women who work as hostesses at the house now don't like to talk much about it.
>
> But sitting in the kitchen, our chairs drawn around the pine table, the doubts and questions gradually emerged. "You either believe in ghosts or you don't," one said. "When I first came to work here I never gave it a thought. I didn't think there was anything unusual here. Now I've changed my mind.
>
> "Things happen that you wonder about," said the woman. "One day, soon after I came to work here, I was talking to a group of children here in the kitchen and one of their clamp boards flew through the air and landed on the table right there. I gave the girl who it belonged to a reproving look. But afterwards she came up and said she hadn't thrown it or dropped it. It was just as if it was pulled out of her hand."
>
> I wandered through the rooms where Mackenzie, that tortured man, had lived, and examined the piano in the

drawing room that the former caretakers swore used to play on its own. I turned quickly and for an instant saw in a dim, faded mirror an image of someone other than myself. The door, with its brass lion's head knocker, banged behind me, and I hurried down the steps.

A guide who worked here in the 1970s said that while she never saw a ghost or witnessed anything spectacular, it was a lot of little things that made her feel distinctly uncomfortable in the house. She found she was avoiding the very old part, the kitchen, as well as the printery. On occasion the printer, working late on special printing orders, would sleep over. One printer said he saw a female figure which he identified from the portrait on the wall as Mackenzie's wife, not his daughter. The figure appeared substantial and walked towards him. Even when the printer did not spend the night sleeping in one of the big beds with feather mattresses, the next morning the guides would find that the mattresses showed signs of having been used and they needed fluffing up.

Stories are legion. Here is one from a visitor. Lawrence J. Fenwick, who paid a visit to the house in 1977, lingered in the printery and watched the printer at work. There was a thick pile of paper ready to be printed. Although the window was shut and there was no draft and the press was not yet at work, the edges of the papers began to flutter all by themselves, an eerie sight.

As Eleanor Darke noted, "There is no way to prove or disprove what someone else said they saw or felt, but the current staff have had no experiences to support any tales of hauntings." Perhaps the last words should be those of researcher Chris Raible: "The ghost of Mackenzie may not inhabit his house, but his spirit and the spirit of his times can still be found there."

1. Mrs. Charles Edmunds

From the first day my husband and I went to stay at the Mackenzie Homestead, we could hear footsteps on the stairs when there was nobody in the house but us.

The first day, when I was alone in the house, I could hear someone clearly, walking up the stairs from the second floor to the top. Nearly every day there were footsteps at times when there was no one there to make them.

One night I woke up at midnight. I couldn't sleep, although I am normally a good sleeper. I saw a Lady standing over my bed. She wasn't at the side, but at the head of the bed, leaning over me. There is no room for anyone to stand where she was. The bed is pushed up against the wall.

She was hanging down, like a shadow, but I could see her clearly. Something seemed to touch me on the shoulder to wake me up. She had long hair hanging down in front of her shoulders, not black or gray or white, but dark brown, I think. She had a long narrow face. Then it was gone. Two years ago, early in March, I saw the Lady again. It was the same — except this time she reached out and hit me. When I woke up, my left eye was purple and bloodshot.

I also saw the man at night, a little bald man in a frock coat. I would just see him for a few seconds, and then he would vanish.

I often saw one or the other standing in the room — at least eight or nine times.

A year ago last April, I told my husband: "I have to get out of here." I had to get out of that house. If I didn't get out, I knew I'd be carried out in a box. I think it was the strain all the time that made me feel this way. I went from 130 pounds to 90 ½ pounds. I wasn't frightened, but it was getting my nerves down.

It was just like knowing there was someone watching you from behind all the time, from just over your shoulder.

Sometimes we'd sit watching the television. My husband might look up all of a sudden at the doorway. I knew what it was. You felt that someone had just come in.

My son and his wife heard the piano playing at night when they were staying with us. When my husband and my son went to look — it stopped.

We could feel the homestead shaking with a rumbling noise some nights. It must have been the press in the basement. We thought at first it might be the subway. But we were too far from the subway ....

I did not believe in ghosts when I went to stay at the Mackenzie Homestead. But I do now. It's the only explanation I can think of.

I wish to say that I would not say anything against the Mackenzies. They were hard-working people and so are we. They were not hard on us ... it's just that the house was a strain on the nerves.

2. Mr. Charles Edmunds

Certain happenings during the three years and eight months my wife and I served as caretakers of the Mackenzie Homestead have convinced me that there is something peculiar about the place.

On one occasion my wife and I were sleeping in the upstairs bedroom. She woke me up in the middle of the night and said that she had seen a man standing beside her bed.

My wife, to my certain knowledge, knew nothing of Mackenzie or his history. All of the pictures in the homestead show Mackenzie as a man with hair on his head. The man my wife saw and described to me was completely bald with side whiskers. I had read about Mackenzie. And I know that the man she described to me was Mackenzie. He wore a wig to cover his baldness. But she did not know this.

On another occasion, just after we moved, in my two grandchildren, Susan (then aged 4) and Ronnie (then aged 3) went from the upstairs bedroom down to the second-floor bathroom at night.

A few minutes later there were terrific screams. I went down and they were both huddled in the bathroom, terrified. They said there was a Lady in the bathroom. I asked where she was now and they said she just disappeared.

On another night my wife woke up screaming. She said: "There was a small man standing over my bed." She described Mackenzie.

Another night, a woman came up to the bed and looked at my missus. She was a little woman, about my wife's height. My wife said: "Dad — there was a woman here." I told her she was dreaming.

Another night my wife woke up and woke me. She was upset. She said the Lady had hit her. There were three red welts on the left side of her face. They were like finger marks. The next day her eye was bloodshot. Then it turned black and blue. Something hit her. It wasn't me. And I don't think she could have done it herself. And there wasn't anyone else in the house.

On another occasion something peculiar happened with some flowers we had in pots on a window ledge inside the house. This was in winter and we had the geraniums inside.

140

We watered the plants twice a week on Sundays and Wednesdays.

On a Saturday morning we found that they had all been watered, although we hadn't done it. There was water spilled all over the plants and the saucers they were standing in were full. There was mud on the curtains, and holes in the earth as if someone had poked their fingers in the earth. There was water on the dressing table. Neither of us had watered the plants, and neither had anyone else.

We often heard footsteps on the stairs. Thumping footsteps like someone with heavy boots on. This happened frequently when there was no one in the house but us, when we were sitting together upstairs.

The whole house used to shake with a rumbling sound sometimes. My wife is convinced that this was Mackenzie's press.

I am not an imaginative man, and I do not believe in ghosts. But the fact is that the house was strange enough so that we had to leave.

We would have stayed if it had not been for these happenings. But my wife could not stand it any longer.

3. Robert Edmunds

One night my wife woke me up. She said she heard the piano playing downstairs. I heard it, too. I can not remember what the music was like, but it was the piano downstairs playing.

Dad and I went downstairs. When we got to the last landing before the bottom, the piano stopped.

It was similar with the printing press in the basement. My wife heard it first and wakened me. I heard it, too. I identified the sound because it was the same as old presses I'd seen in movies and on television. A rumbling, clanking noise — not like modern presses. When Dad and I went downstairs to see about it, it stopped when we reached the same landing.

We heard the piano three or four times, the press just once.

I was not walking in my sleep. I heard them. I don't know what the explanation is. I am not prepared to say I saw any ghosts or apparitions. But I can say that I dreamt more in that house than I ever have before or since.

I do not believe in ghosts. But I find it hard to explain what we heard.

4. Mrs. Minnie Edmunds

When my husband and I were staying at Mackenzie Homestead, I heard the piano playing downstairs at night three or four times.

We discovered that there was no one downstairs to play it these times, and yet I heard it distinctly. Each time, I woke my husband, and when he and his father went downstairs to investigate it, it stopped.

On one other occasion I heard the printing press running in the basement. I woke my husband, and he and his father went to investigate it. It stopped.

It is not possible to operate the press, because it is locked, and on the occasions when I heard the piano, there was no one downstairs to play it. I can find no natural explanation for these occurrences.

East

The Old CBC Building on Sumach

Did a ghost dressed in black enter the elevator every time it stopped on the fourth floor? Many maintenance people wonder about it ....

Site: Former CBC Building on Sumach, currently an industrial warehouse slated for redevelopment

Locale: 90 Sumach Street, south of Eastern Avenue

Period: 1960s

Source: Eileen Sonin, "Great Ghosts of Toronto," *Saturday Night,* January 1968

Long-time employees of the Canadian Broadcasting Corporation used to refer to this six-storey, multi-purpose warehouse built in 1956 in Cabbagetown as the CBC Building on Sumach. It had no other name.

The old CBC Building on Sumach Street in the heart of Cabbagetown is being converted into residential studio loft condominiums. Will the developers be able to evict the black-dressed ghost that is said to haunt the fourth floor and hitches rides on the elevator?

[Josh Goldhar]

Television props were stored here. There were some radio and television rehearsal halls, not to mention the corporation's design centre and its centre for program archives. With the opening of the CBC's new Broadcasting Centre on Front Street West in July 1992, the days of the CBC Building on Sumach and of innumerable other CBC locations in downtown Toronto were numbered. It was finally vacated in late 1993.

What happened to its ghost? Some of the old building's maintenance people steadfastly maintained that the place had a resident spirit that haunted the fourth floor. Apparently, at night, it would be seen to step onto the elevator whenever it stopped on that floor. The ghost has been described as that of a tall, saturnine figure dressed in black. It seemed that it moved in a jerky, disconcerting way, as if ill-co-ordinated or carrying a load. One wonders if the sepulchral figure accompanied the television props in their move to to the new Broadcasting Centre.

The Shuter Street Poltergeist

There may be a mischievous spirit at work in this apartment building. Even worse, the mischievous spirit may be at play!

Site: Private residence, one-bedroom apartment in Cabbagetown

Locale: Apartment building at 295 Shuter Street, near Parliament Street.

Period: From 1983 to the present

Source: John Robert Colombo's *Mysterious Encounters: Personal Accounts of the Supernatural in Canada* (Toronto: Hounslow Press, 1990)

Isabel Germiquet prepared this detailed report of the poltergeist-like disturbances she has experienced over the five or so years while living in her apartment in Cabbagetown. For the record, the apartment is located in the building at 295 Shuter Street in downtown Toronto. She prepared this account of her experiences at my request on 19 December 1988. It takes a hardy soul to endure such disturbances!

I moved into the one-bedroom apartment in which I am now living on August 13th, 1983. As I was moving from a large, two-bedroom apartment, I had too much furniture. So I hung my clothes in the closet in the bedroom, and I put away my things in dresser drawers there, but at first I didn't actually sleep in the bedroom. I could hardly reach the bed for all the furniture and things. Whenever I worked my way through the bedroom to get a change of clothing, I could hear a male voice groaning from within the closet.

During the weeks that I couldn't use the bed, the door was kept closed because the bedroom was such a mess of furniture. In spite of this, I found that the door was frequently open. This happened many times a day, and I knew that I had not left it open. One particular day, when the door was shut, I tried to push it open, but it felt like someone was holding the door tightly shut. Suddenly it gave way, and I stumbled into the room. This was just the beginning. The following is a list of the phenomena that occurred in my apartment over the last five years, and continue to occur to this day.

August-October 1983. The day after I moved in, I began to hear tapping noises in the bedroom whenever I entered it. These noises spread over the entire apartment. Then snoring sounds came from the oven and spread all over the apartment. The first night that I slept in the bedroom, all the coat-hangers in the closet started to rattle for no apparent reason. Snoring came from inside the closet. These sounds continued on a nightly basis. Occasionally, growling noises came from behind the television set.

December 1983 January 1984. My granddaughter and grandson moved from Vancouver to Toronto. They spent a considerable amount of time in my apartment and experienced some of the following phenomena. We were touched on the arms and had our hair tweaked. We heard snoring sounds from the oven and the rattling of the oven-racks. My daughter suggested taking pictures of the open oven. The film showed faces and figures. About this time I was hugged by an invisible presence. On Christmas Day, rapping was heard on the headboard of my bed, and my daughter, sleeping over that night, was struck in the back. Banging was also heard on the inside of the closet door.

My daughter and I saw a male shadow moving out of the dining room. There were no males present in the apartment at the time. The next night, on the advice of the Psychic Centre, we decided it was wise to sleep at my daughter's apartment on Wellesley Street. When leaving my place, we heard footsteps behind us, as we walked down the corridor to the elevator. We turned and looked, but no one was there. While we were at my daughter's, some plastic bags began to rustle, as if someone was moving them.

During this month I read the book *Supernature* by Lyall Watson. It said a man in Sweden was getting spirit-voices on his tape recorder. I decided to borrow a tape recorder from my son. We turned it on and recorded a voice saying, "Strange one, Jimmy. Find me, Jimmy. Jimmy, find me if you can."

April 1984. My daughter moved from Wellesley Street to an apartment in a building next to mine. One night, she left my place at 7:30 p.m. Just after she left, my apartment door opened and closed by itself. At 9:00 p.m., my daughter telephoned to tell me she could hear a man humming in her apartment. At midnight I could hear him humming in my apartment. On one occasion, I heard the sound of someone flicking the light-shade. When I looked up, the light-shade was vibrating.

May 1984. I found an enormous hand-print on the kitchen cupboard A mysterious formation of moisture appeared on the wall without explanation. I called 100 Huntley Street, and a minister came to my apartment. After the minister left, the bottom of the drapes over the sliding balcony door were flung about one or two feet above the level of the floor, and I heard growling and scratching, as if an animal was trying to escape.

July 1984. My eight-year-old daughter and I saw many quartermoon shapes of light moving about the living-room. Later that month I saw two flashes, orange-like flames shooting across the walls. The flames were about sixteen inches by four inches in size. At the time all the doors, windows, and drapes were closed. Also during this month, I sat on the sofa reading and heard a male voice whistling a tune a few feet away.

August 1985. My granddaughter, aged nine, was alone with me one day when I put on the tape recorder. I recorded a male voice that said, "Go out on the twenty-ninth. Look up, Trudy. Don't worry, everyone is coming back — your dad, Ethel, friends." My nickname is Trudy, and my dad and Ethel have been dead for thirty-five to forty years. Another time, when I was alone, I heard a noise. I turned on the tape recorder and a different male voice said, "Come, child ... find thy rest ... ending from thee."

September 1985. While taping, I recorded a woman speaking Italian. I asked three different people to translate the words for me. They all said the woman was telling me to read the books in my library. Later that month, my granddaughter was sitting on the floor watching TV. We heard the noises that generally accompany the phenomenon. Then we both heard a child-like voice saying aloud what sounded like "boak ... boak." We decided that the male voice was saying, "Book ... book."

As I was wrapping gifts, I heard the rustle of a Simpsons bag on my sewing machine. I turned and saw a large hand-print form on the surface of the bag. As I watched, the hand-print on the bag relaxed. On closer examination, I could see the sharp indentations left by the fingernails. A variety of unexplained smells occasionally occurred in the apartment — everything from perfume to rotten meat. On investigation, they did not appear to be coming from air ducts or from other apartments.

February 1986. One day I saw three golden balls of light in the living-room. They were moving around about a foot from the floor.

August 1986. My youngest son was staying over for a few days. One night, while he was listening to music on the tape recorder in the bedroom, I heard the buttons on the machine being pushed, one after the other. I was about to ask him what he was doing, when he shouted for me to hurry into the room. He was very upset and he told me that something he couldn't see was pushing the buttons on his tape recorder. It was now turned off. I turned on the tape recorder and watched as something turned it off again. I could feel a presence in the room, and I shouted at it in anger to go away. There was a swooshing sound and a sharp banging on the inside of the closet door. Thereafter the tape recorder operated normally.

October 1986. One day my son was visiting me and we had a quarrel and I called him a stinker. He left, and a few minutes later I heard a lot of tapping sounds, so I turned on the tape recorder. I recorded a woman's voice saying, "Let stink out the door ... walk in the bare." I wondered if the voice was telling me not to let my son come back.

January 1987. One night my granddaughter was visiting. She wasn't feeling well and went to bed about 9:00 p.m. About five minutes later she started screaming, "Nanny, Nanny, help me! Get me out of here!" When I got to her, she was hysterical. But she told me what had happened. She had turned out the light and pulled up the covers, with the top part folded to about the middle of her chest. Suddenly the covers were yanked down to the bottom of the bed. I looked and I could see the spot where they had been grabbed.

February 1988. I was sitting in the living-room and I saw a bright flash of light in the kitchen area. As I watched, it flashed repeatedly in the direction of the apartment door. The flashes looked like balls of light. They made a whoomp sound, as if they were hitting something. Suddenly the balls of light started to make a sudden, ninety-degree turn and rush straight toward me. They seemed to flatten out a few feet from me, and make the whoomp sound as if they were hitting something there. This continued until seven o'clock the next morning.

One kind or another of the above phenomena has occurred continually in this apartment over the past five years. There has never been a break of more than three weeks between occurrences. Usually, there is an occurrence every night.

The Blonde Ghost of the Don Jail

Does the ghost of a blonde-haired prisoner who committed suicide float about in the main rotunda of the old Don Jail?

Site: The Don Jail, now vacated and unused

Locale: 550 Gerrard Street East, at Broadview Avenue.

Period: Built 1858, rebuilt in 1865 after the fire

Source: Tracey Tyler, "Now Nobody Gets *into* Don Jail," *The Toronto Star*, 9 January 1993

"Designed by William Thomas, who also created triumphant St. Lawrence Hall, the classically inspired Don Jail sits serenely on its rise of ground like a grand palace, entered by one of the noblest doorways in the city." That is architectural journalist Patricia McHugh's evocation of the old Don Jail building, an imposing sight at the intersection of Gerrard Street East and Broadview Avenue.

The Don Jail is an imposing-looking building that is said to be the haunt of a blonde prisoner who hanged herself in the west wing. The gates of the correctional institution were shut and sealed in January 1993.

[Josh Goldhar]

It was a maximum security prison which saw hangings until 1962. The present building, which incorporates the original Toronto Jail, has been shut and sealed since January 1993. A grand old building, it awaits a brand-new function.

The west wing of the original Toronto Jail was reserved for women inmates. It is said to be haunted by the ghost of a blonde haired prisoner who hanged herself in one of its tiny cells in the 1890s. Her spirit has been observed floating through the air in the Don Jail building's main rotunda. In recent years her ghost was reported by Clive Reddin, a guard on the graveyard shift. The journalist Tracey Tyler added that "apparently she has the reputation of being quite violent because she feels trapped in time."

THE DON JAIL GHOST

The "blonde prisoner" of the Don Jail is a hag-like creature in this pen-and-ink drawing by Isaac Bickerstaff.

[Courtesy: Don Evans]

Townhouse Troubles

Does a twentieth-century woman share a modern townhouse with a ghost from the nineteenth century? It would seem that a ghost from the past put in its appearance not just once but on a number of occasions.

Site: Private Residence, Townhouse No. 12

Locale: 1666 Queen Street East, where Queen Street meets Eastern Avenue

Period: 1985

Source: John Robert Colombo, *Mackenzie King's Ghost and Other Personal Accounts of Canadian Hauntings* (Toronto: Hounslow Press, 1991)

Barbara Neyedly is the publisher of the *Toronto Voice*, a monthly community paper for readers in the city's downtown. She is an able and intuitive person who enjoys meeting people and sharing experiences. On 2 August 1990, she responded to my request for "extraordinary experiences" by sending a vivid account of her townhouse troubles. Here is what happened. Make of it what you will.

I couldn't say whether the night's events had anything to do with the street number of the condominium, 1666 Queen Street East, but later I wondered about that. I did find out — much later, as well — that another resident of the townhouse complex, who lived a couple of doors away, also saw a ghost while living there.

I lived at Townhouse Number 12 from 1976, the year the condos were built, until 1986. The houses were on the tall, Elizabethan model, with multiple floors and several small flights of stairs.

It was a blustery winter night, a Saturday, in 1985, when, highly unusual for me, I fell asleep on the couch about 1:00 a.m. The couch was in the living room, which was located on the very bottom floor, facing the front entrance.

I don't now remember the reason I didn't make it up the three flights of stairs to my bedroom before conking out. I only recall being overwhelmed by a delicious drowsy sensation, so overpowering that I fell asleep, leaving several lights on. I had had a few glasses of wine with dinner, hours earlier, but I was not inebriated. In any case, booze has never, before or since, caused me to believe I saw what was not there.

I was not alone in the house. A visitor, who unlike me had made it to bed, was presumably sleeping peacefully four flights above my head.

I awoke suddenly to find all in darkness. I was surprised, as well, to find myself still on the couch. After a few moments, my attention was drawn to the carpeted staircase which led one flight up to the kitchen. A young man appeared and began to descend the stairs a few feet away from where I was reclining, bemusedly watching. I noted a tall figure, serious demeanour, longish coat, slightly long hair. Seeing by his face that he was in his twenties, I concluded that he had been visiting my twenty-year-old tenant, Hayley, whose room was located two flights up. But I had forgotten that she was out for the evening and it was unlikely that she had given the key to anyone.

My faint greeting of "hello" was neither noted nor returned, and later I recalled that this unexpected "visitor" never once looked at me or appeared to see me. Rather, he kept looking to the right, over my head, seemingly at a distant scene, as he walked steadily past me towards the door.

Even stranger, I assumed that he would put on boots at the front door before going out into the elements. But afterwards, try as I might, I couldn't recall that he did, or that he opened the door, walking out, or shut the door behind himself, either.

Instead, simultaneously with this person's disappearance in the direction of the front door, I fell back into a deep sleep on the couch. I was reawakened only by the return of my tenant, Hayley, at 4:00 a.m. Of course, she denied having had a visitor in the house that night during her absence, and it now became obvious to my once-drowsy, now sharply awakened senses that the idea was truly far-fetched, even nonsensical. It had only been a spur-of-the-moment rationalization for coping with the fact of the young man's presence in the house.

At this point, you may be tempted to conclude that I had experienced a very vivid dream while deeply asleep. But the proof that it had been real came from Hayley's news that an electrical power failure had plunged our part of the city into darkness a few hours earlier.

This explained, of course, how I had gone to sleep with blazing lights and how I had wakened up to complete darkness, after which I saw our visitor.

My next thought was that it had been a break-in. We had had three break-ins, such occurrences being more frequent than the appearances of ghosts in the neighbourhood. But when Hayley and I checked the only possible point of entry — the sliding glass back door — we confronted an unbroken surface of sparkling, pristine snow. Not even one footprint! It was only at that moment that I realized that something without an ordinary explanation had happened!

Again, most people would write off my "haunting" as some form of vivid dream state. It's true that many of the details have escaped my memory. But I was definitely awake and I definitely saw the figure, though I was in an unusually relaxed, even languorous, state of mind at the time. I believe it was that very deep relaxation that made my mind receptive to seeing my ghost, and that it helped to lift the curtain to expose what it is that is usually obscured and what most of us glimpse only rarely or never.

Interestingly, a few years later, I had occasion to meet, once again, a couple who had lived only a few townhouses from ours at the same time we lived there. They had also moved away. We got to discussing our old abodes, the people, and the problems. I mentioned, jokingly, that on top of everything else, I had even seen a ghost there.

The wife told me that she had also seen one, but that neither she nor her husband told anyone about it. "They'd think we're crazy," she said. It turned out that one evening she had been seated alone in her dining area, two floors above the ground level, when she was more than startled to see a man, clearly dressed in black, nineteenth-century clothing. His head was topped by a tall, stovepipe hat. He stood there for a moment, and then walked right through the wall!

Before the townhouse complex had been built, there had only been an old service station in that location, about two blocks east of Coxwell Avenue on Queen. Before that, old records show a creek covering the site.

Why it is that relatively new housing units should experience ghosts, a phenomenon normally associated with old houses in which many lives have been lived, is still a puzzle to me. Maybe someday research will reveal the reason.

The Pape Avenue Poltergeist

A family of Newfoundlanders rents a large house in the city's east end only to discover that they are sharing some of their rooms with ghosts or poltergeists!

Site: Private residence in Toronto's east end

Locale: 557 Pape Avenue, at Frizzel Avenue, near Danforth Avenue

Period: 1969

Source: John Robert Colombo, *Mysterious Encounters: Personal Accounts of the Supernatural in Canada* (Toronto: Hounslow Press, 1990)

"Enclosed please find the story of Pape House," wrote Gertie Sequillion in her letter to me dated 23 December 1988. "I hope that this story is all right, as I have not attempted to write for publication before."

An "Apartments for Rent" sign was in evidence in August 1995, when the photographer took this photograph of "Pape House" in the east end. Every exposure on the roll showed what could be construed to be the image of a veiled figure in the front attic window.

[Josh Goldhar]

The story is indeed all right. It is being published here in the writer's own words. Mrs. Sequillion contacted me by phone after I was the guest on Bill Carroll's "Barometer" on Radio Station Q-107 talking about ghosts. She told me this story of living in a three-storey, haunted house at 557 Pape Avenue in Toronto's east end and I encouraged her to write out her experiences and mail the account to me. A week or so later, the six pages of typescript arrived. The events occurred in 1969. The reader is invited to make of it what he or she will!

It all started innocently enough. I was doing the dishes at the sink, like most new mothers-to-be, while waiting for my husband to come home for dinner, when there came a knock on the door and there descended on me my whole family from Newfoundland.

Well, you can imagine my surprise, and all the noise and inconvenience in a one-bedroom flat, with five more people in it! That, however, was not all, as they had news to relate. My mother had sold our family home, which my father had built. My father had had a heart attack over the idea of the move to Toronto. He was still in the hospital in St. John's. Annie, the youngest, was with Mom, waiting for news of his release. Then they too would descend on us, with Dad to follow thereafter.

To save time and confusion later, I will here introduce my family: Dad (Chesley), Mom (Annie Clara), Jessie, who was married and away with the Armed Forces (thank God!), Rod, Chesley Jr., also married and thus saved the ordeal, Ed, who could tell his own story of the place, and Rich who decided to leave rather suddenly, myself (Gert), Marina, John, who was slightly retarded, Lily, Bernice, and Annie, named after my mother and the youngest since our baby sister Celeste had died at the age of two-and-a-quarter years.

Thus we are a big family like steps and stairs. If it had not been so, my experience would have been of more fright, but as the human mind tends to rationalize things supernatural, so did I at the time.

However, I had no idea of this when Rod first said, "Gert, your flat just won't do. Mom wants us to find a place for all of us. That includes you and Fred." I thought, "My husband, poor man, this is something you aren't going to like!"

Most people would say "no" right then and there, but I must confess I was not the "no" kind. I had never said "no" to my mother about anything in my life, so true to form I said "no" in my heart but not in the open. So I found myself with the problem, which to everyone else was so simple. I just had to tell Fred, when he came home, that we were moving. But, oh, how unsimple it was to me!

You see, my husband was not a patient man by any means of the word. He was good-looking, and thus his appeal to me, but patient or understanding of anything but his own comforts he was not. Rather verbal he could be, but not, thank God, to a person's face. Thus I knew the brunt of it would be felt by me alone. Still, he wasn't home yet, so I had time to think just what I'd say. I decided food was my best bet, so dinner turned into something special and lots of it!

To say he was surprised to find a whole houseful of family, all of them mine, is to lighten an otherwise ghastly ordeal. I introduced them much the same as I have to you, with the exception of Dad, Mom, Jessie, Marina, Chesley Jr., and Annie.

"Gert, we don't have room for all these people," he said, and he was amazingly calm. But you just knew he was trying to figure a way of getting rid of them as quickly as possible.

"Honey," I said, as a way of softening the blow, "you can get a newspaper after dinner." Whereupon I was interrupted by Rod who said, "You mean supper, don't you, or have you turned into a bunch of Torontonians?"

This interjection lightened everyone's mood, and soon we were all laughing about the differences between being a Newfie and a Mainlander. This merriment was short-lived, however, when our landlord got wind of the matter and notice to leave was given. Fred, being a man to take care of his money, saw that it would be a profitable venture to move in with my family. Thus the difficult problem for me was solved without me having to tell him anything. And to this day he doesn't know that moving in with my family was already a foregone conclusion.

To us, then, the ad in the paper for the Pape Avenue house seemed a godsend at the time. It read something like this: "Three-storey house for rent in the east end of the city. Kitchen, bath, living-room, and five bedrooms. Immediate occupancy. Phone — — — ."

We called and made arrangements to see the place. It had really large rooms. Everything had been newly painted, and to us the price per month seemed like a steal. Once the first and last months' rents were paid, we still had a little left for more furniture, as ours alone wasn't enough. The packing and moving were done very swiftly. Still, we were not yet all moved in when mother and Annie arrived.

"Happy birthday!" she shouted from behind us, as I was carrying a box out the door. It wasn't my birthday, of course, but she had bought me a gift and couldn't wait any longer to give it to me. It was only the first of May and my birthday was not till the eighth. When it did come, only my brother Rich and I remembered, as his birthday is the same as mine. By then I was in the new house already a week, and what a sleepless one it was!

The house was clean and nice, large enough for all. I don't think we've ever had so much room in our lives. But the noise was driving me crazy.

Let's see. The kids were in the middle bedroom, the one with that awful stain on the floor. Yes, that's right, and Dad and Mom had the larger bedroom across the hall. I just couldn't stand the noise from the kids' room any more, and neither could Fred. I was going to kill the kids if they didn't go to sleep. We had tried to keep quiet about the racket they made, but Fred did have to work in the morning, and as pregnant mother I needed my rest, didn't I? Mom and Dad would just have to be mad at me. Fred was very close to leaving me altogether. Living with relatives is bad enough, but the man couldn't get any sleep at all.

It was the same thing every night, always noises like people fighting, and then running up and down the stairs after one another like a herd of elephants, and then in their bedroom it was like they'd fight and even knock one another down. Sometimes it was as if one of them was seriously hurt. But as the noise kept up all night, I guess they weren't.

Well, tonight it was going to stop or else! That's just what I was thinking that night, but I was not prepared for what I found out. I went into their bedroom, prepared to kill, but like little angels they were sound asleep. In fact, I went all over the house, even up to the third floor, where my older brothers were sleeping. My, it was an eerie place! I felt like someone was watching me, but though I turned around two or three times, the only thing I saw was sleeping men. Still, I got out of there fast. I felt weird up there.

Upon returning to our bedroom, Fred was mad at me. "I thought you were going to quiet them down. Well?"

"Honey," I said, "you and I are the only people awake in this whole house."

"Gert, that's garbage. You can hear that racket," he said, waving towards the stairs.

"Fred, everyone is asleep," I nearly screamed at him. "I'm cold," I added, tucking myself back in bed. "If you don't believe me, you can check for yourself."

Fred grumbled under his breath, but he didn't do anything about getting up. I didn't know what time it was, but I do know I must have fallen asleep from exhaustion, for in the morning, when I awoke, it was nearly ten.

This was the routine, for routine it became, until Fred could take it no longer. He himself decided to go check on the kids. He was cold when he returned and quite determined to leave this house. He said it was the strangest place in the world, where people make a noise and no one is supposed to be doing it.

Telling my mother wasn't going to be an easy chore. But Fred was my husband, and a wife had to go along with her husband, didn't she? So the news was given and accepted with bad feelings all around.

It was about our last night. We all sat at the TV after supper. For that matter, the TV in our place never seemed to be off. Ed mentioned quite jokingly that he would return to the third floor to sleep up there with the other boys. Apparently for the last week he'd been sleeping on the sofa downstairs, because he didn't feel comfortable up there. Rod and Johnny were joking with him about it, and at first he didn't want to tell why, but afterward he did.

"I don't want you guys to think I'm afraid to be on my own or anything, but last night something woke me suddenly, and as I was getting up to see what it was, my face turned to the window and I saw a hideous-looking face staring at me. Well, you know I'm not one to go crying about ghosts or anything, but I don't want some guy looking in at me sleeping either."

Well, what a shock it must have been for him. So it was decided, with a lot of good ribbing, that he'd return upstairs. Funny, no one had mentioned it to us.

Well, the noises never stopped. In fact, they just seemed to us more sinister than ever. So two days later, my husband and I moved out, amid Mother's groaning and reproaches.

My time came and I was finally delivered of a son, healthy, happy, and bawling. After leaving the hospital, my mom was the first to call with the news that they had moved into a new house and I was to come over and show her the baby. So to Mother's house I went, baby and all, that very night, and everyone loved Fred Jr.

It was while we were checking on the baby that Mom and I had a good chance to talk. She wasn't mad at us anymore, and she said so. She then showed us around her new house. "Isn't it marvellous, Gert, and there's no ghosts in it, either."

"What, Mom?" I asked.

"Oh, dear, your father told me not to tell you. But I suppose it is all right to tell you now that the baby's come an' all."

"Tell me what, Mom? What about the ghosts?" I was all questions, and my ears were ready to hear anything, but not what she said.

"Well," she began, "when you left, we took over yours and Fred's bedroom. Honey, we started hearing what you and Fred heard. We were not aware that you were going through so much and hearing so many noises. Your dad recognized it right off, as spirits living in the house. You see, our bedroom wasn't so noisy, but the third floor was terrible, and the boys couldn't stand it up there. Ed and Johnny saw all sorts of things, men mostly, and we tried to keep the knowledge from you, by making you think it was one of us who caused those noises. We were afraid you would be frightened and something would happen to the baby. We didn't want you to move out, though, as we were intending to get another place anyway, when the money situation was a little better for your father.

"Anyway, we didn't know all about the ghosts. We had our doubts, at least until we took over your bedroom. But then we were sure. Your father says there's no such thing as ghosts anyway. They had to be demons, because the living don't come back. Sometimes demons, whoever, try to make it appear as if they did. Realizing it was demons, your father opened our big Bible, but at night the demons seemed to be rustling the pages of it. You could hear them turning in the night.

"So we told one of the Brothers of the Church about it. You remember Mr. — — . He lives down the street. Well, he told us about the house. He said that two brothers had lived there. They had had an argument on the third floor, and a fight broke out, one apparently knocking the other down the stairs, and then ran downstairs to his bedroom, that being the middle one where the children sleep. Well, the other got up and ran after him and found him at the sink, trying to wash or something, and struck him over the head from behind and killed him. There, that is why there's that big stain on the floor there in that room."

"Mom, that sounds just like what we heard," I said. "Are you sure?"

"Yes, dear, I am sure that there was something in that house. I was sure the second I came into this one and that eerie feeling was gone. I knew."

"Well, your father said it's so in the Bible, my dear."

"Yes, honey, we all know that."

Truth, they say, is stranger than fiction, and I know that my mind doesn't want to believe it, but that's just how it happened, and I know. That house is still there today, for anyone to visit and see. I'll show you where it is, and even if necessary take you to the spot, but there ain't no way I'm going back in there.

The House of Presences

Was a poltergeist responsible for the sounds and other disturbances in the old house in Scarborough? What else could account for the strange "effects" and the sense of "presences"?

Site: Old house, now demolished

Locale: 624 Birchmount Road., north of St. Clair Avenue East, Scarborough

Period: 1973

Source: John Robert Colombo, *Mackenzie King's Ghost and Other Personal Accounts of Canadian Hauntings* (Toronto: Hounslow Press, 1991)

Cindy Evanoff and her husband now live in Markham, Ontario, but in 1973 they resided in an old house on Birchmount Road in Scarborough where some strange things happened to them. Learning that I was collecting stories of haunted houses for a book, Cindy prepared this first-person account of what it was like to live in such a house with a poltergeist.

The following is my experience while residing with my husband in a house at 624 Birchmount Road in Scarborough, Ontario, in 1973. The house was an old, two-storey wood-frame, shingled affair nestled on a corner lot across from Pine Hill Cemetery. It was a very serene setting. Looking out the kitchen window, the view was of the cemetery's tall trees and the pretty flowers on the graves. We lived there for two years. It should be noted that the house has since been torn down, and ten new homes have been built on the property.

In 1972, my husband was renting the house and occupying it with two other bachelors who moved out in mid-1973. At that time, strange things were occurring. The mailman brought mail addressed to eight or ten different people who had, obviously, lived in the house in the past. Prior to my moving in, my girlfriend and I — now my sister-in-law — were living together elsewhere. We did not have enough money to buy end-tables for our living-room, so one night we took two large boxes over to the house to spray-paint them in the basement. I painted them on three sides and returned the next night to pick them up. I went downstairs to fetch them and I found both of them upside-down, with the unpainted sides showing.

My husband — at that time my boyfriend — assured me that no one had been in the basement since the night before. I was always puzzled as to why these boxes had been tampered with, especially as the painted sides were not smeared. Therefore the paint had dried before they were turned over. There was always a feeling of someone being there in the basement.

On another occasion, when my husband was going down the stairs to the basement, he felt something grab his leg from behind the open staircase, and fell down the stairs. His shoulder still aches from time to time, even now, fifteen years later. That was the only occasion that "something" physically hurt someone in the house.

After I moved in, in 1973, a number of unexplained things happened. We had two cats who would not go upstairs to the two bedrooms. On a number of occasions, they would sit at the bottom of the stairs and look up and meow strangely from the bottoms of their throats, as if they were scared to death. We had a machete, which sat on the windowsill at the bottom of the staircase. Every morning, for a number of weeks, the machete was on the floor below the window. I would pick it up and put it back on the windowsill. But every morning it was back on the floor. I cannot remember what happened to it. One day it was gone.

Whenever we went out at night for the evening, we would turn on the porch light when we left. As soon as we got in the car to leave, the light would go off and then on again. One time we forgot to turn on the light. When my husband went to unlock the door to switch on the light, it turned on by itself. It was as though someone was saying, "Here, let me do it for you, just leave!"

On two occasions, as we pulled out of the driveway, we both saw a vision in the upstairs bedroom window. It was very eerie for both of us. When we were in the house, we never saw anything or anybody. On numerous occasions, when we returned home, we heard the barbells, which my husband kept in the upstairs bedroom, clanging, as though someone was lifting and lowering them. When we went to check it out, they were on the floor as though they hadn't even been touched.

On one occasion, when my husband was out with his buddies for the evening, I stayed home and went to bed early. Our bedroom was on the main floor and beside the door to the basement. I had fallen asleep but suddenly I woke up. The bedroom door was open and I could look out the doorway. I could see that the door to the basement was open. Who had opened it? We always kept it shut and even had a lock on the outside of the door. When I got up to close it, the door closed by itself before I could reach it. It was as though whoever lived there with us was trying to scare us into leaving.

Needless to say, I took off to the lounge of a nearby hotel where I knew I would find my sister-in-law. I told her what had happened. Some of our friends were sitting there and, of course, they cracked up laughing. We explained that things like this happened regularly in the house. I invited three or four of these people to come back to the house and they did. It was unbelievable. We were only in the house a couple of minutes when the barbells started to clang. You have never seen anything like it. These people literally looked like they had seen a ghost. Their faces drained and were totally white. After that they never joked about what was happening on Birchmount Road. I guess the only thing that kept us in that house and out of an apartment elsewhere was the rent of the house. It was cheaper living there than it would have been to rent an apartment.

We very rarely went down to the basement, as it was not furnished and we just kept odds and ends in storage there. But several times the light in the basement went on by itself, and we would turn it off. The next time it would be on again. We did not have wiring problems, as far as we knew. The other lights in the house did not go on and off like the basement light and the porch light.

Some time after these experiences occurred, we spent the evening in a neighbour's house. A woman was there who had lived for years down the street on Birchmount. She heard our story and told us that several years earlier a woman had lived in that house with her two children. The woman had gone crazy. Apparently she killed and dismembered her two children, threw them in the creek that ran behind the house, and then hanged herself in the upstairs closet. The closet was in the hall outside the bedroom where the barbells were located and where the cats refused to go.

By 1975 we had saved enough money to buy our own house. When we had packed up and were ready to move from Birchmount, my husband said he felt a pat on the back as he was getting into the truck. There was no one behind him. It was as though someone was saying, "Thanks for dropping in!"

We have a friend who is intrigued with the supernatural, etc. After talking to the management that owned the house, they agreed to let her move in. She advised us that she did not experience anything unusual. However, her daughter slept in the upstairs bedroom, where our barbells were kept. The mother said her daughter felt uneasy sleeping in that room, and many a night she would not get to sleep at all. The mother said, too, that her cat and dog, like our two cats, would not go upstairs to the second floor!

A Scarborough Poltergeist

Odd noises, lights going on and off, unexplained cold spots ... these are only a few of the strange things that happened in Apartment 704.

Site: Private residence in Scarborough

Locale: Apartment No. 704, 3 Glamorgan Avenue, north of Ellesmere Road. and west of Kennedy Road.

Period: 1973-74

Source: John Robert Colombo, *Mackenzie King's Ghost and Other Personal Accounts of Canadian Hauntings* (Toronto: Hounslow Press, 1991)

In this account Dan Carter describes a spate of poltergeist-like disturbances that he and other members of his family experienced in an apartment in Scarborough, Ontario. What Carter describes could be the effects created by a poltergeist, a "noisy ghost." A poltergeist is known by its effects, not by its appearance, although at the end of this account "something" does appear.

A series of events made our lives rather interesting over a period of from six to eight months.

On October 1st, my brother and I rented an apartment in Scarborough, on Kennedy Road, near Highway 401. From the time we moved in, odd things would happen. They occurred during our absences from the apartment; e.g., I would come home from work and find all the doors inside the apartment closed, the doors to the bedroom and bathroom, etc. Sometimes lights would be on when I entered and then a short time later they would go off by themselves. My brother and I kept blaming each other for these occurrences.

The linen closet at the end of the hall was extremely cold. We used to keep milk in it as it was colder than the fridge.

We were the first tenants in this apartment for it was a new building.

Sometimes my fiancée, who worked right across the street, would come to the apartment for lunch. One day when we were out, she came over and found the hall light on and every tap in the place on full blast. Thinking it odd, she shut the taps off — the kitchen tap, the taps in the bathroom sink, the tub and shower taps, etc. That evening she asked us why we had left them on.

One night my fiancée and I were watching TV in the living room. There was a loud crash in the kitchen. From the kitchen a cigarette butt flew through the air at great speed and smashed into the back of the front door of the apartment, leaving a black mark from its ash on the top part of the door. I would guess the distance to be about ten or twelve feet. When I went into the kitchen to clean up the mess, I found that nothing was disturbed.

Sometimes bedroom doors would close, either one at a time or all at once, with great force. One time I came home early from work. As I got off the elevator, I heard music playing, very loud music. As I approached the apartment, I discovered the music was coming from inside the apartment. To be sure, I checked the apartments next to mine, above and below, by placing my ear to their doors. The music was definitely coming from my apartment. It occurred to me that my brother had come home from work early and was playing music. I was going to give him a blast for playing the music so loud. When I opened the door to the apartment, everything went dead quiet. My brother was not at home. The only stereo in the apartment was located in his room. It was not on.

When I got married, my wife, my brother, and I stayed in the apartment. Once, she and her girlfriend were preparing to hold a Tupperware party and were cleaning up. When they were doing the dishes, they placed the glasses upside-down on the drain board. The glasses kept flipping right-side up. They did not fall over, but went up in the air, turned over, and landed right-side up. This event was witnessed by three people. They phoned me and said, "Come home now. We will meet you in the lobby." When I got there fifteen minutes later, the girls were in the lobby, white and hysterical. To make matters worse — when they took the elevator from the seventh floor down to the lobby, the elevator went back up to the seventh floor, stopped there, came back down, stopped, and nobody got off.

168

The Tupperware party was held that evening. All the people who entered the apartment that night reported the same thing occurring. Their watches stopped. If they stepped outside the apartment and into the hall, their watches would go again. Re-entering, they would stop again.

We finally decided that there was something else that was living there with us. We also knew that it was out and about, because you could hear the breaking of glass. It sounded like expensive crystal. Suddenly the room would get extremely cold, as cold as the linen closet. We believe it lived in the closet.

At night, when you were in bed but not yet asleep, you could hear the chains on the living room lamps clang against the stems of the lamps. Going out to check on these noises, you could hear them more clearly. But as soon as you entered the living room, they would stop. All the while the windows were closed.

Sometimes, at night, my wife would wake me up and say, "Someone is walking down the hall." Listening, I would tell her it was my brother and he was playing a joke on us. Getting out of bed and listening by the door, I heard something walk past, stepping with one foot and dragging with the other, walking towards the linen closet. Opening the door very gently, and jumping out to surprise my brother, I was surprised to find no one there. My brother's door closed tightly. It was warped. You had to bodyslam it to close it tight.

In March of 1974, I received a call informing me my grandmother had died. My mother and father flew up from Miami for the funeral. My father stayed with his family, my mother stayed with us. We told my mother not to worry about the odd noises. Apartments are noisy places, we told her.

The next morning, my mother informed us she was leaving. When we asked her why, she told us she was lying on the sofa, almost asleep, when she heard glass break in the dining room. Suddenly the room got extremely cold. Reaching for a blanket, something touched her on the shoulder, as if to say, "It's okay. It's only me." She said it was a very warm, loving touch. But she never forgot it.

That night, she decided to prove to herself that something did, indeed, live with us. My mother stood a cigarette on its end on top of the TV set. Sitting on the sofa with my brother and his girlfriend, she spoke: "If there is anything in this room, prove it to me by knocking my cigarette down." The cigarette fell down. My mother then stood the cigarette up again and said, "A kid can do that. I want you to really prove it." The cigarette then flew across the room, as if someone had swatted it. My mother was convinced.

Somehow word got out about our place, and people would come to the door asking, "Is this the apartment with the ghost? Can we see it? Would you like to sublet it?"

The last thing I remember of "the ghost" was this. I was asleep when all of a sudden it was cold in the bedroom, so cold that I woke up shivering. I looked toward the doorway. It was wide open and a dark shadow entered the room. I felt frozen and could hardly move. The only thing I could do was close my eyes and shiver. Then the room warmed up and it, whatever it was, was gone.

Taber Hill Park

Taber Hill was used as an Iroquois burial ground. Was it also used as a native vision-site and a place of renewal?

Site: Taber Hill Park

Locale: Public park, Bellamy Road North, one block north of Lawrence Avenue East, Scarborough

Period: A.D. 1250 to the present

Source: Plaque, City of Scarborough, 1961

Additional information supplied by the Parks Department, City of Scarborough, 15 July 1994

Taber Hill is a mound that rises 174 metres above Lake Ontario, 14 metres above street level in Scarborough. Residential streets in the vicinity bear such Indian-influenced names as Indian Mound Crescent, Longhouse Place, and Rochman Boulevard. The mound itself is covered with grass and crowned with a grey granite boulder with a bronze plaque. The plaque bears the following inscription:

> Site of an ancient Indian ossuary of the Iroquois nation. Burials were made about 1250 and this ossuary was uncovered when farm lands were developed into residential properties in 1956. This common grave contains the remains of approximately 475 persons. Dedicated as a historical site by the Township of Scarborough, October 21, 1961.

An ossuary is a communal burial place for ancestral bones. Taber Hill served as an ossuary for the dead; it may also have served as a vision-site for the living. If so, it was a place where the braves and elders sought guidance from the spirits of the natural world and supernatural realms. To climb to the top of the mound and stand on its crest to survey the scene is to experience the sensation that one is standing on top of the world.

In this vein it is worth noting that Taber Hill Park lies in a mixed-use area of the city. It is surrounded by a residential development, but there are high-tension powerlines to the north and a surprising number of hospitals and elder-care facilities to the south. It is not unlikely that the mound has served as a plateau for visions, a centre for healing, and a place for the transmission of energy.

In this vein, the name "Taber" is close to Mount Tabor in lower Galilee. Biblical scholars recognize Mount Tabor to be the site of the victorious battle of the Israelites over the Canaanites; by Christian tradition, it is the site of the Transfiguration of Jesus.

These four photographs give one a sense of the elevation of Taber Hill Park, Bellamy Road, Scarborough. A natural prominence, it has served as an Iroquois ossuary and doubtlessly a vision site. A boulder marks the summit, an echo of St. Michael's Chapel atop England's Glastonbury Tor. Plaques are mounted on the boulder's western and eastern exposures. The main Taber Hill plaque faces west.

[Josh Goldhar]

173

West

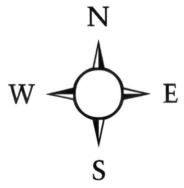

The Euclid Avenue Séances

Did a Toronto physician, poet, and spiritualist establish psychic contact with the spirits of William Shakespeare, Abraham Lincoln, Ralph Waldo Emerson, Lord Tennyson, and Walt Whitman? And if so, what did these spirits have to say to him?

Site: One-time home of Albert Durrant Watson, now a private residence

Locale: 10 Euclid Avenue, at Queen Street, west of Bathurst Street.

Period: From 1910s to 1920s

Sources: Albert Durrant Watson, *The Twentieth Plane: A Psychic Revelation* (Toronto: McClelland & Stewart, 1918)

Albert Durrant Watson, *Birth through Death: The Ethics of the Twentieth Plane* (Toronto: McClelland & Stewart, 1920)

Albert Durrant Watson and Margaret Lawrence, *Mediums and Mystics: A Study in the Spiritual Laws and Psychic Forces* (Toronto: McClelland & Stewart, 1923)

Lorne Pierce, "The Bookman's Page: Albert Durrant Watson," *The New Outlook,* 19 May 1926

Additional information supplied by David Creelman, genealogist, 8 September 1994

Albert Durrant Watson is pretty well forgotten these days. But in the 1910s and 1920s he was one of Toronto's liveliest personalities. He was a man of many accomplishments: a respected physician, author of more than twenty books of prose and poetry, astronomer, spiritualist, and psychical researcher. Everything he did he did with the fresh enthusiasm of the amateur.

Watson was born in Dixie (the Dundas and Dixie area of Mississauga), Canada West, on 8 January 1859. He died in Toronto on 3 May 1926. His last residence is the modest two-storey building with attic at 10 Euclid Avenue. The house was built in 1873 and the wrought-iron fence is original. Watson's name appears in the stained-glass window above the transom. It is unlikely that the present occupants of the house have any knowledge of the fact that for more than a decade the parlour of this house was the setting for a series of well-documented séances. The house is interesting only to the extent that it served at the time as the centre for psychical research, then a fashionable if slightly *risqué* pursuit. Watson's parlour attracted Torontonians of all walks of life — as well as spirits of famous people of the past. Indeed, publisher Lorne Pierce made the following observation in his eulogy for Watson: "No man during this generation in Toronto ever entertained so many strange faces, tongues, sects, systems, enthusiasms, artists, poets, fanatics, sages as he did; no home was more the ante-chamber to the universe."

This three-storey brick house on Euclid Street once served as the residence of physician, poet, and spiritualist Albert Durrant Watson. Lively séances were held in the parlour in the 1910s and 1920s. "Dr. A.D. WATSON" appears in leaded-glass lettering in the window above the front door.

[Josh Goldhar]

Is a trace of mischievousness to be discerned in the features of Albert Durrant Watson? This photographic portrait of the poet, physician, and spiritualist first appeared on the frontispiece of the book *The Poetical Works of Albert Durrant Watson* [1924].

[The Ryerson Press]

"The Humble Ones of the Twentieth Plane" is the name of a group of discarnate entities who agreed to communicate to Albert Durrant Watson through the mediumship of Louis Benjamin. Although he was interested in mediumship, Watson felt he had no psychic gifts, so he sought the services of a self-educated young man named Louis Benjamin. Born in Chicago, raised in Toronto, Benjamin felt himself to be a "sensitive." In New Age parlance, Benjamin was a "channeller." Whether operating an Ouija board which laboriously spelled out messages letter by letter, or falling into a trance and speaking in strange voices in a rapid clip, he acted as a conduit for "The Humble Ones of the Twentieth Plane."

The Humble Ones of Twentieth Plane are the great movers and shakers of the past who find themselves existing in some sense on a spiritual plane far above the gross plane of our earthly existence. Some of these great spirits are interested in mankind and in helping progressive-minded people and their causes. For instance, Benjamin was able to contact the spirit of the long-dead English poet Samuel Taylor Coleridge who so appreciated the work of Watson and Benjamin that he offered to contribute a preface to their second book of psychical research. The offer was accepted and Coleridge's words of greeting were duly transmitted and transcribed. Kathleen Coburn, the Toronto scholar, apparently overlooked this unique post-mortem tribute when she edited the critical edition of Coleridge's collected works.

Coleridge was not the only spirit so moved. So great was the importance of the Watson-Benjamin collaboration that the Humble Ones established a Publication Committee on the Twentieth Plane to further the Watson-Benjamin collaboration. The committee consisted of Abraham Lincoln, Ralph Waldo Emerson, Walt Whitman, and Robert G. Ingersoll. Other literary figures who figure in these séances are John Milton, Thomas Carlyle and Richard Maurice Bucke.

It is a comforting thought to realize that Canadian literature, although it may be ignored on the earthly plane, is widely read on the Twentieth Plane. In the afterlife, John Keats enjoys reading the verses of Canadian poet Robert Norwood. Lord Tennyson, regrettably unfamiliar with the work of W.W. Campbell, appreciates Bliss Carman's verses. Whitman is not reading much of anything these days, but he does bless Helen and Henry Saunders, Toronto-based collectors of his writings. Long unread and out of print are Watson's own books, including his *Poetical Works* (1924); but it is consoling to consider that they are being appreciated by The Humble Ones of the Twentieth Plane.

Lucy Maud Montgomery, the author of *Anne of Green Gables,* was living in Leaskdale, Ont., when she read *The Twentieth Plane.* Although she found it a "good read," she admitted to her diary on 29 March 1919: "It was absolute poppycock — utterly unconvincing. And I was so ready to be convinced ... but my intellect absolutely refused any credence to the so-called 'revelations' of 'The Twentieth Plane' .... There was a certain enjoyment in the book, though, because it is really exquisitely funny — all the funnier because it is so deadly serious."

The Grey Lady of St. Mary Magdalene

Is there a Grey Lady who haunts the interior — and the exterior — of St. Mary Magdalene Church?

Site: St. Mary Magdalene Church

Locale: 477 Manning Avenue, at Ulster Street, south of Harbord Street.

Hours: Open seven days a week, 8:30 a.m. to 5:30 p.m

Period: 1920s to the present

Sources: Norman Gary Johnson, *Healey Willan: His Life and Influences Important to His Music* (Dissertation, Faculty of School of Church Music, 1979)

F.R.C. Clarke, *Healey Willan: Life and Music* (Toronto: University of Toronto Press, 1983)

Interview with Father Harold Nahabedian, Rector, 22 June 1994

Interview with Margaret Harmer, parishioner and former chorister, 22 June 1994

Almost obscured by foliage is the main entrance to St. Mary Magdelene Church on Manning Avenue. The church's Gray Lady has been seen by members of the congregation over the years from the 1920s to the 1990s.

[Josh Goldhar]

Healey Willan, organist and choirmaster, is shown at the organ of St. Mary Magdelene Church, after High Mass, All Saint's Day, 1965. Dr. Willan had no hesitation describing the appearance of the Grey Lady.
[Tom Hyland]

St. Mary Magdelene Church is a neighbourhood church that was erected in the early Romanesque manner between 1888 and 1908. The Anglican congregation has a great appreciation of music. The building and the grounds are said to be haunted by a Grey Lady.

The tradition that it is haunted seems to have started with the peculiar experience of the distinguished musician Dr. Healey Willan (1880-1968) who served as organist-choirmaster to the congregation from 1921 to the year of his death. On many an occasion, when alone in the church, he practised on the organ in the gallery. To make sure that he was alone, he locked the outer doors from the inside. Once, while playing, he looked down, and to his surprise and wonder he saw an elderly woman dressed in grey standing to one side. He immediately stopped playing, descended the stairs, and looked around for her. She was neither there nor anywhere else in the building.

This experience, which occurred in the 1920s, puzzled Dr. Willan for many years and he told the story to many people. Parishioner and chorister Margaret Harmer recalled hearing the story from Dr. Willan. In 1994, in an interview, she added a wrinkle or two. Its seems congregants had reported seeing the Grey Lady before Dr. Willan's sighting. Indeed, the sighting in the church may have been Dr. Willan's second sighting, as Margaret Harmer remembers that he said that in the early 1920s, attending a church garden party on the next-door property, out of the corner of his eye, he noticed an unusual-looking elderly lady dressed all in grey.

These views capture the appearance of the interior of St. Mary Magdelene Church in the mid-1950s. The high altar is flanked by the St. Joseph Chapel and the Lady Chapel. The church's southwest corner is particularly atmospheric; the photograph was taken around two o'clock one winter's afternoon. It is not hard to imagine the locale to be the haunt of the Grey Lady. Both photographs were taken by Tom Hyland, long-time member of the choir.

[Tom Hyland]

When he went to greet her a short while later, she was gone.

The supernatural played a role in Willan's life, as noted by his biographer F.R.C. Clarke. There was the composer's interest in numerology as well as his sightings of the "little grey lady." Willan recalled, "Ghosts are quite common. We have one at St. Mary's — an old girl who used to be the charlady ... I've seen her frequently in the church when I have gone in to practise at night. She doesn't bother me, so I don't bother her. As a matter of fact, I'm rather fond of her, you know — I believe she likes plainchant."

THE GREY LADY

The pen-and-ink drawing by Isaac Bickerstaff turns the Grey Lady into a crabby old woman!

[Courtesy Don Evans]

Musicologist Norman Gary Johnson noted the influence of the High Church in Willan's life:

> Catholicism was a tremendous influence on Willan; however, along with others of the Romantic period, he personally adopted more of a pantheistic religious consciousness than dogmatic, confessional faith. Willan was also interested in the mystical, and psychic happenings held a great fascination for him. He firmly believed in the presence of ghosts, and he often referred to the "little people" — an expression from his Irish heritage. Willan recalled that at his child hood home in England the andirons near

the fireplace moved on occasion. Some exploration in the basement underneath the fireplace area uncovered a skeleton. After the skeleton was removed, the strange noises and and movements ceased. Another time, at his home in Toronto, a series of strange noises were heard over a period of time on the third floor of the house. Willan believed that these disturbances were caused by a ghost and he asked that a priest from St. Mary Magdalene come and exorcise them. After this ceremony was performed, no further disturbances occurred. On yet another occasion, Willan had a vivid dream of a message that he was to deliver to one of his students. The next day he called the student into his office and shared his dream. The student had been terribly upset the night before and she had considered suicide. The message from her dead mother, delivered by Willan, was the solution to a problem known only to the student and her mother.

At St. Mary Magdalene there was a strange "little Grey Lady" who appeared at special times in the church. Willan and others saw her at a distance on several occasions, but no one was able to talk with her or to explain her presence. Mary Mason stated that as she sorted her father's books after his death, she was amazed at the number of volumes dealing with mystical subjects, especially Indian literature (Willan believed in reincarnation). The choir at St. Mary Magdalene were reminded of this mystical part of Willan's personality in a dramatic way the Sunday after his funeral. Prior to his death Willan had scheduled the music to be performed through February. Margaret (Peggy) Drynan, a former student, choir member, and close friend, composed a "Missa Brevis in F Minor" some years before, and Willan asked that she direct her Mass on that particular Sunday in February. In the last four measures of the Mass's "Agnus Dei" the combination of voices brings about an unusual overtone that Willan had always referred to as the "ghost voice." On the Sunday after his funeral, when the choir sang that measure, the door of the Gallery suddenly opened but no one was there.

Dr. Elmer Iseler, the distinguished choirmaster, also saw the Grey Lady. His sighting took place not inside the church building but outside, on church grounds. The figure of a woman stood on the northeast corner of the property. He caught sight of the figure out of the corner of his eye. When he looked again, she was gone. This happened in 1991.

Dr. Iseler recounted his odd experience to the present Rector, Father Harold Nahabedian. Father Nahabedian was surprised for a specific reason. The northeast corner of the property used to serve the purpose of a parking space and Father Nahabedian parked his car there. On a number of occasions, entering or leaving the car, he noticed something odd: the smell of cheap perfume hanging in the air when nobody was there. Father Nahabedian added, "We have since built on the old parking space and the land was blessed before digging. There has been no recurrence of the perfume. Has she gone to her rest?"

The assumption is that the Grey Lady is the spirit of a member of the congregation who for reasons unknown lingers near and inside the church. Perhaps she has an ear for fine music.

In 1984, the small park close to the church at Euclid and Ulster streets was named by the City of Toronto the Healey Willan Park.

Ghost of the Royal Alex

Is the Royal Alexandra Theatre haunted by a trio of ghosts: a man in a beige shirt and brown pants, a prop man, and a member of the audience?

Site: The Royal Alexandra Theatre

Locale: 260 King Street West

Period: 1990s

Phone: For tickets to productions or for tours, phone (416) 872-3333

Source: Unsigned column, "Screams & Whispers," *The Toronto Star,* 31 October 1994.

Additional information supplied by Robert Brockhouse, Royal Alex's literary manager, 6 October 1995.

A jewel-box among the legitimate playhouses of North America, The Royal Alexandra Theatre is impressive in the Beaux-Arts manner. The building was erected in 1906-07, and since then its stage has known all the leading actors and actresses of the time, touring companies and national theatres, as well as local productions like *Spring Thaw.*

The theatre fell on hard times and was slated for demolition in 1963. But that year it was acquired by Edwin Mirvish, merchandiser, producer,

The Royal Alexandra Theatre is often described as a "jewel-box" of a theatre. It is said that a "phantom flyman" appears back-stage. In a novel by Robertson Davies, a member of the audience, sitting in one of these boxes, shouts out during a performance of a magical act, "Who killed Boy Staunton?"
[Royal Alexandra Theatre]

and benefactor, who oversaw and underwrote an extensive restoration to its Edwardian splendour. He and his son David Mirvish now operate it successfully. The same team owns and operates the Old Vic in London (which with its many ghosts has the reputation of being England's most haunted theatre).

Indeed, the majority of the older playhouses in the cities and towns of the Western world are said to be haunted. But the first substantial report of a haunting at the Royal Alex (as it is affectionately known) appeared in print in the Toronto *Star* in a column for Halloween 1994. Until then, the only thing that Royal Alex-fanciers and ghosthunters had for grim amusement was the passage in Robertson Davies's fine novel *Fifth Business* (1970) which vividly describes the action that takes place in the house during a production of a magic show. The performance of the magician Magnus Eisengrim is interrupted when a member of the audience, perhaps someone in a box, demands to know in a loud voice: "Who killed Boy Staunton?"

What follows is the column from the *Star.*

Strange things go bump in the night at the Royal Alexandra Theatre.

Darrin Carter, 29, who operates the electronics board that controls the lighting for *Crazy for You,* claims to have seen a ghost a month ago.

"I was alone at my computer on the fourth floor fly rail, which is open to the stage so that I can look down on the actors," he recalled for "Screams & Whispers."

"It was dark except for my little reading light; I was reading a book. There is just one door to this fly rail and anyone going out would have to walk by me. Then, just before intermission, I saw a man from the neck down cross my field of vision above the top of my book, wearing a beige shirt and brown pants. I looked up. There was no one there and the door wasn't swinging shut. All the hair stood up on my arms and the back of my neck right until intermission."

Carter thinks he may have seen the ghost of a "flyman" who was accidentally killed at the theatre about twelve years ago. Another ghost said to haunt the place is that of a woman, a member of the audience, who died many years ago in the second balcony. "We've all had a feeling of a presence here," Carter says.

Was he terrified by the experience? "I wasn't scared so much as exhilarated."

The Ghost of Colborne Lodge

Does the ghost of Mrs. Howard maintain its lonely vigil, staring out the sec-ond-floor bedroom window of Colborne Lodge ... watching over the burial-place of her beloved husband, John Howard?

Site: Colborne Lodge

Locale: Colborne Lodge Drive, south entrance to High Park in the city's west end

Hours: Early January to March: weekends from noon to 5:00 p.m. April to May: September to mid-November, Tuesday to Friday, 9:30 a.m. to 5:00 p.m.; weekends from noon to 5:00 p.m. June to August and mid-November to early January: Tuesday to Saturday, 9:30 a.m. to 5:00 p.m.; Sunday noon to 5:00 p.m.

Period: First reported in 1970

Sources: Herbert A. Graham, "Old Houses Remember," *Fate*, October 1971

Interview with Bette Shepherd, former museum worker, 27 June 1994

Additional information supplied by Betty Roodhart, historian, 27 June 1994

Colborne Lodge is a graceful Regency-style villa that bears the name of Sir John Colborne who served as Lieutenant-Governor of Upper Canada from 1829 to 1836. The lodge, complete with period furnishings, was deeded to the city in 1873. It is now a museum administered by the Toronto Historical Board

John Howard, English-born surveyor, architect, and engineer, designed and built the lodge for himself and his wife. He lived here and died in the lodge on 3 February 1890. Rich in public spirit but poor in heirs, he donated 120 acres to the City of Toronto in 1873 and bequeathed the remaining forty-five acres plus the lodge to the city to be developed and maintained as a public park. He called it High Park in reference to its high viewpoint over Lake Ontario. Across from the lodge stands an elaborate monument that is surrounded by a fence, the front portion of which is wrought iron from St. Paul's Cathedral in London. Here is the final rest-ing-place of John and Jemima Howard, united in death.

Here is an exterior view of Colborne Lodge, taken in 1976. Does the spirit of Mrs. Jemima Howard from time to time peer from the second-floor bedroom window? Witnesses claim that someone or something does!

[Collection of the Toronto Historical Board, Toronto, Canada]

These two photographic portraits show Mrs. Jemima Frances Howard and Mr. John G. Howard. They were taken about 1870.

[Collection of the Toronto Historical Board, Toronto, Canada]

The florid painting of Mrs. Howard hangs in the parlour of Colborne Lodge. Do the subject's sad eyes stare out the upstairs bedroom window?

Howard's professional life was one of achievement; his personal life was marred by the poor health of his beloved wife, Jemima. She died at the age of seventy-five in 1877, predeceasing her husband by thirteen years. She spent her last years confined to the second-floor bedroom and in great pain. As historian Betty Roodhart has noted, "To help kill the pain of what we think was breast cancer, the doctors gave her morphine and laudanum, an opium derivative, which probably was hallucinogenic. This probably explains why some people thought she may have been insane." Her last days were spent staring disconsolately out of the bedroom window at the plot of land where she would be buried.

Was she gazing at what she knew would be her own grave? Or was she gazing at the future burial-place of her dear husband? Does her spirit continue the melancholy vigil to this day? Details are sketchy, but the ghost of Mrs. Howard was first reported by a police constable who was patrolling the park on his motorcycle late one night in 1969. He slowed down as he approached the lodge, then stopped. Framed in the second-floor bedroom window was the silhouette of a woman. He checked the doors and groundfloor windows of the lodge and found them secure. Then he reported the odd sight. Since then other people — passers-by and visitors to the lodge — have reported seeing a ghostly figure in the window that overlooks the burial-place of John Howard. Some have seen a silhouette, others the full face of a woman who is described as suffering great pain and anguish.

Writer Herbert A. Graham described the interior of the lodge and its eerie ambience in 1971:

The house has four upstairs bedrooms — one large master bedroom at the front, two smaller ones at each side of a hall and another at the end of the hall toward the back. Having visited this last one many times, I long had known that it has a strange atmosphere but on this visit it felt particularly weird The room was empty of any living entity. It contained nothing more than its usual four-poster bed, bureau, washstand and, beside one window, a table on which lies an open Bible. Yet I was certain I shared the room with somebody — somebody I couldn't see but whose presence I felt. An odd smell pervaded the air like that of a bedroom too long slept in with the windows shut. For once I did not linger but quickly went downstairs.

Roodhart pointed out a discrepancy between Graham's account and the historical record "Mrs. Howard died in the sick room at the back of the house, but the quote clearly describes the master bedroom at the front of the house."

Sceptics maintain that the lodge is not haunted and that what the policeman reported was a trick of lighting or the silhouette of the caretaker seen through the window. Psychics report that the lodge is the haunt of "presences." Roodhart added, "The staff have never seen or felt any ghostly presence."

Mrs. Howard's vigil seems likely to remain a ghostly tale about a love that conquers sickness and death.

The burial site of Mr. and Mrs. Howard is enclosed by an iron fence. To this day, it is said, the spirit of Mrs. Howard watches over the monument.

[Josh Goldhar]

The Grenadiers of Grenadier Pond

Did a group of Grenadier Guards drown in Grenadier Pond? Is the little lake haunted by the ghosts of these youthful soldiers to this day?

Site: Grenadier Pond

Locale: Southwest corner of High Park, Bloor Street West at High Park Avenue

Period: War of 1812

Source: Raymond Souster, "Death of the Grenadiers" (1959), *The Colour of the Times* (Toronto: The Ryerson Press, 1964)

Interview with Raymond Souster, poet, 9 July 1995.

No doubt the ripples of Grenadier Pond in High Park are caused by the action of the wind and the waves. But the story persists that the turbulence is the result of the restlessness of the souls of drowned Grenadier Guards.

Grenadier Pond is a small lake in a large park. The large park is High Park in the city's west end. The small body of water may be glimpsed from the Gardiner Expressway, from Lakeshore Drive, from Ellis Drive, and from

Ellis Park Road. Boating is popular in the summer, skating across its frozen surface in winter. Throughout the year visitors enjoy feeding the ducks and swans.

In the late eighteenth century, at the time of the Indian wars, the story goes, a regiment of the Grenadier Guards gave chase to a band of hostile Indians. The Indians fled across the icy surface of Grenadier Pond in single or Indian file. The Guards, close on their heels, attempted to cross after them, but they did so four abreast in their regimental marching step. The thin ice gave way, and a number of their company drowned in the pond's frigid depths. The souls of the drowned Guards haunt the pond to this day.

THE GRENADIERS

Here is Isaac Bickerstaff's pen-and-ink drawing of the drowning of the Grenadier Guards in Grenadier Pond in High Park.

[Courtesy: Don Evans]

Apparently this story was current in the west end of Toronto in the early years of this century. The city's unofficial poet laureate, Raymond Souster, made imaginative use of the tale in his poem "Death of the Grenadiers." In the poem, published in 1959, he wrote that the "lonely soldiers" keep watch from the depths of the pond. "And girls have told me / they've felt that someone / was looking up their legs / as they skated the pond."

The Legion Ghost

Does the ghost of an old soldier haunt the attic of a Canadian Legion hall in the west end of Toronto? Journalist Kathryn Newman resolved to find out for herself.

Site: The Royal Canadian Legion Hall (Mimico and Humber Bay Branch No. 217)

Locale: 515 Royal York Road, near Queen Elizabeth Boulevard, Etobicoke

Period: From the 1960s to the present

Sources: Kathryn Newman, "A First-hand Encounter with Henry's Ghost," *The Oakville Journal Record*, 31 October 1979

John Robert Colombo, *Mysterious Canada* (Toronto: Doubleday Canada, 1988)

The ghost of a soldier is said to haunt the attic of the Royal Canadian Legion Hall in Etobicoke. The building, with its stark white cenotaph, is shown here.

[Josh Goldhar]

Some people's faces brighten with the mention of the word "ghost." Other people's faces darken at the mere suggestion of a "spirit" or a "spectre."

The face of Kathryn Newman lights up when she hears about ghosts and spirits. She is a freelance journalist who learned about the haunting of the Royal Canadian Legion's Hall on Royal York Road below the Queensway. She was told that the ghost of a young soldier, whose first name is said to be Henry, is trapped in the hundred-year-old building.

She and a friend decided to devote one night of their lives to seeking him out. Her description of the event and her account of the experience was published as "A First-hand Encounter with Henry's Ghost" in the columns of the *Oakville Journal Record*.

The face of singer Donna Dunlop also brightens when she thinks of the ghost of the young soldier ....

Ghosts have always been a part of my life.

As a young child I would sit at my grandmother's knee and listen to her weave stories of haunted spectres and eerie happenings. At the end of each story, she would tell me that when you are dealing with ghosts, you have to be ready for the unexpected.

As a freelance writer, I have learned to expect the unexpected. However, no amount of stories, training, or experience could have ever prepared me for spending a night in "the haunted Legion Hall" on Royal York Road.

Originally the structure was built and named Eden Court by Edward Stock. The Stock family was one of the first families of settlers to populate the area which is west of Bloor West Village in the west end of Toronto. In its heyday the building was an attractive house with a sprawling porch, verandah and beautiful gardens.

There is a shadier side to the Stock House. During the 1930s it was used as a gambling hall and meeting place for the criminal element. Gangster Abe Orpen owned the building, and when it was renovated in 1966, bullet holes were found in the doors.

When Harry MacIsaac, the assistant steward at the Legion, informed me that permission had been granted for me to spend the night looking for the ghost of Henry, I almost jumped right out of my skin. The veterans and staff at the Legion had named the ghost Henry after a boarder who at one time resided in the attic.

I immediately recognized that I needed someone to

accompany me on my adventure. It would have to be a person who could verify any ghostly phenomena and not jump to conclusions. My first and only choice was Sylvia Peda. She had a background in journalism, and we had worked together on many stories. Armed with notepads, a tape recorder, pens, talcum powder, and a flashlight with new batteries, we stepped through the legion door into the unknown.

Bill Lazenby, president of Branch 217 Legion Hall, escorted us through the building and up onto the third floor. This was the floor that had the reputation of being the most haunted.

"There is something I should tell you. The light switch is at the end of the hall, and you have to walk down in darkness to turn it on. The only escape is by the main staircase. If you are cornered, you have had it."

Thankfully, the president turned on the switch for us and wished us luck. We were on our own.

Sylvia smiled one of the sly smiles that she is most famous for. With a gleam in her eye, she reminded me that we would probably be found with our heads at the bottom of the stairs, our faces frozen in hideous expressions of terror.

Despite Sylvia's bizarre sense of humour, I was glad that she was with me. I would not want to be in this place alone. Besides, when the atmosphere became too weird for my liking, I could always send Sylvia into the darkness to switch on the light.

We had to decide whether we wanted to conduct our investigations in the dark. After much discussion, we both decided that it might be wiser to leave the light on for the time being. While we were debating the issue of the light, we both became aware of a noticeable chill. It became intensely cold, and then Henry turned out the light. We tore down the stairs sensing Henry at our heels. It was then that I realized that I had left some of my equipment upstairs.

The second floor is set up as an entertainment area. Small tables are scattered along the side of the large room. At the back is a stage. We felt comfortable there. We convinced ourselves that we were safe and that nothing could happen on this floor. We relaxed.

We needed to gather our thoughts. "There is so much history here," Sylvia commented.

"Yes," I responded. "But it's more than that. When you think of what could have happened here with the gambling. Hey, maybe Henry's still up there in the wall," I chuckled uneasily.

There is a fine line between fantasy and reality. It was important to try to restrain my imagination. We needed facts, and we both knew it was time to go back upstairs and face Henry head on.

With courage and determination, we marched up the stairs. A ghostly green glow shone in the hall, and the doorway to the third floor was cloaked in darkness. Somewhere between the second and the third floor, I lost my courage. But it was my turn to brave the hall and turn the light on. I tried not to notice the room getting colder. I switched on the light and then I heard footsteps and thumping right behind me.

Sylvia sprinkled talcum powder on the floor, and we ran for our lives. This time I remembered my equipment. A cold breeze passed by us in the entrance on the second floor. We stood for a few seconds, trying to determine its direction, and then we returned to the safety of our table in the entertainment area.

Traditionally, the witching hour is the time when spirits are said to be most active. As the clock on the second floor ticked towards midnight, I wondered just how much more activity I could endure in one night.

For the next half hour we listened to the building creak and moan. Cold breezes invaded our space. Unusual noises and whispers were heard coming from the second-floor bar. I experienced itching on my hands and feet. It felt like I had been exposed to fiberglass.

Sylvia became so cold that she was forced to put her winter jacket on. Then, at 12:30 a.m., she was touched on the head by an unseen entity. It took her several seconds to recover from her encounter with the ghost.

We began to discuss our next move, and just as we were about to enter the stairway hall, the toilet on the third floor flushed by itself. Sylvia and I grabbed hold of each other's arms for support. We held our breath. "I didn't know ghosts went to the bathroom," Sylvia commented.

The hours ticked away. We began to discuss our departure. We had seen enough ghostly phenomena to last a lifetime, and we both sensed it was time to go. It was important to leave the building the way we found it. That meant all the lights in the building needed to be shut off.

For the last time we climbed the stairs to the third floor. I felt the ghost's presence ahead of me. I was not nervous. In fact, I sensed a sadness. Sylvia did not sense the same thing. Her sense was one of a spectre who was lost, caught between worlds.

White powder footsteps had formed in the talcum which we had sprinkled on the floor. The steps started on one side of the room, travelled in one direction, and stopped suddenly. I flipped the light off, and darted through the hallway, and down the stairs. I did not look back.

One by one we turned off lights until we reached the rear door of the second floor. That was the way out. I felt relieved to be outside the building. It was good to feel the cold fresh air. I turned, and waved goodbye to the upper back windows of the building. I knew somehow that Henry was watching us leave.

As I drove the car to the front of the building, I decided to stop to take a few pictures. Sylvia and I climbed out. I was fiddling with my camera, when a circular flash of blue light shone from behind the centre curtained window on the third floor. Several seconds later the curtains on the second floor parted ever so slightly.

Upon reflection, Sylvia and I both believe that this was Henry's way of saying goodbye. One thing is for certain. Whoever Henry is, he gave us an experience neither of us will ever forget.

Trick or treat.

In the early stages of her musical career, singer-songwriter Donna Dunlop performed solo in the Legion's downstairs Club Room on several occasions. She knew about the house's prohibition background, but not its reputation as a haunt. She first performed there one Saturday night before Christmas 1985. During a break she climbed three flights of well-lit stairs to a dark storage room on the top floor of the old house. It was about 11:00 p.m. Was there a ghost among the dust and the Remembrance Day memorabilia?

"I was alone, sitting on the very stop stair reading, with my back to the room, when I sensed another presence behind me. It was quite sudden. I turned around. I think we sensed each other. In my mind's eye the presence seemed to be a young man, a soldier. Although I was chilled, I felt he was sympathetic. Even so, it was an eerie experience!"

She mentioned her experience to no one. Some months later, invited to perform again in the Club Room, she overheard a group of Legion members discussing the ghost, just as she was packing up her equipment to go home around 1:30 a.m. They spoke of "footsteps, a young man ... a soldier."

Singer-songwriter Donna Dunlop has her own story to tell about the Legion Hall's soldier-ghost. This photograph was taken in High Park by the noted photographer Paul Orenstein.
[Donna Dunlop]

"I performed many times in that Legion Hall. I even returned to the third floor again, but usually I'd only go halfway up. And I could never sit with my back to the top of the stairs, although I frequently glanced in that direction. In those days, and at that Legion branch in particular, I would sing "The Ghost of Bras d'Or," a folksong by Charlie MacKinnon from the compilation album *Calling All You Nova Scotians*. It tells the very moving and simple story of one Canadian whose spirit returns home from the war as a ghost. Before he was a soldier, he had been a musician. Whenever I sang the song, I would think about that young man, that soldier."

The Phantom Ship of Etobicoke

A young sailor is astonished to see the apparition of a Great Lake steamer from Etobicoke Creek. Detail is not lost as he recalls the experience more than fifty years later.

Site: Lake Ontario

Location: Etobicoke Creek, west end of Toronto

Period: August 1910

Sources: Rowley W. Murphy, "Ghosts of the Great Lakes," *Inland Seas,* Summer 1961

Dwight Boyer, *Ghost Ships of the Great Lakes* (New York: Dodd, Mead, 1971)

As a young sailor in 1910, Rowley W. Murphy experienced one of "the mysteries of the sea." Fifty years later, a veteran seaman and marine historian, he was still cherishing the memory of the sight of the strange steamer in Lake Ontario off Etobicoke in the west end of Toronto. Was it a vision? A sighting? A spectre? According to his own account, written half a century after the initial encounter, Murphy remained of two minds about the nature of the "ghostly lake steamer."

> My father, a cousin, and I were on a holiday cruise around the west end of Lake Ontario, and as we were late getting underway from Toronto Island, and were running before a light easterly, decided to spend the night in the quiet, sheltered and beautiful basin at the mouth of the creek, spelled "Etobicoke" — but always pronounced "Tobyco" by old timers. (This seems hard for present residents of that area to tolerate, as they insist on trying to pronounce each syllable.)
>
> In 1910, the Tobyco Creek was really a small river which made an abrupt turn westward and widened into a small lake, with a good beach held by poplar trees, between this harbour and the Lake. There was perfect shelter in this excellent harbour from wind from any direction, though in a hard easterly, it was not easy to reach Lake Ontario through the narrow harbour entrance.

At the date of this cruise, there was one brick farm house to the west of the harbour entrance and no buildings at all among the walnuts and oaks on the lovely grassy banks of the creek, except one ancient landmark, known as "The Old House," from the veranda of which Lieutenant Governor Simcoe is said to have shot a deer in 1794. This house was in good condition, when a few years ago it was torn down to increase parking space for a supermarket! The whole area is now completely built up, but in 1910 the beautiful grassy plains contained no buildings from Lake Ontario to the Lakeshore Road, except the landmark mentioned.

Our cruising yawl, with a larger sister of the same rig and a still larger Mackinaw (one of several "fish boats" converted to cruising yachts with great success), were the only occupants of the harbour this perfect night. The crews of the three yachts numbered eleven in all, and as is generally the case, after dinner was over and dishes done, gathered on deck in the moonlight to engage in the best conversation known to man.

All hands turned in earlier than usual, there being no distractions ashore, and by midnight were deep in happy dreams, helped by the quiet ripple alongside. At what was about 1:30 a.m., the writer was wakened by four blasts on a steamer's whistle. After waiting for a repetition — to be sure it was not part of a dream — he put his head out of the companionway.

There, flooded by moonlight, was a steamer heading about WSW — at about half speed, and approximately half a mile off shore. She had a good chime whistle but not much steam — like the *Noronic* on that awful night of September 17, 1949, who also repeated her four blasts many times.

But who was she? On this amazingly beautiful night, with memory strained to the utmost, it was difficult to do more than think of who she was not! She was considerably smaller than the three famous Upper Lakers, *China, India,* and *Japan* (about this date under Canadian registry, known as *City of Montreal, City of Ottawa,* and *City of Hamilton*). She was not as small as *Lake Michigan,* but like her, did not appear to be of all wooden construction. However, there were many in the past, of quite related design and size. The vessel seen had white topsides and deckhouses, and appeared to be grey below her main deck, like the Welland Canal-sized freighters (at this date, the big wooden steamers of the Ogdensburg Line of the Rutland Transportation Company). *Persia* and *Ocean* were like her in size and arrangement, but were all white and came to known ends, and of course *Arabiana* was of iron, and was black.

In this appearance off "Toby Coke" (a variant of spelling), the starboard light, deck lights and some seen through cabin windows, had the quality of oil lamps; and her tall mast, with fitted topmast, carried gaff and brailed-up hain-sail. Her smokestack was all black, and she had no hog beams — but appeared to have four white boats. Her chime whistle was a good one, but was reduced in volume as previously mentioned, and was sounded continuously for perhaps ten minutes. Very soon all hands now watching on the beach decided that something would be done. So a dinghy was quickly hauled over from the basin, and, with a crew of four made up from some of those aboard the three yachts, started to row out with all speed to the vessel in distress, to give her what assistance might be possible.

As the boys in the dinghy reached the area where something definite should have been seen, there was nothing there beyond clear and powerful moonlight, a few gulls wakened from sleep — but something else, impossible to ignore. This was a succession of long curving ripples in a more or less circular pattern, which just might have been the last appearance of those caused by the foundering of a steamer many years before on a night of similar beauty. In any case, the four in the dinghy returned in about an hour, reporting also small scraps of wreckage which were probably just old driftwood, seldom seen with any fresh breezes blowing.

But something more there was. This was the appearance to the visual and audible memory, which those on the beach and those afloat had seen and heard, of something which had occurred in the more or less distant past, and which had returned to the consciousness of living men after a long absence.

Whatever the cause, the experienced crews of the three yachts mentioned were of one mind as to what had been seen and heard. At least eleven lake sailors would be unlikely to agree on the character of this reappearance without good reason! And the reason was certainly not firewater working on the mass imagination, as no one of the three yachts had any aboard. So, reader, what is the answer?

The Etobicoke Poltergeist

How to account for the footsteps and the screeching laughter in the attic, when there was nobody in the attic? How to explain the waves of cold air running through the house? Could it be a poltergeist?

Site: Private residence in Etobicoke

Locale: 184 Prince Edward Drive South, at Sunnydale Drive, south of Park Lawn Cemetery Bloor Street West

Period: May 1968

Sources: John Gault and John Downing, "Eight Flee Home's Screeching Ghost," *The Toronto Telegram*, 8 May 1968

           Betty Lou White, "An Evil Poltergeist in Etobicoke," *Fate*, March 1969

           Eileen Sonin, *ESPecially Ghosts* (Toronto: Clarke, Irwin and Company, 1970)

Thick bushes and trees seem to protect this clapboard house from the gaze of passers-by. In May 1968, this house on Prince Edward Drive in Etobicoke attracted spiritualists and investigative reporters who described poltergeist-like happenings that were taking place on the upper floors.

[Josh Goldhar]

The so-called Etobicoke Poltergeist was a dweller in the attic of a large, three-storey clapboard house on Prince Edward Drive in Etobicoke in the west end of Metropolitan Toronto. The house was built as a farmhouse in the 1890s when the district was rural. Today the area is suburban. The house in question is well maintained, somewhat shielded from the street by shrubs and trees, and occupied by a family with no connection with the happenings reported in 1968.

John Gault and John Downing, two investigative reporters, covered the events that took place in the house in the columns of the *Toronto Telegram*. At the time of the poltergeist-like disturbances, early May 1968, there were eight people in the house. The upstairs apartment was occupied by Roy and Carol Hawkins and their two young daughters, Sherry and Trudy. Stephen, their nine-month-old son, was in the hospital and a source of family concern. The main floor apartment was occupied by Carol's parents, Mr. and Mrs. Albert Cracknell, and their ten-year-old daughter Shirley. The basement apartment was rented to a bachelor English schoolteacher named Archie Nishimura. There was also the house cat Fluffy.

Roy and Carol Hawkins and their children were rudely awakened one night the first week of May by footsteps and screeching laughter. The sounds came from the attic, but a search found nothing. The next morning Carol felt that someone was standing over her but nobody was to be seen. Then she experienced a sudden chill. Two nights later there was a repetition of the footsteps and laughter. These sounds were heard throughout the house by the Hawkins and the Cracknells. Fluffy the cat advanced toward the attic door. There was a loud noise as if somebody or something had whacked the cat. Fluffy screamed, then there was a human scream and then the sound of laughter.

The next afternoon, footsteps in the attic were heard, the first time there were sounds during the day. Again there was a search of the attic but nothing untoward was found. John Gault and John Downing of the *Toronto Telegram* received permission to spend the night in the attic to determine whether anyone or anything was walking across the attic floor. They even sprinkled flour on the floor. At 3:30 a.m they heard the phantom footfall, but when they checked the flour-covered floor, they found no footprints.

The Reverend Tom Bartlett and his wife, the Reverend Pat Bartlett, of the Star of Progress Spiritualist Church were called in to perform an exorcism at midnight the following evening. Gault and Downing interviewed Tom Bartlett who, considering the evidence, had come to the conclusion that there was a female spirit in the house. He recalled ascending the attic stairs:

At the head of the stairs, I stopped and willed whatever it was to appear. I saw a brown oval of light, a cocoon. Brown means the spirit is still linked to the earth.

I think the spirit is near transition — that's what we call death. She must be very ill or has taken a bad turn in her mind. She has some obsession to come in this place. She probably once lived here and was happy.

Pat Bartlett, the minister's wife, also a spiritualist minister, joined him and described what she saw and felt: "I saw a band of brown light. I then got a terrible pain in my stomach and chest. This person is suffering some serious illness — perhaps cancer."

At the foot of the attic stairs, reporters and other observers heard thumps overhead. Mrs. Hawkins saw a light at the top of the steps. There were reports of a sudden cold. The the rite of exorcism was performed. By 4:00 p.m., the footsteps were heard no more.

Reporters returned the next evening and everyone heard the footsteps again and felt a series of cold waves passing through the house. Mrs. Cracknell smelled perfume and broke down. A crowd collected outside the house and four policemen were dispatched to keep order. Shortly thereafter the families moved out of the house and all manifestations ceased.

What to make of the Etobicoke Poltergeist? No one knows for sure. It was the opinion of the Bartletts that the disturbances were caused by an elderly and eccentric woman, very much alive at the time of the disturbances. Apparently she had once lived in the house, now lived elsewhere, but wanted to "keep the house for her son." It is difficult to know what to make of this explanation.

John Gault and John Downing, while neither embracing nor dismissing the supernatural explanation, expressed concern and sympathy for the Hawkinses and the Cracknells. They noted: "We experienced some of the things they did. We spent two nights in the house, and two evenings and two afternoons. There is something there that is strange."

The Haunting of Cherry Hill House

Does the ghost of sixteen-year-old Miranda haunt this restaurant, or is it the haunt of aboriginal spirits whose resting place has been disturbed?

Site: The Cherry Hill House Restaurant

Locale: Public restaurant in historic house, 680 Silvercreek Boulevard, Mississauga; Silvercreek Boulevard is one block north of Dundas Street West off Cawthra Avenue

Hours: Open Monday to Friday for lunch and dinner; open Saturday for dinner only; closed Sunday. Phone (905) 275-9300

Period: Built in 1822; reports from 1973 to the present

Sources: Frank Jones, "Visiting Our Restless Spirits," *The Toronto Star,* 26 October 1980

Stefan Scaini, "Buildings that Hold the Souls of the Dead," *The Toronto Star,* 14 January 1984

Mitch Potter, "Halloween Haunts of the Witch and Famous," *The Toronto Star,* 28 October 1988

Interview with Tom Skrela, owner and general manager, Cherry House Hill Restaurant, 17 June 1994

Cherry Hill House, an historic ranch-style country house, is the oldest building in Mississauga. In 1973 the house was converted into a restaurant; there is a dining room with seating for seventy-five guests as well as a basement pub. The Cherry Hill House Restaurant is furnished in the early Victorian manner. Since 1985 it has been owned and operated by Tom Skrela.

The frame house was erected by Joseph Silverthorne in 1807 and occupied by his descendants until 1932 when it was rented to a Scottish family named Lindsay. The last member of that family died in 1972, whereupon the house went vacant. It was acquired by the Triomphe restaurant chain and moved eight hundred feet to its present location, 680 Silvercreek Boulevard, off Cawthra Avenue north of Dundas Street West. It opened its doors as an elegant restaurant on Halloween 1973. That was when the problems started.

"In that year," wrote journalist Frank Jones, "a security guard, Ron Land, was sitting outside the deserted house guarding it one night when he saw a white figure rise out of a pile of earth, brandishing a sword. Land jumped out of his car, and his dog Cindy ran towards the figure. The dog shied away, and as the figure came towards him, Land too turned and fled. Police, the next night, kept watch, but saw nothing."

Allan Blue, an early manager, reported a number of strange experiences. While the house was still boarded up, tools left neatly stacked at the end of the day were found scattered around the next morning. A Scottish carpenter working in the attic fell down the stairs and broke his wrist. "I was pushed," he said. One night Blue slept in the building to allow plumbers in early the next morning. It was a strange night, Blue recalled. "I didn't know whether I was dreaming or waking, but I saw faces of old Indians floating out of the fireplace towards me. I got up and went and made myself a cup of coffee and sat up until the plumbers came." Blue later heard that the house had been built on an Indian burial ground. Perhaps the move disturbed the spirits.

Once the Cherry Hill House Restaurant opened, the staff began to report hearing footsteps. One woman said she heard her name, Elizabeth,

The spirit of "the girl in white" is said to haunt Cherry Hill House Restaurant. The heritage building is located north of Dundas Street West, Mississauga.

[Josh Goldhar]

being called by a figure in a shawl in the upstairs dining room. "There is a strangeness here," Jean-Louis Orsacchino, who succeeded Blue as manager, told Jones. "Sometimes I hear a sound like children's feet running upstairs, but when I go up, no one is there. One of our people saw a little girl sitting on the stairs, but when he turned, my gosh, she was gone. One night the pub manager came up here and he could hear people talking inside, but the door was locked. When he went in, no one was there, and as you can see, there is no other entrance."

The journalist Stefan Scaini reported, "On several occasions, the staff claimed to have seen the image of what appeared to be an old Indian. He would float quietly in the darkness, then slowly disappear. Others have seen him come down the stairs, and once a carpenter who had been working in the attic felt a hand grip his shoulder. He turned in time to see the old man vanish."

Scaini went on to note, "There may be a reason for these images of Indians in Cherry Hill House. An archeological study done a few years ago discovered that the foundation blocks that support the house came from a nearby field that was once used as an Indian burial site." A subsequent manager, Sandro Julita, remembered hearing about a vision that dates from that time. "The building was moved here from just down the street. While the construction for the move was under way, a security guard on the site swears he saw a girl on a horse inside the house. The horse was white, the girl was wearing white." On another occasion a medium was brought in and she reported that "the girl in white" is the spirit of a sixteen-year-old girl called Miranda, who apparently was burned to death in the house years ago while making candles.

Today's general manager, Tom Skrela, acquired the restaurant from the Triomphe chain in 1985. He knows all about the long tradition that Cherry Hill House is haunted. "People feel there is something here, some sort of presence. They sense it and they see it," he explained. "I myself have neither felt it nor seen it, perhaps because I am here all the time and they stay away from me!"

Is the ghost good for business? "I suppose so. We don't draw attention to it, but guests sometimes talk about it. Members of the staff tell me they feel things and see things. For instance, they hear footsteps coming from the ceiling when there is no one on the second floor. And in the basement pub, sometimes the juke box plays all by itself. Guests seem to find it interesting."

The Mississauga Blob

What was the unexplained flaming "blob" that crashed into the picnic table in the backyard of the home of the Matchett family of Mississauga?

Site: One-time home of the Matchett family

Locale: Private residence, 789 Melton Drive, north of the Queen Elizabeth Way, west off Cawthra Road, Mississauga

Period: 26 June 1979

Source: Dwight Whalen, "The Mississauga Blob," *Pursuit*, First Quarter, 1981

Traven Matchett and his daughter Donna were plainly mystified when a blazing blob plummeted down and landed on the picnic bench in their backyard in Mississauga, on a Saturday afternoon in June 1979. Was it a "flaming frisbee"? No satisfactory explanation has been forthcoming.

[Inland Publishing Co. Ltd.]

About 5:00 p.m. on Saturday, 26 June 1979, something flaming plummeted and landed with a thud onto the picnic table in the backyard of the home of the Matchett family then living on Melton Drive in Mississauga. In its descent the "blob" almost hit nineteen-year-old Donna Matchett on the head. With a garden hose she extinguished the glowing, intense, reddish-orange cylindrical "blob" which measured about eighteen inches high by eight inches wide. It solidified on the picnic table into a flat, dark green mass with a fibrous, pock-marked texture. Donna's father Traven Matchett sought help by phoning the Toronto International Airport, the Canadian Armed Forces Base, the University of Toronto, and the Ontario Science Centre but to no avail. Then he phoned the *Toronto Sun* newspaper which dispatched a reporter who published an account in Sunday's paper. There was immediate media reaction from close at hand and from around the world. "This place was like Grand Central Station," Traven Matchett said, referring to the phone calls and visits from the media. The Ontario Ministry of the Environment sent an inspector. The Peel Regional Police arrived and questioned everyone. The authorities concluded that the substance was common plastic and that someone had thrown a "flaming Frisbee" into the Matchett's backyard. Yet the Mississauga Blob is what anomalies collector Charles Fort has called "a skyfall." Specifically it resembles *powdre ser*, the Welsh term for "rot of the stars." To this day nobody really knows the peculiar nature of the mysterious Mississauga Blob.

North

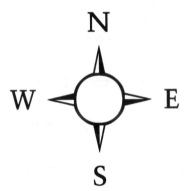

Mulholland's Apparition

Did Henry Mulholland's apparition appear to his wife and children one afternoon at their homestead in Upper Canada ... while thousands of miles away he was drowning in the North Atlantic?

Site: The old Mulholland Homestead

Locale: Lawrence Plaza, northwest corner of the intersection of Bathurst Street and Lawrence Avenue; Asbury and West United Church, 3180 Bathurst Street; Bagot Court off Varna Drive, north off Lawrence Avenue West; also Mulholland Monument, Manorpark Crescent, southeast of Leslie Street and Sheppard Avenue; all sites in North York

Period: 11 May 1833; 1963

Sources: F.A. Mulholland, *The Mulholland Family Tree* (Toronto: Ontario Publishing Company Limited, 1937)

Patricia W. Hart, *Pioneering in North York: A History of the Borough* (Toronto: General Publishing Company Limited, 1968)

Eileen Sonin, "Great Ghosts of Toronto," *Toronto Life,* January 1968

Eileen Sonin, *More Canadian Ghosts* (Toronto: Pocket Books, 1974)

Harold Hilliard, "North York's Heritage," *The Toronto Star,* 5 January 1981

Jeanne Hopkins, "Our Yesterdays," *The Toronto Star,* 2 April 1991

The story of Mulholland's apparition is inseparable from the early history of the City of North York, and thus a part of the history of Metropolitan Toronto.

The pioneer couple Henry Mulholland and Jane Armstrong emigrated from County Monaghan, Ireland, and received Crown land in 1806 in "East York," near the present-day intersection of Sheppard Avenue East and Leslie Avenue. They farmed the land but felt isolated. In 1812, they acquired 375 acres of land at "the Bathurst and Lawrence crossroads" in "West York." Here, from local materials, they built their large, two-storey farmhouse and furnished it in the Colonial style. They felled the trees, farmed the land, and raised ten children. Mulholland took part in the War of 1812 and helped blaze the trail that became Forest Hill Road. Mulholland's appearance was sketched in words by one of his descendants, F.A. Mulholland:

> Henry Mulholland was a typical Irishman — red-haired, grey eyed, musical, and humorous, with the true fighting spirit of an Ulsterman. His death, at the age of forty-four, no doubt robbed a young community of a valuable leader and enterprising pioneer. But he left behind in the person of his wife, Jane, a woman somewhat stern, but brave and capable, who survived him by sixteen years ... From the property she gave a site on which was erected a Wesleyan Methodist Church in 1845, called "Asbury" in honour of a leader in the Church.

Here is an account of Mulholland's tragic end:

> Henry made two or three return trips to Ireland to induce other emigrants to come to the new country. In 1832 he sailed with the added purpose of borrowing money to purchase more land. The following year he set sail once more from Belfast on *The Lady of the Lake*. But he never reached Canada again. On May 11th, 1833, in Lat. 46.50 N. and Long. 47.10 W., at 5:00 o'clock in the morning the ship ran into a field of ice and at 8:00 a.m. an iceberg struck the bow of the vessel which sprang a leak. All efforts to prevent the impending disaster were unavailing and soon the boat was well under water. Only one life-boat was launched. Into it, thirty-three persons climbed, with no oars and no provisions. The last that was seen of the brig was about thirty persons were clinging to the rigging. Perhaps Henry Mulholland was one of those. For after three days the occupants of the boat (now reduced to fifteen in number) were picked up by a passing brig and brought on to Quebec, and Henry was not among them.

Finally there is the description of Mulholland's apparition:

The story goes (and it is a good illustration of the some what eerie insight of the Irish) that one evening about the time of the wreck of *The Lady of the Lake* the youngest Mulholland children were playing outside their home when they saw their father coming up the land. They ran into the house and told their mother, who went out and she, too, saw him. But suddenly he vanished from sight. Going back into the house she sat down and said, "Something has happened to your father." Not long afterwards the news came that he was drowned.

In passing, it is interesting to note that death by water was not an uncommon fate for the Mulhollands. For instance, two of Henry Mulholland's great-grandchildren drowned in Georgian Bay in separate boating accidents in 1882: Robert in the burning of the *Manitoulin* in Manitowaning Bay, William in the wreck of the *Asia*.

The "crisis apparition" that involved the drowning of Henry Mulholland caught the fancy of artist and illustrator Isaac Bickerstaff.

[Courtesy: Don Evans]

Eileen Sonin, writer, broadcaster, and psychic, was intrigued with the story of Mulholland's apparition. In 1963, she knocked on the door of a modern home, part of a subdivision of the Mulholland property, close to the old Mulholland Homestead (erected in 1926, demolished in 1950).

The modern home is located on Bagot Court off Varna Drive, north from Lawrence Avenue West, west of Bathurst Street.

At the door she was greeted by Mrs. Evelyn Leonard who complained that there was another presence in the house, someone staring at her from the stairway. Her husband, too, felt someone was watching him. Their ten-year-old son Peter refused to go upstairs to bed alone because of "the strange lady in the white dress." Then all of them heard footsteps. Sonin continued, "I ran to his bedroom and just as I reached the doorway, I experienced an intense cold such as I have never felt before. The hairs on my arms stood up, my scalp was tingling and I was shaking with this terrible cold. I could see nothing in the room, although I was certain someone or something was there." She added that she "received a mental picture of a woman in a long white gown and a cap with frilled lace around it. I was not scared, as the spirit seemed to be very shy and quite harmless."

Is there any connection between Mulholland's apparition of 1833 and the watcher in the Leonard home 130 years later? Sonin thought there was a link, but she was at a loss to know what it was. Such links are tenuous at best. The Mulholland family has given the present many tangible reminders of the past.

In October 1937, a memorial was dedicated to the memory of Henry Mulholland and Jane Armstrong by the descendants of the eight branches of the Mulholland family. The memorial, a plaque embedded in a tall stone cairn, was originally raised on the Henry Farm, near the intersection of Sheppard Avenue and Woodbine Avenue, now a subdivision. This was the farm of the Mulhollands' great-grandson George S. Henry, Premier of Ontario in 1930-34. The Henry Farm was part of the original Crown grant to the Mulholland family. In 1966, to make way for the Don Valley Parkway, the monument was moved to the park on Manorpark Crescent, across from the old Henry House.

The inscription on the plaque reads as follows: "Dedicated to the memory of Henry Mulholland and his wife Jane Armstrong, pioneers of this district who emigrated from Ulster in 1806, and took out the original grant of four hundred acres from the Crown. He fought in the War of 1812 and later returned to Ireland to induce further immigration. While returning he was drowned in the wreck of *The Lady of the Lake* in the Straits of Belle Isle in 1833." Alas, the inscription makes no reference to the tradition of Mulholland's apparition.

Here is a view of the Mulholland Monument, which stands on Manorpark Crescent, North York. The imposing structure was erected in 1937 in memory of pioneer settler Henry Mulholland, his wife Jane Armstrong, and their family. The inscription on the memorial makes no mention of the "crisis apparition" associated with Henry Mulholland's death at sea, 11 May 1833.

[Josh Goldhar]

At Night at the Ritz

Apparently more than mere movies were to be seen at the old Ritz Theatre, even after the last patron left ....

Site: The old Ritz Theatre, one-time name of the Vaughan Cinema (building demolished in the 1980s)

Locale: 550 St. Clair Avenue West, west of Vaughan Road

Period: From 1947 to the late 1970s

Sources: Kathleen Kenna, "Something Weird," *The Toronto Star*, 26 September 1983

Information supplied by researcher, Cinemateque Ontario, 22 June 1994

Interview with Gerald Pratley, film historian, 23 June 1994

Interview with Richard Gotlib, cinema enthusiast and lawyer, 24 June 1994

It was only a generation ago that every district in Toronto had its neighbourhood movie theatre. Hardly any of these film palaces remain today. Most, like the Ritz, are places of happy memories.

The Vaughan Cinema was a neighbourhood movie theatre that was erected on the north side of St. Clair Avenue West and opened in 1947. Like so many other independent theatres in the late 1970s, the Vaughan fell on hard times, changing its name and managers as business went from bad to worse. In the 1980s it was known as the Ritz Theatre, in 1984 as the Fine Arts, and at the end as the Heritage Theatre. The wrecker's ball levelled the building. The site is occupied by a mixed-use commercial and corporate structure that suggests not a single ghost or spirit.

When it was known as the Ritz, the theatre was said to have two resident spirits. Staff members working there at night reported seeing a woman dressed in clothes suggestive of the 1930s and a man dressed all in black. In 1983, journalist Kathleen Kenna sought out Anthony Mancini who had worked at the Ritz as a member of the night staff and quoted him as saying, "It's getting very embarrassing ... I'm not a believer in ghosts at all, but I saw something that made my hair stand on end and gave me goose bumps."

According to Kenna, "Theatre patrons say one of the ghosts might be a man who hanged himself by a sandbag rope behind the stage curtain on opening night in 1947. As well, there was a funeral home next to the theatre until 1932."

Haunting of the Willan Residence

Was the long-time residence of Healey Willan haunted by two spirits whose footsteps were heard time and again? His daughter thinks so ....

Site: One-time home of Healey Willan and family

Locale: Private residence, 139 Inglewood Drive, west of Mount Pleasant Road

Period: From 1920 to 1968

Source: Interview with Mary Mason, actress and writer, 24 June 1994

Mary Mason is an actress and writer as well as the daughter of the late Healey Willan, composer and choirmaster of St. Mary Magdelene Church. From her birth in 1921 to her marriage in 1943 she lived in the Willan Residence at 139 Inglewood Drive. The family sold the three-storey house following Dr. Willan's death in 1968. In an interview in 1994, Mary Mason recalled how the spirits of the house affected her and the rest of the family.

So often people feel they're in control of their lives, but it seems as though there is something evil abroad that we cannot control because of our reliance on something called "science," which is really another name for knowledge, and nothing else seems to count. There is a loss of spiritual cognizance. It is a tremendous loss.

I first realized there was a "presence" in the house when I was five. It happened one day in 1926. I had had scarlet fever and was in isolation in my bedroom on the second floor. I was awfully bored. The window of my room was closed so the door of my room was open all night. I distinctly heard footsteps descending the stairs from the third floor. I sat up in bed. I had a narrow view of the hall but I could see nothing there. I thought it's my youngest brother who was then in the cadet band at Upper Canada College. He was coming to visit me before early practice and I would have someone to talk to. The footsteps continued coming down the stairs and along the hall and approached my room where they stopped. That was it.

The attractive brick house at 139 Inglewood Drive was the residence of Healey Willan and his family. Family members reported that on many an occasion they heard the fall of phantom footsteps along the hall and down the stairway.

[Josh Goldhar]

Dr. Healey Willan, composer, conductor, and choirmaster, is shown enjoying his pipe in this photograph taken in the mid-1950s by long-time friend Tom Hyland.

[Tom Hyland]

There was no one there. It was very odd. This happened a number of times. The door was no barrier. There was a nasty feeling. I felt awful and frightened.

My mother and father had both heard the phantom footsteps on other occasions. "Don't tell anyone," Mother cautioned me, "we may want to sell the house!" Sometimes I woke rigid with fear; I felt a disembodied presence beside me. I couldn't see anyone in the room with me, yet there was someone there. Mother spoke to Father

Hiscocks, the rector of St. Mary Magdalene, because she knew I was disturbed. He came and had tea with us and then spoke to me privately. "Let me tell you about the time I was the vicar of the little Anglican church at Cannes. It had been part of a Catholic monastery years before. Every Sunday evening the people came for vespers and sometimes we saw a little monk coming up the centre aisle. He floated up the aisle and seemed to be searching for something. He disturbed the service and I had to do something. So I addressed the congregation. 'We all know someone else is here, a little monk looking for something. Let's all pray that he finds whatever it is he seeks.' So we bowed our heads and prayed in silence. We didn't see him again. So try to pray for this soul who is troubling you." What Father Hiscocks said helped a lot.

One time my eldest brother had a party and one of the entertainers was a psychic. When it came time to have supper, everyone went downstairs to the dining room. So I asked her if she had been offered anything to eat. When she said no, I took her a tray of food. We began to chat and she said, "I see you lying flat on your back in bed and you are frightened. You know someone is in the bedroom with you. That someone is troubling your brother too. Don't worry. Your grandfather is looking out for him. Grandmother is looking out for you. They are guarding you. Don't worry." I found what she said comforting. Both my grandparents had died before I was born.

It was not limited to family members. The cleaning woman once told me, "Mary, someone is walking about in the house upstairs when nobody else is here." I suggested it might be the dog but she would have none of it.

Once, when I was fourteen or fifteen, everyone went to a concert and I was left alone in the house with our dog, Nicky, a collie. I heard footsteps descending from the second to the first floor. The footsteps were heavy, as if someone were carrying something. Our dog leapt up on the sofa beside me, every hair on his body sticking straight out. He stared at something, eyes wide, watching something coming down the stairs. It was horrifying.

One Sunday afternoon I was in one of the third-floor rooms studying for exams. Downstairs, afternoon tea was being served. The door of the room was closed. I heard footsteps coming right up to the closed door. They were light-footed steps. I thought it was my young nephew. There was nobody there.

They surprised you when you had no thought of them in your head. I felt they were mean-spirited. Our house was the original house in the area. It had been a farming area. Perhaps one or more of the early occupants of the house had committed a crime. Maybe the heavy-footed one and the soft-footed one were compelled to repeat their actions. It might be what purgatory or hell or damnation is. I think there's a retribution there somewhere.

I left the house when I married in 1943. I have three brothers. After the Second World War, my middle brother returned from England with his war bride. Sheila is Irish and she sensed there were spirits in the house. Mother called Father Brain, the rector of St. Mary Magdalene. He exorcised the house, going in a procession around the outside, praying. What the neighbours thought of the "bell, book, and candle" routine I do not know! The rite helped but did not put the spirits to rest completely.

Basically the family ignored the disturbances. We never gave the spirits names. You don't want to assign them personalities.

After my father died in 1968, the house was sold. The new owners gutted and renovated it. I wonder what happened to the spirits. If people want to say I'm crazy, that's their privilege. Mother and Dad and my brothers were well aware of the haunting but we were all philosophical about it. If anybody tries to tell me that once the body stops breathing the spirit dies, I disagree. It is obvious to me that such a person has not had these experiences. For those of us who have, it is not a laughing matter.

The Houses of the Man of Mysteries

Here are houses that are not haunted ... at least they are not known to be haunted ... except that they were at different times the residences of Canada's leading ghosthunter, R.S. Lambert.

Site: Private residence, 210 Douglas Drive (late 1940s and 1950s)

Private residence, 52 Kildeer Crescent (1960s)

Locale: 210 Douglas Drive, near Glen Road, Rosedale

52 Kildeer Crescent, north of Eglinton Avenue West, east of Laird Drive, Leaside

Period: Late 1940s and 1950s; 1960s

Source: R.S. Lambert, *Exploring the Supernatural: The Weird in Canadian Folklore* (Toronto: McClelland & Stewart, 1955)

John Robert Colombo, *Mysterious Canada* (Toronto: Doubleday Canada, 1988)

Information supplied by Jessica Riddell, Ottawa, 29 June 1994

Additional information supplied by Richard T. Lambert, Emsdale, Ontario, 20 July 1994

Everyone who shows an appreciation of major and minor mysteries of the world remains indebted to those researchers and investigators who explore the unexplained and write books about their findings. Without the work of a folklorist like Andrew Lang or a journalist like Elliott O'Donnell, to give two instances, there would be little recognition of the energy and variety of the British ghost story.

The person responsible for researching and popularizing the supernatural in Canada is R.S. Lambert (1894-1981). In the late 1940s and 1950s he lived with his second wife, Joyce, at 210 Douglas Drive, and in the 1960s at 52 Kildeer Crescent. There is nothing remarkable about these houses except that Lambert lived in them.

Richard Stanton Lambert had a distinguished career in adult education before immigrating to Canada. Born in England in 1894, a graduate of Oxford, he established the British Institute for Adult Education, taught at

R.S. Lambert, author and broadcaster, was especially knowledgeable about psychical research. The pen-and-ink drawing was done by artist and illustrator Isaac Bickerstaff.

[Courtesy: Don Evans]

the Universities of Sheffield and London, and joined the British Broadcasting Corporation. In 1928 he founded the weekly paper *The Listener*, which he edited until he left the BBC in April 1939. During those years he acquired a reputation as a tireless psychical researcher.

Emigrating to Canada in 1939 with his wife Elinor and their children, he joined the Canadian Broadcasting Corporation which was able to make great use of his transatlantic contacts to further wartime broadcasting within the Empire and around the world. After the war Lambert served as supervisor of school broadcasts. In his spare time he wrote over forty books and won the Governor General's Award for Literature. He retired from the CBC in 1959; eleven years later he moved to Victoria, B.C., where he died in 1981.

He was living on Douglas Drive when he wrote the basic book of Canadian mysteries, *Exploring the Supernatural: The Weird in Canadian Folklore* (1955). Originally published in London and in Toronto, it has remained popular through the years. It is one of those engrossing books that should be read in a summer cottage or isolated farmhouse before a roaring fire on a dark and stormy night. It demonstrates the author's great skills as a taleteller, his deep understanding of human nature, and his keen appreciation of the interplay between individual experiences and the customs and traditions of entire peoples.

Lambert was of the generation of psychical researchers who felt that their studies held the key to an understanding of the nature and fate of man. In Lambert's footsteps followed parapsychologists like A.R.G. Owen who felt that the discipline of parapsychology was principally a pursuit to be conducted in scientific laboratories with random-number generators and statistical tables. One consequence of the shift of emphasis from psychical research to parapsychology has been that experienced researchers have pretty well abandoned the greater part of the field, leaving it to amateurs and enthusiasts, psychics and channellers. Today there is little organized research of such subjects as ESP (Extra-Sensory Perception) and RSPK (Recurrent Spontaneous Psychokinesis). The latter embraces such matters as apparitions, ghosts, and poltergeists. Given the current climate of opinion, R.S. Lambert remains Canada's leading and last "ghost-hunter."

The Homes of the Amazing Randi

Few people appreciate the fact that the performer known as the Amazing Randi was born and raised in Toronto. He went on to become not only an outstanding conjurer and escape artist but also the world's best-known debunker of psychic claims.

Sites: Private residence, 18 Roe Avenue (1928-40)

        Private residence, 27 Rumsey Road (1942-45)

Locales: 18 Roe Avenue, off Avenue Road, south of Wilson Avenue, North Toronto

        27 Rumsey Road, east of Bayview Avenue and south of Millwood Road, Leaside

Periods: 1928-40; 1942-45

Sources: John Robert Colombo's *Mysterious Canada* (Toronto: Doubleday Canada, 1988)

        Interview with James Randi, performer and author, 29 May 1987

James Randi is a Toronto-born illusionist and escape artist who performs as the Amazing Randi. He is also a founder of the Committee for the Scientific Investigation of Claims of the Paranormal [CSICOP]. He holds in his hand a cheque for $10,000 which he will present to anyone who performs any paranormal phenomenon under controlled circumstances.
[the Toronto *Star* Syndicate]

There is nothing haunted about these private residences. No ghosts or spirits linger in their attics or basements, at least none that have been reported. Yet these modest residences are of interest to all ghost-hunters because they served as the boyhood homes of James Randi, the conjurer and escape artist who achieved show-business fame as the Amazing Randi.

Randi is the worthy successor of the late Harry Houdini. Like the master illusionist, Randi performs death-defying escape acts; like his mentor, Randi has devoted considerable time to debunking claims of the paranormal. Randi's exposure of the faith-healer Peter Popoff on Johnny Carson's *Tonight show* is a classic instance of the use of reason to lay bare deceptive practices.

Randi was born Randall G. Zwinge at the Toronto General Hospital in 1928. He spent his early years in the family home at 18 Roe Avenue in North Toronto. He lived there until 1940 when the family moved to Hamilton (where he resided at 14 Edgecombe Drive). When the family returned to Toronto, they moved into the house at 27 Rumsey Road in Leaside. Later, he accompanied the family on its move to Montreal in 1945. At the age of seventeen, writing as "Zo-Ran" (for "Zodiac-Randi"), he contributed a fake astrology column to the tabloid *Midnight*. Thereafter, he made his stage debut as a conjurer in a Montreal night club and occasionally returned to Toronto to perform, notably at the Canadian National Exhibition. He was in his twentieth year when he immigrated to the United States in 1948.

Today Randi resides in Sunrise, Florida, but he is seldom at home, for he travels widely, performing his illusions on campuses, in theatres, and on television, as well as lecturing on the supernatural and dispelling illusions about the paranormal. His first book was *Flim-Flam!* (1980); since then he has written important books on Uri Geller, faith healers, and Nostradamus.

If Randi decided to investigate any of the haunted sites in Toronto, he would begin by referring to them as "haunted" sites. He would use quotation marks to indicate that there is no proof of the existence of such things. "There's an awful lot of evidence for the existence of Santa Claus," he once told Bryan Johnson of the *Globe and Mail*. "The problem is that none of it happens to be very *good* evidence."

During a return visit in 1987 to attend a meeting of the Committee for the Scientific Investigation of Claims of the Paranormal (CSICOP), he maintained he did not "grow up" in Toronto. "I did not grow up and I never plan to grow up. I am having too much fun doing what I most want to do." He recalled that as a youngster he had explored the ravines of the Don Valley. On one occasion he came upon a rock with some graffiti written on it. The graffiti read: QUESTION AUTHORITY! Randi was impressed. He thought for a moment, then added a line of his own: WHY SHOULD I?

The Ghost of the Star Lab

If you were a ghost and you wanted to haunt the Ontario Science Centre, would you become the star of the star show? Maybe one did!

Site: Star Lab, Ontario Science Centre

Locale: 770 Don Mills Road, intersection with Eglinton Avenue East, Don Mills

Hours: Seven days a week, 10:00 a.m. to 6:00 p.m. Phone (416) 696-3127

Period: 1980-90

Source: Ivan Semeniuk, researcher in astronomy, Ontario Science Centre, 9 August 1994

The last place where anyone would expect to encounter a ghost is in the Ontario Science Centre with its interpretive and interactive exhibits of scientific principles and technological achievements in the areas of space and earth sciences, environment, physics, chemistry, psychology, human biology, and engineering. The showplace centre has welcomed visitors from around the world since 1969, but until someone there creates an exhibition on the paranormal, the only place you'll hear the word "ghost" mentioned is in the Star Lab.

Star Lab is the OSC's planetarium. Located in the Hall of Space, with room for fifty viewers, the self-enclosed theatre of the night can demonstrate the movement of the stars and planets across the northern heavens with startling realism. The illusion is accomplished with an array of special effects projectors, able to reproduce any spectacle from meteor storms to the aurora borealis on the domed ceiling. Live presentations are offered daily by OSC hosts who operate Star Lab's computerized console and provide narration.

The human element in the presentation is especially important when the host must compensate for an unexpected technical glitch and keep the show smoothly on track without alerting the audience. Such glitches are inevitable from time to time, but they were especially pronounced in Star Lab's early days. "Before the show was computerized in 1985, it ran on a maze of wiring and manual switches," explained OSC astronomer Ivan Semeniuk. "There were so many projectors, dimmers, and motors all wired together that they began to interact in unexpected ways. Images might appear out of turn, or superimposed, or even upside-down for no apparent reason. Music and lighting would turn on or stay off at inopportune moments.

"Although the audiences may not have been aware of what was going on, the OSC hosts certainly were, so much so that they began to blame the glitches on the Star Lab Ghost. They would begin each show in a state of anticipation, always wondering if the ghost was preparing a trick or two to play on them."

Happily for the OSC hosts, but unhappily for visiting ghosthunters, most of the glitches have long since been programmed out of the Star Lab. "But we won't let our guard down," Semeniuk says. "Every time we add a new component to the system, we test it out thoroughly to make sure the ghost hasn't found a new way to slip back in among the stars."

Vision of a Crime

Driving alone on a busy thoroughfare in 1987, a motorist observes a woman and a child as they step out of a parked car and enter a field. He slows down, pulls over ... and watches a crime that was committed in the year 1956!

Site: Farmer's field off Warden Avenue

Locale: West side of Warden Avenue, south of Highway 7

Period: January 1987

Source: John Robert Colombo, *Extraordinary Experiences* (Toronto: Hounslow Press, 1989)

Is it possible for someone who is living today to "tune in" to the events of the past and witness them now as they must have unfolded decades ago or even centuries ago? It would seem this is what happened to Allen Goldenthal, B.Sc., D.V.M. Dr. Goldenthal is a veterinarian with the City of Scarborough as well as the owner-operator of the Birchmount-Steeles Animal Clinic in that city. His account comes from a letter dated 9 June 1987.

In January of 1987, I was driving north up Warden Avenue towards Highway 7. Suddenly, up ahead, on the west side of the road, a south-bound car pulled over. It was an old car, lime to faded green in colour. The driver of the car was a man. A woman got out of the car, pulling a child behind her. The woman was about six feet tall. She had a build that was almost masculine. She wore a long black dress and a high collar. The dress went down to her ankles. She had silver-platinum hair, a high-up hairdo, done in a fifties style.

At first I thought she was taking the child into the field to pee. But then I noticed the child struggling and trying to pull away. The child's hair was cut short, almost in what they used to call a Prince Valiant hair style. I placed the child between four and six years of age. Then the woman started dragging the child across the road to the field on the east side. I could hear the child yelling for help, even though my windows were up. At one point she paused in the centre of the road and looked directly at me. Even though I was in the northbound lane doing seventy kilometres, I did not seem to be getting any closer to her. It began to bother me that the cars in the southbound lane were passing by this scene as if nothing was happening.

When I came alongside the parked car, the man in the driver's seat turned to face me. He was Greek or Italian in appearance, with an oblong head, full moustache, and balding pate. His eyes were dark and cold.

Finally I had driven past the scene. I was about fifty yards down the road when the strangeness of everything suddenly dawned on me. I turned the car around and stopped. There was no one there and no longer any car. Then the name of the car — BelAir or Belmont — suddenly hit me. I don't know why, because I am not at all familiar with these automobiles.

The next day I related what had happened to me to some friends and inquired of them what I should do. Their reply was that if I had witnessed a crime I could expect to read about it in the papers in a day or so and then I could give my information to the police. Obviously nothing had happened, or at least nothing had appeared in the newspapers, so I stored the scene in my mind. I could no longer sleep well at night, however, as I was troubled by the events I had witnessed.

It dawned on me that what I had witnessed might have occurred in the past, long ago. Nevertheless I refused to tell anyone else about the vision, even though it weighed heavily on my mind. There is a certain amount of fear connected with talking about such things. As a public servant, I have to consider what my clients' reactions would be if I talked about such things. So I kept quiet about it for four months. By April I knew that I would no longer be at peace with myself unless I investigated the matter more fully. So I resolved to act.

One of my clients was a constable with 41 Division, as I remember. I asked him to do me a favour and investigate the first vision for me. I told him I believed that it took place in the time period between 1956 and 1960, that some crime or other was committed farther into the field on the east side, and that I believed the child was a boy between four and six years old.

Constable Adams did some inquiring for me and got back to me a few days later. He had created quite a stir because the oldest officer in York Region had only had twenty-five years of service on the force. But the officer did recall coming onto the force with an unsolved murder in the files. My client protected my interests by not telling him why he was interested in this case and where he had received his information about it until he had talked to me.

The facts of the case are these. On January 9th, 1955, young Judy Carter was abducted from her Toronto home on Sherbourne Street and taken to Warden and Highway 7 where she was murdered. She was six years old. Her body was found on January 11th beside the creek that at one time flowed past Warden which, at that time, was only a concession road. Somehow I had witnessed a crime that had occurred four months before I was even born! The Chief of Police for York who investigated the crime was Harvey Carps and he retired without ever closing the case. Constable Adams informed Metro Homicide that I was willing to talk about the case I had seen. He told me that they would call me in the future for what information I could give. But that was some time ago. I'm still waiting, but at least I can sleep at night.

The Famous Television Séance

A television station in Scarborough served as the setting for the world's first televised séance and the most notable séance held in modern times.

Site: Studio One, CFTO TV Limited

Locale: 9 Channel Nine Court, Scarborough, off McCowan Road north of Highway 401

Period: September 1967

Sources: John Leo, "Pike Asserts He Got Messages from Dead Son at TV Séance," *New York Times*, 27 September 1967

Allen Spraggett, *The Bishop Pike Story* (New York: New American Library, 1970)

Allen Spraggett, *Arthur Ford: The Man Who Talked with the Dead* (New York: New American Library, 1973) written with William V. Rauscher

Additional information supplied by a member of the production team of CTV's *W5*, 15 July 1994

In the 1960s and 1970s, Allan Spraggett was the country's most popular broadcaster and writer about "the unexplained." He is shown here in the fall of 1976 on the set of his popular CBC-TV show *Beyond Reason*. The show's guest is the late Mrs. Virginia Morrow, who was publicly known as Virginia Tighe; she is most widely remembered as the woman who under hypnosis recalled details of a previous existence as an Irish woman called Bridey Murphy.

[Memory Lane, CBC]

The most notable séance to be held in modern times and the first séance ever to be televised was conducted in Studio One of CFTO TV Limited, 9 Channel Nine Court, Scarborough. Studio One is the station's main production studio, the one that originates local newscasts. CFTO is the flagship station of the CTV Television Network. The landmark séance broadcast was part of the long-running public-affairs show W5. The host was Ken Cavanaugh, and the program in question was first seen on the national CTV network the evening of 17 September 1967.

What viewers saw was about thirty-five minutes of the full three-hour séance that had been videotaped two weeks earlier. The videotaping session, held on September 3, was supervised by Allen Spraggett, religion editor of the *Toronto Star,* who introduced the direct-voice medium Arthur Ford and James A. Pike, a maverick Episcopalian bishop then very much in the news for his criticism of U.S. involvement in Vietnam. Pike was in distress following the recent suicide of his son.

Ford fell into a trance and contacted Fletcher, his guide, who was said to be the spirit of a French-Canadian Catholic soldier who fell in World War I. Speaking through Ford, Fletcher gave Pike information about his son which Pike felt could be known to no one else. Pike was visibly moved and arranged for a second sitting with Ford at a later date. Pike then declared himself a spiritualist.

The televised séance met with considerable press response. "Pike Asserts He Got Messages from Dead Son at TV Séance" was the headline on the front page of the the *New York Times.* Because it was so widely reported, this séance rivals in influence the most famous séance of the nineteenth century: the reported levitation of the medium D.D. Home at Ashley Place, London, 16 December 1868. Yet for all its influence the televised séance is eclipsed in significance by the private, makeshift affair held on the evening of 31 March 1848 in the parlour of the family cottage in Hydesville, N.Y., by Maggie and Katie Fox, the famous or infamous Fox Sisters. They were born at Consecon, Canada West, and had been in New York state about half a year when they discovered their talent for spiritualism. Indeed, it was their séance that inaugurated the Spiritualist Movement itself.

Allen Spraggett later researched and wrote biographies of Pike and Ford In the latter book he showed that at least some of the information that Ford offered Pike was derived from research and not from Fletcher. Spraggett concluded that Ford was a "gifted psychic who for various reasons, scrutable and inscrutable, fell back on trickery when he felt he had to." But to Spraggett must go the credit for having arranged the most famous séance of modern times.

The Most Beautiful Woman in the World

Visions are reportedly seen by people of all ages, of all countries, and of all cultures. Visionaries who are Roman Catholic behold the Blessed Virgin Mary. Protestant mystics often catch glimpses of Satan. In the Western world, technologically minded witnesses may report sightings of spacecraft piloted by alien beings. But sightings of sirens or alluring women are decidedly less common in the 1990s than they were, say, one hundred years ago. But from time to time just such a vision is reported by a believer or non-believer. Here is one account of just such a vision.

Site:	Jogging trail
Locale:	Foot of Blythwood Road, between Mount Pleasant Road and Bayview Avenue, North York
Period:	"A long time ago"
Source:	Robert Hoshowsky's "The Most Beautiful Woman in the World," *Toronto Voice*, October 1992

Robert Hoshowsky is a freelance writer who lives in Toronto. "The Most Beautiful Woman in the World" is an amazing ghost story. It has all the qualities of imaginative fiction, yet the author maintains that it is a complete and accurate depiction of what he saw early one morning when he went out jogging in North Toronto. It first appeared in the October 1992 issue of the community weekly *Midtown Voice* — the Halloween issue.

> A long time ago, before it became fashionable, I was a jogger. Not just a block or two, but five, ten, even fifteen *miles* each and every night. Initially, I was joined by friends. The three of us huffed and wheezed our way through the labyrinth of streets and alleyways known as North Toronto a couple of hours after dinner, long after the sun had dipped below the horizon and the food in our stomachs had settled enough so we wouldn't puke. With our lungs straining for the next breath, we savoured every second of our run with youthful enthusiasm.
>
> After a while, however, one friend after another dropped off and sought other pursuits. Tyler discovered the joys of poker, and became forever lost to gambling away his pock-

Robert Hoshowsky has never been able to forget the oval face of the spectral figure of "the most beautiful woman in the world." She appeared to him, ever so fleetingly, as he jogged on Blythwood Road. In 1995, he sketched her figure from memory. The photograph of Hoshowsky was taken by the photographer Lydia Pawelak.

[Robert Hoshowsky/Lydia Pawelak]

et change after class. Dwight formed a heavy-metal band, and pretended to bite the heads off stuffed parakeets in the high-school auditorium during lunch. Since I had no musical abilities whatsoever, I kept running, alone.

One night, feeling especially adventuresome, I decided to try twenty miles. No stopping, not for pain or traffic lights. This was in August, and there are surprisingly few people awake at three in the morning.

Dressed in a ratty old muscle shirt and shorts that looked like they'd been washed ten thousand times, I was ready. And, up until the time I saw her, I was having a pretty good run. She was about half a mile away, on the other side of the street. I rubbed the sweat from my eyes and kept on running. At first, I thought she was a disheveled housewife, wandering around looking for her cat. That is, until I noticed a few little things.

Her bare feet weren't touching the ground.

I stopped so suddenly that I nearly fell flat on my face. The "housecoat" she was wearing was a nightgown, a very old-fashioned one, adorned with a high lace collar and white material that reached to her ankles. Her hair was loose and hung around her slender shoulders in thick black ropes.

What shocked me the most was her body. It was translucent, not like anything I had seen before. With every passing second, sections of her appeared and disappeared at the same time. She seemed just as astonished to see me as I did her, looking at me like I was intruding on her territory. Yet she was striking, with firm, high cheekbones and a lovely oval face. She couldn't have been more than thirty.

Her entire appearance suggested nobility, as if she had just drifted off the canvas of a Pre-Raphaelite painting. Long, slender hands, the supple neck of a swan, and enormous dark eyes which seemed to occupy most of her exquisite face. I fell in love with her in an instant, despite the fact she was a ghost. Never before have I wished so hard for one thing: for this woman to be truly alive, with warm human flesh and the breath of the living, not the wind of the dead. By the way she was dressed, she had been that way for at least a hundred years.

As I walked towards her, I felt my knees turn to water and stopped, not out of fright but of fear — of myself. We stood on opposite sides of the road staring at one another for an eternity, a supernatural breeze blowing the nightgown around her naked form. She was trapped, a prisoner caught in the never-world between life and death, a place I could not enter, and a land she could never leave.

I turned and ran, stopping only when I reached the top of the hill. The instant I turned to look at her, she swirled around, her body slowly disappearing into the darkness. The look of sadness hadn't left her eyes, and won't until the day I am dead, when we can meet again, not as strangers, but lovers.

She was, and forever will be, the most beautiful woman I never met.

Printed in the USA
CPSIA information can be obtained
at www.ICGtesting.com
JSHW012025140824
68134JS00033B/2888

9 780888 821850